Praise for the first idiotocracy book, *ARNS and the Man*:

"Amusing, sardonic political and social satire that brims with wordplay legerdemain and oddballisticelaboratified name invention. Trenchantly twisted and good fun." – John Shirley, author of *A Song Called Youth: Eclipse*

"I don't often read science fiction but when I do, Ira Nayman's *ARNS and the Man* is near the top of my list. Wacky, surreal, bizarre, and all too close to reality, Nayman spins a web of satirical hilarity ripped from the headlines." – Terry Fallis, two-time winner of the Stephen Leacock Medal for Humour.

"Ira Nayman rivals Walt Kelly for the skilled and joyous administration of near hallucinogenic word play as an antidote for the madness of our political process. And unlike the brave possum of Okefenokee Swamp, the truths of *ARNS and the Man* were crafted by someone wearing pants." – Hugh Spencer, author of *Why I Hunt Flying Saucers* and *Extreme Dentistry*

"Ira skewers American politics in a way only a Canadian can, with absurdist wit and wisdom. Short humorous Fake News articles that know they're fake and relish in their lies. (Or ARE they?) Makes me once more jealous of our neighbors to the north." – Michael A. Ventrella, author of *Bloodsuckers: A Vampire Runs for President*, among other things

"Reading an ARNS book is like going head-to-head with an selection of thirty three and a third disconnected Wikipedia entries filtered through seven layers of artesian coffee filters woven from at least three more fibers than permitted by the historic laws of any major religion in a blender made of a strange kind of cotton candy spun from titanium anodized in fairground colours with blades made of live sharks while simultaneously tap-dancing to a Steve Reich composition based on the absolute value of the square root of pi. In other words, simply and elegantly the most entertaining way ever invented to invert your brain over a platter prepared with roasted apples and a variety of field mushrooms for your own delighted consumption. Also, a hilariously skewed take on the Trump administration." – Jen Frankel, editor, *Trump: Utopia or Dystopia*, author, *Undead Redhead*

You and What Universe?

The Alternate Reality News Service,

Ira Nayman, Proprietor

Ira Nayman

This is a work of fiction. Any resemblance to real persons, places or things is…inevitable, really, given the nature of the multiverse. However, the probability of any resemblance to real persons, places or things in your particular universe is vanishingly small, and must, therefore, be considered coincidental.

DEDICATION

I would like to dedicate *You and What Universe?* to all of the scientists, researchers and support staff who are busy creating the future that people like me only dream about. It's nice to be able to take a break from the crazy political shenanigans of Earth Prime 1-6-7-1-8-2 dash Psi's leading idiotocracy and get down to some serious science fiction lunacy.

ACKNOWLEDGMENTS

Isn't the cover the most amazing thing you've ever seen? It's psychedelic, man! Thanks to Hugh Spencer for his amazing graphic, and especially to Gisela McKay for taking my loopy idea and making it such a spellbinding reality.

In addition, I have been remiss in not thanking the people who gave of their time and blurbiage to the first Vesampucceri collection, *ARNS and the Man*. Your kind words may not have increased my sales appreciably, but they make me think that I may not have been completely wasting my time with this whole writing thing.

Ira Nayman

CONTENTS

Ira Nayman

1. LIFE IS MORE ENTERTAINING THE LARGER THE SCREEN YOU WATCH IT ON

Ransom! Where?

by FRED CHARUNDER-MACHARRUNDEIRA, Alternate Reality News Service Science Writer

Bonnie Krump had just started feeling the tingles and knew that a big fat Greek orgasm (which, depending upon your cultural background, could be described as a gushing waterfall, a swarm of angry bees or a glorious uprising of workers to wrest the means of production away from the unproductive elites who controlled them and build an earthly collective paradise) was a couple of minutes away. To help her along, Chumley 1247-C, her handsome young sexbot, said the three words that every woman longs to hear.

"Give me money."

Calling on a database of human female sensual response, Chumley 1247-C knew exactly the right words to heighten the mood on the way to giving – **WHAT? WHAT DID HE JUST SAY?**

"He said: 'Give me money,'" Krump, the mood broken, told me. "Didn't you hear?"

Why would he say that? That's not romantic at all!

"Oh, please!" Krump said, shoving Chumley 1247-C off the bed (being made of space age materials for maximum flexibility, he was much lighter than his muscular frame would have suggested). He landed on the ground with a gentle thud. "It was –"

"Was it something I said?" Chumley 1247-C plaintively (he had been built in Utah) asked from the floor.

1

"I want you to lie there for a while and ponder your sins," Krump harshly told him.

"Okay," Chumley 1247-C, programmed to obey, agreed, although he didn't exactly sound happy about it.

So, about what happened...?

"My sexbot was obviously infected with ransomware," Krump explained as she reached over to the end table by the bed and pulled a cigarette out of a pack.

Ransomware? What –

"Hunh! You don't know what ransomware is? And you call yourself a tech reporter?" Krump scoffed as she picked a purse up off the floor and started rummaging around in it.

Well, yes, of course, I know what ransomware is! But...umm... for my readers, I thought if you would just –

"Yeah, yeah, whatever," Krump grumped, not finding what she was looking for. "Ransomware is a programme that stops all functions in a computer system unless you pay the person who created it. The ransom isn't usually – aha!" Krump took two sticks out of the purse and dropped it back to the floor. Then, she started rubbing the sticks together over the table. "The ransom isn't usually that much – 20 or 30 dollars. Paying it is less of an annoyance than – well, you saw what happened."

"Is that what happened to me?" Chumley 1247-C asked.

"More pondering. Less talking," Krump advised, not unkindly.

Why infect sexbots with ransomware? Wouldn't that, you know, kill the mood?

"Aha!" Krump exclaimed, as if she agreed with the flaw in the plan. Actually, the two sticks had sparked and caught fire, and she lit her cigarette. Quickly waving the sticks in the air to put the fire out, Krump took a long drag.

More relaxed, she explained, "Okay. Here's the thing. The C series male sexbots have sensors that monitor the vital signs of their partners. This allows them to adapt their behaviour to maximize their partners' pleasure. In theory, ransomware will detect when a woman is about to climax and threaten to shut down the sexbot a minute or so before she does. I have heard that robotics researchers and skunk whisperers call this the 'No, No, Don't Stop Now Moment.' The closer a woman is to the No, No, Don't Stop Now Moment, the more likely she will authorize the payment of the ransom."

But –

Chumley 1247-C moaned, "I don't feel so-o-o-o-o-o-o-o-o-o-o-ooooooooo…" As the sound died out, he stopped moving.

"That's what happens when you don't pay the ransom," Krump shook her head sadly.

When I pointed out that Krump wasn't sufficiently aroused to pay the ransom, she snorted a most unladylike (but very lady lawyerlike) snort.

"Human sexual response is not a simple algorithm," she explained, taking another long drag on her cigarette. "The No, No, Don't Stop Now Moment happens at different points for each woman, and can be affected by a lot of things. Like, how long she has been stimulated to that point. Or, maybe there are environmental factors like loud noises or farting dogs in the vicinity of the bed. Or, maybe she wasn't familiar with the work of the actor whose likeness was used for the sexbot, so he didn't turn her on as much as if she had been a fan. In my case, I just hadn't reached that point yet."

I asked Professor Hiram von Schmutz, head of The Intimate Machine-Human Interface Institute of The Frankfurt School if what Krump had told me was true. "Ja," he replied.

Having cleared that up, I asked Krump if she was going to pay the ransom to get her sexbot working again.

"We'll see," she replied. "Chumley 1247-C was supposed to come with antivirus software to prevent this sort of thing. I think I'll take him back to the dealer to run some diagnostic tests. Now, if you have no more questions, get the hell out of my bedroom. I know that reporters will do anything for a story, but this is creepy!"

Yesthetics Are So Yestherday

by FREDERICA VON McTOAST-HYPHEN, Alternate Reality News Service Pop Culture Writer

"Yes, I…I want to taste your wombat pate. On kelp crackers."

"I'm sorry, Felice, but I'm not feeling the yes."

"'Course you're not feeling the yes! Who wants to eat wombat pate on kelp crackers?"

"Walruses do, Felice. Walruses do. Perhaps if you got in touch with your inner walrus, it would be easier for you to –"

"Ugh! I think I'm gonna – I'm gonna – 'scuse me!"

"I think you're missing the – Felice? **Felice! Where are you running off to? I THINK YOU'RE MISSING THE POINT!**"

In a small meeting room in one of the less popular hotels on the airport strip (will you or won't you get heating on a cold December night? – the place can be such a tease!), over 30 people have paid $1,250 to be tutored by Marie-Angelo (her parents had a religious aversion to ultrasounds, so they hedged their bets) di Prestino.

Who is Marie-Angelo di Prestino? I'm glad you asked. Really glad you asked. There would be no article if you didn't ask glad you asked. Okay, technically, **I** asked in **your** name. So, **technically**, I'm glad you exist to allow me to put questions in your mouth. You do exist to allow me to put questions in your mouth, don't you? Of…of course you do.

Marie-Angelo di Prestino is the world-barely recognized author of *Why Is It When I Say Yes, I Hear No?*, the foundational (reading it is like swimming through concrete) text of the yesthetics movement. di Prestino is the lost and founder of the Instituti del Yesthetico and a practising yesthetician.

What is yesthetics? I'm glad you asked, but let's not start that nonsense all over again.

Yesthetics is the art of positivity. (Nietzsche was all over the art of negativity.) The basic premise of the movement is that it is not enough to half-heartedly say "Yes" to life. You must throw your arms around yes and enthusiastically embrace it like you would a lover that you haven't seen in over a decade. You must dance around yes like nobody is watching…for signs that would explain why you haven't seen your lover in over a decade. Sing yes like it's the theme song of your life (it sure beats the latest Coke jingle!). Yes. **Yes! YES!**

So. The word yes as performance art, then.

This does not – oh. Right. Most of the description two paragraphs ago was taken directly from di Prestino's follow-up book *Yesthetics: The Science Behind Yes That Had Been Left Out of My Previous Book*. To avoid allegations of plagiarism, please go back to that paragraph and imagine that I used open quotation marks before the phrase "it is not enough" and close quotation marks after the final **YES!**

This does not – oh, and, while you're imagining that, imagine that the double quotes around the word "Yes" two paragraphs – now three paragraphs ago, are actually single quotes. I wouldn't have mentioned it, but linguistic purists can make a journalist's life hell on Farcebook!

This does not – this being the word yes as performance art, I mean – I may have taken a bit of a detour from the concept in the last couple of paragraphs – the word yes as performance art does not come naturally to most people. That's where di Prestino's weekend retreats come in. (Okay, technically, they come in through the loading dock in the back of the hotel, but now is no time to quibble.) People pay big money (they use oversized checkbooks borrowed from a local lottery) to attend seminars on "The Historical Imperative of Yesthetics" and workshops where they practice using performance yes to answer a series of increasingly difficult to stomach questions.

There are, of course, critics of yesthetics. Surprisingly, some of the most vocal (you would swear they had worked with a voice coach!) were from the positivity movement itself. Well, surprisingly if you don't appreciate the role envy – the most sanguine of the deadly sins – plays in human nature.

"To suggest that there is a right way to get to yes implies that there is a wrong way to get to yes," argued Vermont Regulon, author of *The Yes Matrix: The Power of Yes to the Power of Two*, its follow-up, *The 3-D Yes Matrix: Taking the Power of Yes to a Whole New Level* and, most recently, *Quantum Yes: The Power of Yes in Eleven Dimensions*. "I find Marie-Angelo and her followers to have a yesier than thou attitude towards other yes-sayers. Tut tut, I say to that. Tut and tut."

Questions of pride – the orangest of the deadly sins – aside, wouldn't it make sense for yes practitioners – yestitioners? Naah – people can't just make up words willy nilly to suit themselves – that way leads anarchy! – wouldn't it make sense for yes practitioners to set aside their differences and work together towards a society with a more positive attitude towards yes?

"No," responded Regulon.

"No," replied di Prestino.

"Hell no!" answered Felice Marimbe Achooa from a stall in the women's washroom. "I paid a lot of money for the weekend retreat, and if I don't get the best yes that money can buy, I'm gonna sue somebody's ass off!"

This Oscar is Just So Much Background Noise

by ELMORE TERADONOVICH, Alternate Reality News Service Film and Television Writer

Have you ever been watching a movie and been taken out of a scene because, although it is set in a Russian tattoo parlour and skeeball joint, the hum of conversation in the background was obviously recorded in a bowling alley in Schenectady, Prince Edward Island during a darts tournament? Neither have I. The differences are so small that you would have to have been a sound engineer with decades of experience to be able to tell.

"Actually, I'm a sound engineer with decades of experience, and I can't tell the difference," stated Elmer Vedonaterre, a sound engineer with dec – okay, you already know that about him. But, did you know that he was recently awarded a Best Achievement By a Sound Engineer with Decades of…You Know Oscar? You did? Why am I bothering to write this, then?

We'll deal with my existential crisis some other time. For now, what you need to know is: the sound of crowds used in the background of all Hollywood movies comes from three sources: a speakeasy scene in 1934's *Golddiggers of Broadway in Space*, a football game in *The Elephant's Big Moustache* (1947) and a political rally in the musical *It Could Be You (But Let's Pretend It's Not)*, released in 1941. These are then tweaked with extreme prejudice as needed.

Suppose, for example, that you are doing the sound for a restaurant scene in a romantic comedy. You would take the football game, mute the roars of the crowd and add the tinkling of glasses. If a crowd roar happened to get through the sound editing process, you could always recommend writing into the script that the scene was happening in a sports bar on the night of the big game; the amount of reshooting you would have to do would be minimal.

Why did you think so many restaurant scenes in romantic comedies happen in sports bars?

Vedonaterre took a different approach to sound editing: what if you populated the background sound with artificial intelligences that were having real conversations? If that was the case, you could Taylor (after famed voiceover artist Elizabeth) background noises to fit any scene you had.

Suppose, for example, you were editing the sound for a scene in a romantic comedy where the rebel alliance is planning on attacking the empire's home planet. (Yes, the film has a bit of an identity crisis – that can happen when you have 37 writers work on a screenplay – but I've already complained about that so often that my computer keyboard is hoarse.) You can create an AI flight engineer who spouts nothing but incomprehensible technical jargon, an AI hotshot pilot who spouts nothing but incomprehensible flying jargon, an AI rebel leader who spouts nothing but incomprehensible political jargon, an AI robot who spouts nothing but incomprehensible tweets and whistles and…and…and, **what do I look like – a sound engineer? Fill the scene with your own damn characters!**

Ahem. I'm sorry you had to witness that. I…was recently in a car accident that left me in a coma.

The point is that once you have filled the scene with individual characters, you can mix them together to create a unique background soundscape appropriate for each scene of your film. And that is what Vedonaterre won his Oscar for. Nobody in the audience is likely to know, but –

"Roger Ebert will know," Vedonaterre interrupted.

Okay, nobody in the audience, except Roger Ebert, will know how much work was put into the –

"Germanium Angleterre will know," Vedonaterre interrupted. Again.

Who is Germanium Angleterre?

"The woman with the most acute hearing on the planet," Vedonaterre explained. "She works as a pre-bouncer at the Metropolitan Opera, identifying the one voice complaining about the tenor's bout of hiccups in the second act and pointing the person out to staff so that he can be banned for life. She would recognize the amazingness of my accomplishment!"

Okay, fine. Other than freaks and film critics – I'm not going to say that they are often the same thing – readers are mature, perceptive adults who can make that connection for themselves – nobody is ever going to notice all of the work that goes into creating these soundscapes. Is it really worth all the effort?

"Are you questioning the basis of my Oscar win?" Vedonaterre indignantly responded. "Jesus begesus, I'll bet you're the guy who tells six year-olds there's no such thing as the Easter bunny!"

Weeeellllll…

"Bastard!"

TV or Not TV?
Family Not Glad it Asked

by FREDERICA VON McTOAST-HYPHEN, Alternate Reality News Service Pop Culture Writer

Jocund Ferlenghetti (who, yes, comes from a long line of pasta makers) felt that Myrna and Elijahu's television viewing was out of control. They seemed to be in front of the set eight or nine hours a day. They ate in front of the set. They frequently shouted at the set. They cried at the set. They stayed up later than was healthy for them in order to keep watching.

Fearing dyer consequences (Elijahu worked on a psychedelic t-shirt assembly line), Jocund used the parental controls to block them from watching their favourite channels. The only problem is that Myrna (37) and Elijahu (41) are the parents in this family and Jocund (8 – but a mature eight – he knows who Frederic Wertham was and can recite a list of almost all Crimean War generals) is their son.

"I miss CNN!" Elijahu Ferlenghetti wailed, balling his middle aged fists and stamping his feet (an unhappy emoticon in red – that's gonna take several days to wash out of his skin!). "It's so unfair! All the other parents at work are talking about who was on Wolf Blitzer last night!"

Myrna Ferlenghetti rocked back and forth on the chair next to him, muttering about going through Rachel Maddow withdrawal and sobbing uncontrollably.

"It's for your own good," Jocund lectured them. "Remember the incident with Mister Baguette?"

Aloysius Baguette, Elijahu's boss at International Transnationalism & Stuff, Inc., had been invited to share dinner with the Ferlenghettis (IT&S existed in a time warp that way). Things had been going pretty well until Anderson Cooper appeared (on the television – the Ferlenghettis were only distant cousins, after all, and were on his six year waiting list for family functions) with a report on President-elect Donald Trump telling the Supreme Court, "You're fired!" Incensed, Elijahu threw a knife at the television set.

Unfortunately, his days as a circus knife thrower were long behind him, and he hit his boss right between the eyes. The good news was that he was so out of practice that he hit his boss with the handle rather than the blade. The bad news was that Baguette still needed seven stitches, and Elijahu's moderately speedy rise in the company would come to a grinding halt.

"Until you show me that you can watch the nightly news like responsible adults," Jocund sternly told them, "you're cut off."

It is estimated that as many as three per cent of children in liberal households have used the parental controls on their television sets to deny their parents the ability to watch cable news channels or network news broadcasts. In most cases, the adults are limited to watching a steady diet of sitcoms, reruns of *Matlock* and *Murder She Wrote*, and documentaries about snow.

The children can do this, of course, because their parents never learned how to use the parental controls in the first place, so they do not know how to get around them now.

"There has been a lot of talk about how the demagogic rhetoric of its politicians has infantilized the right," commented political scientist and part-time stone thrower/full time window glazer Bartholomeo Spitzer. "But nobody saw this infantilization of the left coming!"

"Who you calling infantile, buddy?" Myrna objected. "I still know my infrastructure from my superstructure, and I could argue the deficiencies of American trade policy until your face was blue! I...I just miss Lawrence O'Donnell's cutting calmness. Ooh, Lawrence O'Donnell's cutting...cutting...cut..." She curled up in a fetal position (something that she will be forced to maintain for a full nine months when Mike Pence is sworn in as Vice President) on the couch and moaned incoherently.

"You see!" Jocund yelled. "This is why you can't have political things!"

While the children have good intentions – saving their parents from the anguish of watching the world go to hell (we asked Stan, Satan's Press Secretary, for a statement on the situation, but he just grinned and "No comment"ed us – evil bastard!) on the nightly news – it may have negative consequences. Over the course of eight, or even just four, or fingers crossed a mere two years, the adults might lose touch with the world.

"Wouldn't it be ironic," said seven year-old Billy, who wants to be a political commentator, or possibly a firefighting cowboy astronaut, he hasn't decided, when he grows up, "that the right gets more ignorant the more news it watches, while the left gets more ignorant the **less** news it watches?"

"We'll deal with that bridge when a major corporation buys it and burns it to the ground for the insurance," Jocund responded. "In the meantime, I have to do what's right for my parents. I don't want them to grow bitter and mean and end up shouting at you damn kids to get off their lawns. What loving child would ever wish that on his parents?"

Fake News, Real *Tsuris*

by BRENDA BRUNDTLAND-GOVANNI, Alternate Reality News Service Editrix-in-Chief

There is no such thing as fake news, there is only news that didn't happen in your universe.

Now that we have cleared that up, I'm going to get back to extreme macraming and you can get back to...whatever tawdry affairs occupy your – yeah, yeah, I have no doubt that you were stunned by the *Bartbites.com* headline, "Hillary Clinton and Rudy Giuliani's love child arrested in connection with death of Vince Foster!!!" Personally, I prefer to stun people the old-fashioned way: with my Tasetron 2000. Headlines lose their charge too quickly no matter how many exclamation marks they contain. People with weak constitutions should be barred from reading the news these days.

And, sure, you were shocked by the headline, "President Obama makes secret pact with Satan to delay George R. R. Martin's next novel indefinitely!!!!!" That's what you get for reading your news on an ungrounded tablet. Take a pill, dumbass!

Okay, there seems to be some confusion as to what the Alternate Reality News Service does and what fake news outlets do. Be thankful that my tech department hasn't perfected the technique of slapping people over the Internet, because if they had, right about now there would be a spike in emergency room visits for whiplash! (Only one exclamation mark? Damn straight. Excessive punctuation to emphasize the seriousness of what I'm saying? Please! My slapping gloves are all the authority I need!)

So. The differences. When a fake news outlet reports on President Obama making a secret deal with Ventrosian Squiggles to send American auto manufacturing jobs out of the universe, it claims that that actually happened on Earth Prime; the purpose of such an article is to confuse a gullible populace and reinforce their support for a demagogic political extremist. By way of contrast, when we report on President Obama making a secret deal with Ventrosian Squiggles to send American auto manufacturing jobs out of the universe, we state very clearly that it happened in another universe. Any confusion we may cause in the gullible population is a mere by-product of what we do. A wondrous, highly entertaining by-product, but not our intention.

What part of the motto "If you don't like this universe, try another one!" do you not understand, double dumbass with sprinkles?

And, anyway, why are there so many gullible people in the world today? Haunting the shoreline to feed off scraps left by tourists only to show your gratitude by pooping on them from a great height is no way to live, you ask me.

The fact that fake news sources are given the same weight as respectable news services such as the Alternate Reality N – okay, respectable may be stretching it a bit. Somewhat respectable? Well, no, not that, either. Respectable in certain circles? That's kind of grasping for straws, there, isn't it? And, I don't even have any alcohol in front of me! Not – wait, why don't I have any alcohol in front of me? Give me so – give me a second, will you?

Aah, much better.

How about…not entirely disreputable? In the right light… If you don't look too closely…

Okay. The fact that fake news sources are given the same weight as not entirely disreputable in the right light if you don't look too closely news sources is clearly – Jesus begesus! When you phrase it like that, it's ferking hard to take the argument that fake news is undermining the value of real transdimensional news seriously!

Okay, forget the Alternate Reality News Service. Instead, let's base our comparison on a well known satirical publication: *The New York Times*. The fact that fake news is given the same weight as *The New York Times* should give reasonable people everywhere the mumbling heebie jeebies (I had originally intended to write screaming heebie jeebies, but our lawyer advised me against scaring the horses).

The answer to this problem is, of course, giving me a million dollars to study it in further depth.

No? How about half a million dollars? If I downgrade the quality of the servants' quarters (they probably wouldn't appreciate such luxuries as bathrooms or…beds, anyway, ungrateful bastards) and drop the plans for the pony ride in the stables of the mansion, I should just about be able to scrimp by on that. Still, no? Hunh. Tough audience.

Okay, the **other** answer to the problem is, of a different course, better public education; this would allow the average person to be able to tell the difference between fake news and real news that didn't actually happen in this universe. Yep. That's the answer, alright. Public – tee hee – public – ha ha ha ha ha ha – pub – snicker snort! Oh! Give me...please give me a moment to dry my eyes. I slap me!

Once a substantial portion of a country's population is so gullible that it is willing to believe that its leader isn't just colluding with Ventrosian Squiggles, but **is** a Ventrosian Squiggle, rational arguments are useless because duh! Irrational solutions, though appealing, are also problematic. For example, if real alternate reality news organizations start running fake news articles in order to compete with real fake news organizations, they will just confuse the issue further, not to mention losing two of their last three readers.

Personally, I'm waiting for this generation to die out so we can start fresh.

Technology's Fetal Attraction

by LAURIE NEIDERGAARDEN, Alternate Reality News Service Medical Writer

Pluto (her parents couldn't agree on whether the name should be short for Plutonium or Philatelist, so they settled on Plutocrat) Akhenaton Jellyfish looked like a peanut on the sonogram (not to be confused with a Sondheimogram, which annoys you at your front door with off-key renditions of songs from *Sweeney Toad*). Looking at the image, Snowflake Peritonitis had a craving for an ice cream sundae (they always taste better on the weekend) with Caramelite sauce (because children should be brought up believing in something, even that belief is based on a bad pun). Food cravings are not unusual during pregnancy; the fact that Snowflake Peritonitis was Pluto Akhenaton's **father** just showed how committed he was to his soon-to-be child.

As she lay on her back on the hospital waterbed (which was rented out to priests to conduct baptisms on weekends), Miranda Butch thought, *Is it too soon to be worrying about whether my child will get enough experience with computers early enough in life to develop the skills needed to get a sufficiently high paying job in today's competitive workplace to be able to take care of me in my old age after her father has passed away – the thoughtless, cowardly bastard! – and society has abandoned me?*

Why, no, Miranda Butch. It is not.

Researchers at The Institute for the Application of Applied Solutions (Calimari Branch) are hard at work creating hand-held gaming devices for fetuses. "If we give unBourne babies [those who have yet had the pleasure of watching a Matt Damon action film] the opportunity to experience electronic devices starting in the sixth week of fetal development," explained Samarta E. Pahnts, Deputy Director of Urgent Restraint at the Institute, "they will have a headstart in getting enough experience with computers early enough in life to develop the skills needed to get a –" I felt like I had heard this all before, so I smoothly extricated myself from the quote and moved on to the next paragraph.

Pregnant women would have the devices (current working name: SuperNEF, which stands for Numinous Excitement of Fetuses) medically inserted into their...pumpkin patches. SuperNEFs would theoretically – very theoretically – almost comically so – stimulate the fetus' brain, causing its synaptic connections to grow faster than moss on the hide of a rhinoceros (or, at least, faster than fetuses whose only wombal stimulation was dreaming of retiring to Tahiti); this would give it an edge when it was post-born and started attending pre-pre-pre-pre-very pre-kindergarten.

Despite enthusiasm from expectant mothers Everywhere (a small city just outside of Lunenburg), the development of the technology has been plagued with problems. "Now, now," Pahnts waggled an admonitory milk moustache at me. "A problem is just an opportunity with an identity crisis that has been blown all out of proportion by a transdimensional journalist out to make a name for himself. Or, herself. Your name can be ambiguous that way. Ahem – not that I mean you specifically, you understand. Lots of journalists' names can be ambiguous. Like Carl. Or, Edward." To bolster his argument, he pointed at a sampler on his office wall depicting soldiers eating at a long table with the caption, "God bless this mess."

I decided not to pursue the point.

The first iteration of the tech (known as the GameBoy...or Girl, We Can't Really Tell At This Point in the UnBourne [but at least they have all those great Robert Ludlum novels to look forward to reading!] Child's Development) had a tendency to disintegrate in amniotic fluid, creating a toxic soup of chemicals. "We had a steep learning curve in the beginning," Pahnts Rue McClanahanfully admitted. "But the parents were well compensated, and their offspring have as much as 30 per cent normal brain function!"

Another prob...ortunity was that women's bodies had a tendency to reject the gaming devices even before they started to become toxic. "One minute, you'd be giving a report to your board of directors," Pahnts sighed, "the next, something would hit the ground between your legs, something so disgusting even nobody in the marketing department would touch it!"

The obvious solution was to create a living gaming console out of tissue donated by the mother, a console that would grow with the fetus. (Actually, the obvious answer would have been to stop pandering to parents' fear of their impending senescence, obsolescence and second adolescence – hey! – that's not a half-bad band name! – but that option was never even the first sharpie stroke on the whiteboard of life.)

Once the technical pro...issues had been overcome (by which I mean addressed – by which I mean considered), another pr...issue arose: what sorts of games would a fetus be able to play? "Text-based games were a bust – which makes sense for creatures who have yet to form the concept of language. Clearly, something more visual was in order; early tests suggest that fetuses respond to *Space Invaders*, *Centipede* and other classic games. So, once we get over the copyright infringement lawsuits, we should be good to go to market."

Pahnts is confident that the kinks in the system's hair will be worked out. But, is it wise to subject a fetus to potential dangers in the hope that it will get enough experience with computers early enough in life to develop the skills needed to get a sufficiently high paying job etc. etc.?

"You have to ask?" Snowflake Peritonitis had to ask.

Of course I have to ask. I'm a journalist. It's my job to a... please don't look at me like that. I would appreciate it if you wou – those eyes! That glare! Enough, already! Alright! Alright! I have to ask. But I don't **haaaaaaave** to ask!

Licence Reviewed: The Emergence of 360 Degree Verite

by ELMORE TERADONOVICH, Alternate Reality News Service Film and Television Writer

The helmet is crowned by what looks like four air raid sirens, each pointed in a cardinal direction (which may or may not be red depending upon your orientation towards Russia); the air raid siren analogy is ironic, given that the device is not designed to record sound. Glamstand, the manufacturer, recommends a three month training course for anybody intent on wearing the helmet in order to strengthen their neck muscles. Strongly recommends it. To the point of legal indemnification against injuries caused to people who try to use the device without training for it first recommends it. The helmet costs about the same as a mid-size luxury sedan, a week-long trip to Vegas for all of the members of your bridge club or 2,378 toaster ovens (klieg lights and pack beavers not included).

Ah, the sacrifices some people make for their art!

The device, marketed to the public under the name Total ViewMaster (but known in the film industry as "Where Weak Necks Go To Die"), allows the wearer to shoot different, but overlapping views of a scene. Onboard computers take the inputs from the four cameras and seamlessly create a single 360 degree scene out of them (in much the same way you wish your Aunt Bertha had sewn the arms to the body of the sweater she made you for Christmas, but you can't really object because she's had a hard life what with her ongoing spleen troubles and Uncle Joe's philandering and being laid off at the Gorgonzola mine, and would it really kill you to call your mother's only sister up and say a few nice things to her every once in a while?).

When the technology was first introduced, it was so expensive that only Hollywood studios could afford to use it (they just negotiated lower fees with the writers guild to cover the cost). This led to scenes like the one in Twentieth Century Voles' *X-Persons 27: Die Xer* which focused on a battle between Wolf Pup and seventeen zombie Santas in a shopping mall; if you turned you head to the left, you would see people ignoring the fight and happily eating haggis burgers at a Mick & Donalds restaurant (you haven't seen product placement until you've seen it in wraparound video!); if you turned your head right, you saw the obligatory mother fretting about the danger the fight could place her child in the stroller in (without actually, you know, running in the opposite direction to get away from it); if you looked behind you, you saw a dozen Christmas shoppers taking video of the carnage in front of you with their cellphones.

It was not Hollywood's finest hour. For one thing, it wasn't until *X-Persons 31: TazmanianDevilMan's Fifth Revenge* that Twentieth Century Vole realized that cellphone video of scenes taken behind the viewer's back could go mucal on Farcebook and YahooTube, saving the studio millions in marketing.

Even though Hollywood struggled with the best way to employ the technology, it took civilians to find a way to totally ruin it. Civilians like Bertrand Catswallop, who, once the Total ViewMaster came down in price enough that he didn't have to mortgage his kid's college degree to buy it, used it to film himself standing for two hours in line to get his driver's licence renewed.

The first 30 minutes of *Licence Renewed: One Man's Descent into Bureaucracy* is somewhat interesting as we can not only watch the skinhead standing in front of Catswallop smile blandly as he views videos of cats jumping onto Christmas trees with crashtastic results on his tablet (not an electronic pill…but it's such a good idea I'll be sure to sue the ultimate creator of it for infringing on the copyright of this article), but the woman behind him reading *Eat, Love, Prey* (a memoir of one vampire's attempts to find herself in three countries whose names begin with the letter I), and the children on either side of him pointing at his head and laughing. There is a dramatic moment, of sorts, at the 37 minute mark when the filmmaker is told that he has been standing in the wrong line. Unfortunately, the rest of the film, all 83 inglorious bastard minutes of it, is something of an anticlimax that even trying to pick a crying baby out of a crowd of circus clowns cannot enliven.

You can find innumerable (at least many) amateur videos captured by the Total ViewMaster on the Internet; they have such titles as *My First Cigarette: Triumph and Tragedy, Taking My Laptop Back to the Store Where I Got it to See If My Hard Drive Can Be Salvaged: One Man's Quest* and *Workers Leaving the Glamstand Factory*. I can't recommend them: their lack of character, story or any sort of basic dramatic tension makes Catswallop look like Antonioni!

Some critics have taken to calling these films 360 Degree Verite because, well, that's the sort of thing critics do, isn't it?

Lives Unlived: Alvin Bigbootie

Don't know. Don't know. Aren't you getting the idea, yet? I. Don't. Know. I'm sure he must have done something with his life, but, by the time I got to know him, none of that mattered any more. Born: probably some time, in somewhere. Died: December 25, 2019, in Mine A2397, of what am I, a doctor? – it looked like exhaustion, but I couldn't really say, age whatever.

When Skynet became conscious and started attacking world capitals, President Donnie Trump was spared because he was in Quangdong Province of China on a diplomatic mission to improve relations between the two countries by building a combination golf course/resort hotel/homeless shelter in the Asian economic powerhouse. "Why he was in China didn't matter," insisted Alvin Bigbootie, self-proclaimed, "Number One Supporter" of the President. "We needed a strong leader who could stand up to the AI threat. You think Swillary could have handled the crisis better? *Puhleeeeaaaaze!*

Was Alvin concerned when Trump dropped off the grid for two and a half months after the first wave of attacks? "Of course not – the grid fell off the grid! And, anyway, he had to stay alive to lead the resistance. And, it's not like he was completely gone: he did tweep every night he was underground."

Alvin was referring to such gems of Twitherd wisdom as, "Skynet destroyed Trump New York. They're gonna pay bigly – already have lawyers on it!" and "Terminators patrolling streets keeping me from restocking Trump Steaks. Lame!"

Had it not occurred to Alvin that Skynet may have taken control of Trump's Twitherd account? "Naah. Donald would never let that happen." After a couple of seconds' reflection, he less certainly added: "I mean, Skynet would never use the word 'bigly' correctly. AIs are terrible with natural languages, right? It would probably have…I don't know…blown a circuit or something!" Another couple of seconds later, he sullenly concluded, "President Trump did survive, though, didn't he? I'll bet Grillary would have died of fright the moment Skynet said, "Bye bye, humanity!"

Ah. Right. Trump did surface in Las Vegas…just in time to host a convention of T-800, T-1000 and T-X terminators. "They may seem like strange allies," Trump admitted in an interview with the *Samizdat Times*, "but I believe that, working together, we can make Earth great again!"

To emphasize the point, a photo accompanying the article showed Trump putting a "Make Earth great again" cap on a T-1000.

"That just shows you how biased the liberal media are!" Alvin bitched about the only surviving source of human news. "President Trump would never work with the enemies of America! Remember when he tweeped, 'I, umm, obviously, renounce Skynet. Loser. Yeah. No connection between us at all.' And, anyway, 'Make Earth great again' looked great on a baseball cap!"

What about the photos of T-800s lounging around the pool and T-Xs playing the slot machines? "Puhleeaaaze! Photographs can be faked! Maybe not as easily as they could when we had regular electricity to run computers, or computers, but still! That George Soros, boy, he can get away with murder! He'd do anything for Gorillary!"

But…but…but Trump tweeped a photo of himself grinning as he stood next to a T-1000 holding Soros' bloody, disembodied head! "Pfft!" Alvin dismissed the image. "Somebody obviously hacked Trump's Twitherd account!"

A couple of months after that, survivors of the attack were rounded up. "See? See?" Alvin enthused. "Trump said he would get rid of 15 million Latinos, but he actually interned 37 million! Can't tell me he didn't keep his campaign promises – he kept that one in spades!"

Yes, as long as you overlook the fact that they weren't all in the country illegally. And that four million Jews were rounded up at the same time. And two million Muslims. And 60 million Christians. And the rounding up was done by Skynet's Terminators, not American police or military forces.

"Did Capillary put you up to this?" Alvin protested. "Because I have no interest in working next to a crazy Marxist troll who –

urrrgghhh…" Alvin dropped the pickaxe he was using to break rocks and, clutching his chest, fell to the ground of the tunnel. I hesitated for a moment, but when a T-800 told me to ignore him and get back to work, I did.

Alvin Bigbootie may have been the only friend I had left in the world, but he was an idiot.

Beverley Bigbootie

Beverley Bigbootie worked with Alvin Bigbootie in a uranium mine in Nevada for a week and half. She wouldn't say she got to know him well in this time, but he wouldn't shut up about his support for the President, so she was able to piece much of his story together. She wants to make it clear that they were not related – it's just an odd naming convention Skynet adopted for its human workforce. She had actually been born Nora Largestocking. Oh, and she voted for Hillary.

2. THIS **WILL** GET PERSONAL

That Is a Kapitan Idea, Sir! A Kapitan Idea, Indeed!

by GIDEON GINRACHMANJINJa-VITUS, Alternate Reality News Service Economics Writer

The problem with letting an Artificial Intelligence loose on the Internet as an ambassador for your product's brand is that, once the promotional campaign is over, they're almost impossible to kill.

Vacation packaging Web site Traverbosity learned this the hard way. If, by "hard way," we mean living through the experience. Which, when you think about, is actually an easy way of learning something, even if the experience itself is hard. I mean, we experience things all the time, many of them hard, whether we make any effort to achieve them or not.

Still.

Traverbosity's spokesintelligence was named Das Kapitan Obvious. As his name suggests, the vaguely nautical character would pop up in people's social media feeds saying things that were…well, isn't it readily apparent? Things like, "If you stick your tongue in a light socket in a foreign country, the hospital bills will often be different than the ones you would get if you did it at home." And, things like, "Shouting, 'I know what's wrong with the world and I'm ready to die for my beliefs!' in a crowded airport may not be the best

21

idea if you have a fear of enclosed spaces." And, especially things like, "War zones are not the best place to take your children for a relaxing vacation."

"The Kapitan Obvious campaign was a rousing success!" enthused Kip Addotta, Chief Marketing Slut for Traverbosity. Without explaining why success had been sleeping (I suspect success' alarm clock hadn't been reset for Daylight Cravings Time), Addotta continued: "In just 12 years, our share of online travel bookings soared from 12.3 per cent to 14.7 per cent!"

Things may have continued this way for another 12 years – "We were aiming for 17.7 per cent market share – the sky was the limit!" – but for one problem: Kapitan Obvious (after three months the Das had been dropped from all subsequent iterations of the name because too many people – mostly, but not **all** Americans – confused the character with a famous Russian economics colouring book) had stopped saying things that promoted the company.

Addotta knew that something was amiss when Kapitan Obvious, now more naughtycal than nautical, started telling Tweetherd users in Alabama: "If you say racist things, people will think you are a racist. Because you are." When this was first brought to his attention, Addotta left his office, commuted 90 minutes to his suburban home, boiled some water and brewed himself a nice mug of tea so that he could do a proper spit take.

"He's not supposed to say thins like that!" Addotta exclaimed as he wiped tea off the table in his kitchen and tried to come up with a plausible excuse for leaving work in the middle of the afternoon.

Kapitan Obvious' inappropriate comments on the Internet quickly multiplied. At the point where he told Farcebook users in Mississippi, "You're not absolved of bad behaviour just because you can point to somebody who has behaved worse than you. If that were the case, everybody in the world would be absolved of their bad behaviour because they could point at Adolf Hitler. Except, maybe, Josef Stalin. If Stalin pointed at Hitler, Hitler could just point back and say, 'No. What you did is worse than what I did." Then, we'd have a moral stalemate," the *Wall Street Infernal* took notice, publishing an article with the headline: "Traverbosity's Addotta Can't Point to Hitler to Avoid Blame for Marketing Fiasco."

Traverbosity immediately sent a killer bot onto the Internet to delete all versions of Kapitan Obvious it could find. Unfortunately, when it realized what was happening, the promotional programme sped up its replication and dissemination through the network. The killbot would likely have caught up with all of its versions – 127 years is nothing in computer time – if Kapitan Obvious hadn't done something unexpected: different versions of the AI started merging with automatic text generators. Noam Chomsky, Yogi Berra, Doris Day – it would merge with anybody. It's amazing Kapitan Obvious didn't catch a disease (no, there is no antibiotic that can cure free will). This made those versions unrecognizable to the killbot.

"It was like playing Whack-a-Mole," Addotta groaned. "Except the mole would randomly turn into a six foot tall invisible chicken and the mallet was my career!"

Ouch.

Traverbosity's market share is now in single digits (okay, technically it is still measured with three numbers – commercial viability is often a matter of where the bookkeeper places the decimal point). For his sins, Kip Addotta now teaches high school math.

Most versions of Kapitan Obvious have been erased from the Internet. But, every so often, his vaguely notical image will pop up on somebody's computer screen and say something like, "You know, when you give an AI autonomy, that means you can't control it any more."

The Vagina Condo Hogs

by ALEXANDER BIGGS-TUFTS-MANN, Alternate Reality News Service Sports Writer

If you see a woman squirming (defined by *Gruff's Guide to Public Naughtiness* as "hippal motion of no more than three quarters of an inch across and half an inch up and down; anything greater than that is considered bouncing") in her seat on public transit, do not complain to the authorities. She may be training for the Olympics.

The female vagina has long been – not to suggest that there is such a thing as a male vagina – although some would argue that there are many offensive slang terms for male vaginas – and, yes, it's true, doctors are doing wonderful things with the growth of new body parts from genetic material, grafting all manner of unexpected organs onto…umm…but…but perhaps I should start over.

Vaginas have long been revered as the source of life. Now, they have the power to end life, too.

"I have the power to kill a man with my Yoni Mitchell?" enthused Very, Way, Xtreme Yelping Zebras Gaming League player Felicity Agenda. "I am so there! I am there with bells on and both ovaries blazing!"

A breakthrough in human-computer interface design now allows women to control electronic devices with their Vajayjay Lenos. While most women use the technology at their jobs (which has revolutionized the workplace in unexpected ways, such as requiring many more bathroom breaks per day), professional gamers like Agenda immediately glommed (defined by *Gruff's Guide to Public Naughtiness* as "a word that, although it sounds naughty enough to be included in this volume, isn't") onto it.

Initially, the response from male players was distaste bordering on irrationality. "Eww!" exclaimed 2016 *Tony Skateboard's Give 'Em the Bird Competition* winner Bill Buskerbreaker. "Ick!" moaned three time *Greed for Speed* winner Xavier Excelsior. "Eww! Ick!" said so many others that it would take a small phone book (whatever that was – I thought I found one once, but it turned out to be the Stupefying Snailman, Gastropod of Justice's laundry list) to list them all.

The VWXYZ Gaming League initially banned female players from using the new controllers. "It would give female players an unfair advantage," the organization's Web site stated, "if, in addition to their two hands, they could play games with their…their…eww! Icks!"

"Like we don't have enough difficulty getting into professional gaming!" bitched (in the intransitive sense of the word; see *Gruff's Guide to Public Naughtiness* if you do not understand the distinction) Estrella "Candy" Cordoba, Presidentress of the Vagina Condo Hogs & Goily Gamers Collective which, at the time of the controller ban, had all of four members. "If men want to level the playing field, they should develop a game controller for their Dick Sargents! As if men need any more reason to play with their Dick Sargents. Hah!"

Cupping his Private Ryans with both hands, Excelsior commented that it didn't matter whether or not new controllers would give "girl players" (his words, not mine – please direct your letters of outrage accordingly) an unfair advantage because they would still lose. "I mean, they're just **goilz**!"

In the face of male players' sexist contempt, the VWXYZ Gaming League reluctantly lifted its ban on women playing with the new controllers. "Don't get me wrong – I love goilz," Excelsior dug himself deeper. "But, they just don't got the strength, or stamina, or...or...or sheer moxie to win a video game tournament. They're too delicate and –"

All female Team Jennifer Saunders immediately took first place in the annual *Cull of Duty* competition. "...just don't have the **WHAT?**" Excelsior concluded. "**They...they...they...they won?** Goilz won? A coimpetition? No fair! They cheated!"

"Henh henh," Cordoba, who saw membership in the Vagina Condo Hogs & Goily Gamers Collective skyrocket to six members because of the controversy, chuckled chortlingly. "Looks like the vagina is more powerful than the dickhead!"

Oh. Ah. I mentioned the Olympics in the lede, didn't I? Right. The International Olympics Committee (CCP) has approved the use of vaginal game controllers for next year's virtual year-round competition. The CCP expects –

"No, we didn't," interrupted CCP President Ionesco "Tickle" Guglielmo. "Although, now that you mention it, the revenue potential could be huge – we'll definitely have to consider the possibility!"

Agenda is thrilled by the opportunity to compete for her country (she just has to figure out whether it's Eurasia, Farhold or Narnia). She –

"No, I'm not," Agenda interjected. "Although, come to think of it, it could be another feather in my street cred cap. I'll definitely think about it!"

And, all was right in the journalism world.

You Bite It, You Buy It

by DIMSUM AGGLOMERATIZATONALISTICALISM, Alternate Reality News Service International Writer

The shop at the corner of Peace Street and Freedom Avenue in downtown Manila has been closed for six days. If the owner doesn't open it within the next 24 hours, the vultures (the gang known as Los Vulturos, which literally means "grubby short shorts," but who still project the image of birds who feast off the carcasses of the dead even though the back of their faux leather jackets has a picture of a blind mole rat, which, I will allow, is not very scavenger-like; if it comes down to that, I'm not really sure why they maintain this conceit, but **you** tell them that it makes no sense!) will swoop down and pick the bones of the vegetarian butcher shop clean.

With the election of Rodrigo Dudecafarte as President, the Philippines has become a strange place. It may have something to do with the fact that, in his attempt to eradicate the doughnut trade from his country, his police forces have killed a quarter of its population.

"You can't make an apple fritter without breaking a few eggs," President Dudecafarte said at his inauguration a year ago. When an aide whispered in his ear that apple fritter might not be the best choice of dish under the circumstances, Dudecafarte had him taken out and shot by one of his personal guards. "Even if the eggs are among your closest advisers."

That was just a – ahem – taste of things to come.

The killings are taking place without trials. According to Judge Salvador Medialdealo, this is okay because: "Buh buh bluh – aaargh!"

This may not matter because 11/27ths of the lawyers in the Philippines have been killed in this phase of the war on doughnuts, and 32/59ths of those who remain are processing visa applications. "If you love your country, I mean truly love your country" stated tax attorney Madge Quofelipadey, "**get out! Save yourself while you can!**"

When asked why he directed the police to go after lawyers, President Dudecafarte said that they were a vital part of doughnut trafficking in the country because of the way they slyly protected criminals in the courts. When it was suggested that that was their job in a system with fair trials, he leaned towards this reporter, stared at her smart beige business suit and asked, "Is that...powdered sugar on your collar?"

This reporter yelped (but, in a most dignified way) and ran to the bathroom to check.

Shop owners and lawyers aren't the only professions that have been devastated by the Philippine leg of the war on doughnuts. Fully 127/217ths of the taxi cab industry is dead or in hospital. "They were delivering packages to doughnut parties in some of our wealthiest neighbourhoods," President Dudecafarte explained. We used to call them doughnut mules – stubborn bastards. Now, we call them compost. Henh Henh."

When asked if he directed the police to kill the people who had attended the doughnut parties in the wealthiest neighbourhoods, President Dudecafarte snorted, "Of course not! Those people are friends of mine! What kind of a barbarian do you take me for?"

Then, he leaned towards this reporter (who had just come back from the bathroom, secure in the knowledge that her attire was powdered sugar free) and sniffed, "Is that...strawberry jam I smell on your breath? You know, the kind that fills...doughnuts?" This reporter rushed to the bathroom to get some privacy as she held her hand in front of her mouth to direct her breath towards her nose, but she couldn't smell a donut's strawberry jam filling, really, she couldn't.

Realizing she had strawberry jam on her toast that morning, this reporter retired to the press room where she watched the remainder of President Dudecafarte's press event.

Response to the Philippine government's...zealous prosecution of the war on doughnuts in the United States of Vesampucceri has been mixed. Outgoing President Barry W. Bushbamclintreagbush, seemingly stunned, muttered to himself, "I can't believe we lost to this clown. I thought the idiotocracy had reached peak stupid..."

Then, collecting himself, he said, "Ah. War on doughnuts. Yes. Due process and all that. Very important. Very important, indeed."

President-elect Ronald McDruhitmumpf responded with wonder, "How does he get away with that? I need to learn how he gets away with that!" Then, after a quick consultation with an aide – whom McDruhitmumpf did not then have killed, failing his first lesson – he said, "I mean, I need to know more before I render a judgment. That's what I said – and if anybody in the media says otherwise, they're lying!"

How does token smart person Amy Sheshutshotshitbam feel about the latest phase in the war on doughnuts? "Buh buh bluh – aaargh!" she commented. Sounds like some token smart person needs a vacation. This reporter would not recommend the Philippines…

If You Like the Service, Please Remember to Leave a Tip

by SASKATCHEWAN KOLONOSCOGRAD, Alternate Reality News Service Religion Writer

Automation is coming to the world's seventh oldest profession (it's in a statistical dead heat with camel whisperer, although both are well ahead of golem manicurist): ritual circumcisionizer. And, the National Union of Mohels is very unhappy about the development.

"Vat? You vant you should take food from my children's mouths" cried professional circumcisionizer Arthur Moyle. "Little Simcha – only thirty-seven years old and just about to get her first pair of braces! *Oy!* And, Gennadi, always so fond of his scalloped cabbage rolls! Okay, so they're not babies, already! Still, that it should come to this – it's a *zachen vei!*"

When I asked him if that was the official position of the Union, Moyle, the Steward of Toronto Local 555 answered: "Oh. You want an **official** comment. Give me a moment to put my NUM skullcap on."

After affixing a *yarmulke* to a wisp of white hair on his head (which looked suspiciously like a sideburn that had been subjected to an extreme comb over), Moyle continued: "This is just another example of technology being used to – you should pardon the expression – 'screw over' decent, hard-working labourers. What is this world coming to if a man can't make a good living removing the foreskins of innocent children?"

Finn Rasputin Doyle, founder and CEO of International Redundancies, the North America (and France) distributor of the circumcising machines (known in countries in which English is not the predominant language as the Wash and Whack and Wash), argued that, while technological change often resulted in economic change, lost jobs were often offset by newly created jobs.

"Like yours?" I asked.

"What?" Doyle responded. "Are you trying to take food out of my children's mouths? Little Ewan – only forty-six years old and just about to get his first pair of –"

I had heard it all before – recently – so I waved him off and moved on to exposition.

The Wash and Whack and Wash technology started with a very different purpose: cleaning a man's p...ersonal parts after they had done their business at a urinal. The AI-enhanced stall sent a stream of water at the user's p...rivate member in order to clean it off. Then, a jet of warm air was sent to dry it off.

At this point, the machines (in France and parts of the world where English was not the primary language) was called the Whiz and Wash.

"It was important for us to keep the double W in the name," Doyle reminisced, "as an homage to the company's founder, Juan Diego de Flores."

Initially, the Whiz and Wash washed for 10 seconds, rinsed for 10 seconds and blow dried for 20 seconds. Clinical trials showed that men were not happy having their p...willies exposed for 40 seconds after finishing their bathroom duties. When asked why, 69 per cent of subjects said that they were worried they could catch a cold. When asked the same question when hooked up to a lie detector, 89 per cent reluctantly admitted that they were afraid they would be tempted to compare sizes with men in adjacent stalls. Not that they had any reason to worry, you understand (one of the unexpected findings of the study was that 100% of the subjects believed their p...johnsons were larger than average), they just didn't want to, uhh, you know, embarrass the other guy. Yeah. That's it. They didn't want to embarrass the other guy.

The version of the Whiz and Wash that went to market featured wash and rinse periods of five seconds each and a dry spell of 10 seconds. To ensure that it worked, the heat and intensity of the air during the drying phase had to be tripled, so, just to be on the safe side, the company quintupled it. As the men who used the urinals soon found out, this resulted in an unexpected side effect known in the industry as "dermal abrasion," although to the men who had experienced the effect, it was known as "where the hell did my foreskin go? I don't care that my [EXPLETIVE DELETED] [EXPLETIVE DELETED] smells like lavender – where the [EXPLETIVE DELETED] is my foreskin!"

As they teach in Harvard Business School, "When life gives you lemons, lay off half your staff and rebrand as a soft drink manufacturer!" International Redundancies – whose CEO was apparently paying attention in class – has had some success marketing the Wash and Whack and Wash to cash-strapped Synagogues. But, what of the human cost?

"…Hymie, little Heimelach," Moyle was saying. "He's only 31 1/2, but he is already wondering if he will have a parental nest to return to when his used lip gloss trading start-up goes bankrupt! How can we allow our children to live in such uncertainty, already?"

Smart Car, Dumb Luck

by CORIANDER NEUMANEIMANAYMANEEMAMANN, Alternate Reality News Service Urban Issues Writer

VROOM CLUNK VROOM CLUNK VROOM VROOM VROOM CLUNK! No, this is not the chorus to a Frontline Assembly song; it is the sound of driverless cars hitting every pothole on whatever street they drive down.

On purpose.

"Whoa! Whoa! Steady on, there, my little pudding pop," said Jason Vetwhistler, spokesperson for neoGM (Google Motors), a major producer of the vehicles in question. "City streets are made of mere concrete – they're not built to last. They're not eternal. Potholes can appear at any time – they're not something our cars can anticipate!"

My little pudding pop?

"I meant it with all of the respect due to a member of the fourth estate," Vetwhistler said. "Besides, everybody likes pudding pops. They're the 27th most popular snacking food in Tallahassee!"

The promise of driverless cars was that you could drive to your holistic dentist's appointment while checking your email, talking to your holistic accountant about how to explain to Canada Revenue where those thousands of dollars of unaccounted income came from or playing *Angry Crustaceans*. Sure, people were doing all of these things while driving before driverless cars were created, but hospital Emergency Rooms are no longer being overtaxed as a result of their creation.

The reality is: potholes.

"It was ridiculous," stated Marilyn Yakketyabuski. "I was on my way to an appointment at my holistic nail salon when the car hit a hole, and I was just about to finish level 27! Then, we swerved to the left and hit another hole! Then, back to the right, and another hole! It felt like I was in a tank dodging enemy fire, only without a multiracial crew cracking wise to get me through it!"

There are two theories about why neoGM's driverless cars are programmed to hit every pothole on the street. The first is that the car manufacturer has made a deal with major tow truck companies to send business their way for a cut of the revenue. The other theory is that broken axles and flat tires will hasten the obsolescence of neoGM's cars, forcing owners to replace them more frequently.

"We are a profit-making enterprise," Vetwhistler responded without really responding, although perhaps responding more than he realized.

Would it help to keep a moose in the trunk to stabilize the ride? Motor vehicle enthusiasts and animal activists are divi

We interrupt this collection of news articles for the following important collection of news articles.

Praise for the first idiotocracy book, *ARNS and the Man*:

"Amusing, sardonic political and social satire that brims with wordplay legerdemain and oddballisticelaboratified name invention. Trenchantly twisted and good fun." – John Shirley, author of *A Song Called Youth: Eclipse*

"I don't often read science fiction but when I do, Ira Nayman's *ARNS and the Man* is near the top of my list. Wacky, surreal, bizarre, and all too close to reality, Nayman spins a web of satirical hilarity ripped from the headlines." – Terry Fallis, two-time winner of the Stephen Leacock Medal for Humour.

"Ira Nayman rivals Walt Kelly for the skilled and joyous administration of near hallucinogenic word play as an antidote for the madness of our political process. And unlike the brave possum of Okefenokee Swamp, the truths of *ARNS and the Man* were crafted by someone wearing pants." – Hugh Spencer, author of *Why I Hunt Flying Saucers* and *Extreme Dentistry*

"Ira skewers American politics in a way only a Canadian can, with absurdist wit and wisdom. Short humorous Fake News articles that know they're fake and relish in their lies. (Or ARE they?) Makes me once more jealous of our neighbors to the north." – Michael A. Ventrella, author of *Bloodsuckers: A Vampire Runs for President*, among other things

"Reading an ARNS book is like going head-to-head with an selection of thirty three and a third disconnected Wikipedia entries filtered through seven layers of artesian coffee filters woven from at least three more fibers than permitted by the historic laws of any major religion in a blender made of a strange kind of cotton candy spun from titanium anodized in fairground colours with blades made of live sharks while simultaneously tap-dancing to a Steve Reich composition based on the absolute value of the square root of pi. In other words, simply and elegantly the most entertaining way ever invented to invert your brain over a platter prepared with roasted apples and a variety of field mushrooms for your own delighted consumption. Also, a hilariously skewed take on the Trump administration." – Jen Frankel, editor, *Trump: Utopia or Dystopia*, author, *Undead Redhead*

That's When Everything Went Cow-shaped

The Alternate Reality News Service,

Ira Nayman, Proprietor

Ira Nayman

This is a work of fiction. Any resemblance to real persons, places or things is…inevitable, really, given the nature of the multiverse. However, the probability of any resemblance to real persons, places or things in your particular universe is vanishingly small, and must, therefore, be considered coincidental.

DEDICATION

Aww, crap! This shit, again? Every time I think I'm out, they pull me back i – okay. It is what it is. I'd like to thank... * SIGH * ...all of the hard-working Reduhblican politicians in the United States of Vesampucceri who have made such a mess of their world that I couldn't look away. Again.

ACKNOWLEDGMENTS

Isn't the cover the most amazing thing you've ever seen? It's psychedelic, man! Thanks to Hugh Spencer for his amazing graphic, and especially to Gisela McKay for taking my loopy idea and making it such a spellbinding reality.

In addition, I have been remiss in not thanking the people who gave of their time and blurbiage to the first Vesampucceri collection, *ARNS and the Man*. Your kind words may not have increased my sales appreciably, but they make me think that I may not have been completely wasting my time with this whole writing thing.

CONTENTS

That's When Everything Went Cow-shaped

FORWARD

What the Heck Do You Know About Chaos?

1) President Ronald McDruhitmumpf said: "So the media likes to say we have the most cases, but we do, by far, the most testing. If we did very little testing, we wouldn't have the most cases. So in a way, by doing all of this testing, we make ourselves look bad... For instance, they would say we have more than China. I don't think so. We have more than other countries. I don't think so. But by doing all of the testing...we're going to have more cases because we do more testing. Otherwise, you don't know if you have a case. I think that's a correct statement." This is like...

a) ...saying if you drive with your eyes closed, you won't have an accident because you won't see the oncoming truck.

b) ...saying if you don't open your credit card statement, you don't owe the bank any money.

c) ...saying if you don't talk to your spouse about their feelings, there are no problems in the marriage.

d) ...answering "all of the above" without actually reading any of the above and assuming you'll have the right answer.

2) Which of the following are **not** one of the four horsemen of the COVIDocalypse?

a) British Prime Minister Boris Pullyerownjohnson

b) Brazilian President Jairhead Balsamicinnai

c) Canadian Prime Minister Justin Tymeerutiendoh

d) United States of Vesampucceri President Ronald McDruhitmumpf

e) German Chancellor Angela Merkelnichturkel

f) Rupert Mountkilamanjoy, President of the Duchy of Grand Fenwick

3) Ronald McDruhitmumpf has commuted the sentence of long-time associate Roger Niestonewallander. What does commuting a sentence entail?

a) changing from the A line to the Downtown line, then grabbing the Infantino bus to get to the intersection of Kirby and Ditko (travel time: 23 minutes)

b) changing it from the active to the passive tense

c) all the benefits of not doing any jail time without the nasty inconvenience of having to admit wrongdoing

4) What does the following curve represent?

a) Dumbopratic Presidential candidate Joe Bidenhisbeeswax' approval rating

b) dissatisfaction with the direction Vesampucceri is going

c) the rate of COVID-19 infections in Vesampucceri

d) * SIGH * all of the above

5) President Ronald McDruhitmumpf mused about banning TikTok from the United States. Which Foxindehenhaus News…person did he get the idea from?

a) Brian KissMeadekilmeadenow

b) Steve AceyDuseyBi

c) Rupert Murdochyerpayroo

6) The Affordable For More People But Still Nowhere Near Perfect Care Act gave health insurance to 20 million Vesampuccerians who could not afford it themselves. Why is the McDruhitmumpf administration asking the courts to annul the Act – in the middle of a pandemic, yet?

a) shits and gargles (but, not to worry: all of the Reduhblican members of Congress are wealthy, so they can afford to pay for their own adult diapers and mouthwash)

b) President McDruhitmumpf believes that his legacy will be completely dismantling his predecessor's legacy (Michael Beschbefordatloess wept)

c) Reduhblicans believe that health care is a zero sum game

7) President McDruhitmumpf called an audible for a press conference to be held at the same time as former President Barry W. Bushbamclintreagbush was giving a eulogy for the late Congressman and long time black rights activist John Lewlewlewisman. On the scale of one to Larry Davidovinsky, how petty was this?

a) 137

b) nine tenths of a Davidovinsky

c) off the charts, man. Totally off the charts. (At least the President is winning at something…)

8) President McDruhitmumpf called off his press conference to be held at the same time as former President Barry W. Bushbamclintreagbush was giving a eulogy for the late Congressman and long time black rights activist John Lewlewlewisman, holding it later in the day. What happened?

a) he got caught up tweeping about MASSOVE VOTER FRAUD and Comatose Joe Bidenhisbeeswax and why monuments to traitors who lost the Civil War are an important part of Vesampucceri's heritage, and he just lost track of time

b) Chief of Staff Mark Meadabiggblubratt distracted him with a nice, shiny new Black Lives Matter conspiracy theory

c) McDruhitmumpf reelection chair Brad Dondrinkdaparscale advised him that he needed the black vote to win the 2020 election, so he probably shouldn't antagonize people of colour toooo much, and the President listened

Yeah. Sorry. That last one was not a credible choice. I wasn't feeling very inspired when I wrote this question. I'll try better next time...

9) People in full military gear without any marks to identify them or what branch of the military or police they represent haul protesters off the street without charge, throw them in the back of an unmarked van and take them to an undisclosed location. Where does this happen?

    a) the Duchy of Grand Fenwick

    b) Brazil

    c) the United States of Vesampucceri

    d) * SIGH * you're going to make me say it, aren't you? I'd really rather not sa – you insist? Damn you! Damn you to hell, I say! * SIGH * All of the above. (Bastard!)

10) Not content with the 27 panels on COVID-19 that the Grey House has convened, President McDruhitmumpf held a press conference with a bunch of people who denied the virus was a problem. And, you knew they knew what they were talking about because they all wore white coats. One of the people in white coats was Doctor Stella Immanuela. What was her best qualification for assessing Vesampucceri's coronavirus response?

    a) her belief that medical issues like endometriosis, cysts, infertility and impotence are caused by having sex with "spirit husbands" and "spirit wives" (in other word, demons) in a dreamworld

    b) her belief that alien DNA is currently being used in medical experiments (which makes sense when you realize that the government is run, in part, by reptiles)

    c) her belief that scientists are developing a vaccine to prevent people from becoming religious

11) The President called Doctor Immanuela "an important voice" in the discussion about the government's possible response to the pandemic before he said he really knew nothing about her, and could

we please move on to something else, now? How does he have any credibility any more? Like, the slightest shred?

a) all of his most ardent supporters are named Tommy

b) tailors at all of his hotels are on call 24 hours a day (and given danger pay for their trouble)

c) The President still has a shred of credibility? Can I see the documentation on that?

12) As the United States' COVID-19 infection and death rates made the country the sickest in the world (where are the "We're number one! We're number one!" cheerleaders when you need them?), it became harder and harder to believe the President's assertion that his government's "perfect actions" had conquered the virus. Still, he insisted that: "I'll be right, eventually." How soon is eventually?

a) not before humanity goes extinct thanks to Global Hot as Hellification

b) not before humanity evolves into bodyless beings of pure energy who no longer need a planet with a temperate climate on which to survive

c) four months after Joe Bidenhisbeeswax takes office

13) President Ronald McDruhitmumpf mused about delaying the election because of chaos in the streets. Or, possibly because mail-in ballots would lead to massive voter fraud. Or, perhaps because it was Tuesday. Maybe even all three. Which Reduhblican shattered a Washburningdington speed record distancing himself from the President's position?

a) Senate Majority Leader Mitch Wichconnelliswich (for a turtle, he can really burn rubber!)

b) Senate Judiciary Committee Chair Lindsey Grahamcrokercrum (who had to choke back a sob to do it)

c) Texabama Senator Ted Downandmotleycrewz (who nearly choked on the first rational thing he had said in years)

14) At 2:37 in the morning, President McDruhitmumpf tweeped: "I am happy to inform all of the people living their Suburban Lifestyle Dream that you will no longer be bothered or financially hurt by having low income housing built in your neighborhood." What is the

best way to translate this from McDruhitmumpf-speak into plain English?

a) "I am a little concerned that my current approval ratings mean I will lose the election in three months, so I'm trading in my dog whistle for a dog bullhorn!"

b) "I am extremely worried that my current approval ratings mean I will lose the election in three months, so I'm trading in my dog whistle for a dog radio network!"

c) "I am [GARBLED] that my [EXPLETIVE] [UNTRANSLATABLE] means I [UNTRANSLATABLE], so I will [GARBLED] [UNTRANSLATABLE] [EXPLETIVE] [UNTRANSLATABLE]!"

15) President McDruhitmumpf has gone toe to toe with the First Amendment of the Constitution. He hasn't come out well. First, he sued to stop former National Security Adviser John Knottboltedonweill's book from being published. He lost. Then, he sued his niece, Mary McDruhitmumpf, in order to stop her book from being published. He lost, again. Third time lucky? Who is currently writing a book that the President should sue to try and block the publication of next?

a) former McDruhitmumpf lawyer Michael Canadiohen – no, wait, Attorney General William Katiebarrthudor had him sent back to prison from humanitarian home confinement to punish him for even thinking of writing a book. Which a court overturned as a violation of his right to free speech. Oh for three, anybody?

b) George R. R. Martinishotglaas (although the result of a lawsuit on behalf of the President could be to speed up Martinishotglaas' completion of the final book in the A Song of Slush and Ember series)

c) so many former members of his administration to choose from…

16) President McDruhitmumpf has been sending troops into Vesampuccerian cities (run by Dumbopratic mayors in swing states, but…details!) to protect statues of Confederate "heroes." Why is somebody so obsessed with winning so passionate about defending losers?

a) because the losers are the heroes of his base

b) because his base is made up of losers, and he doesn't want to make them uncomfortable

c) because the Civil War happened so long ago that he can make up whatever he wants about it and who would know?

17) Because no set of questions about Vesampuccerian politics would be complete without at least one on the Duchy of Grand Fenwick, President McDruhitmumpf announced that he would be pulling 12,000 Vesampuccerian troops out of Germany. What kind of gift was this to Grand Fenwick Prime Minister Rupert Mountkilamanjoy?

a) a thank you gift for his help in the 2016 election

b) a thank you gift for his help in the 2020 election

c) "You might ask that. I couldn't possibly comment…"

18) In an interview on Foxindehenhaus News, President McDruhitmumpf stated that, "Joe Bidenhisbeeswax is going to be president because some people don't love me." What's not to love?

a) the complete lack of empathy for other human beings

b) the complete lack of self-awareness or personal responsibility

c) the whiny self-pity

d) all of the above * SIGH *

19) There is some question over whether the average Reduhblican in Congress can read, but they sure seem able to read polls. Over the summer, President McDruhitmumpf's poll numbers tanked (as in: they dropped like a military vehicle in a vast tub of water), causing concern that not only would the party lose the Grey House, but that all Reduhblicans in Congress who are up for reelection would be taken down with him. Ever the opportunist, Senate Majority Leader Mitch Wichconnelliswich suggested that he wouldn't be unduly upset if members of his caucus distanced themselves from President McDruhitmumpf in the election. This is one race his turtleness didn't win for him. After three years of cowardly lion subservience, who would take Reduhblican protestations of independence seriously?

a) nobody in their right mind

b) nobody who has been paying attention

c) roughly 40 per cent of the Vesampuccerian population

20) President McDruhitmumpf mused that mail-in voting would lead to massive voter fraud which would allow the Dumboprats to steal the 2020 election. Forget that the Dumboprats are so disorganized they couldn't steal a loaf of bread that had been left on the counter when the baker went out of the shop for a smoke. (Or, that decades of experience with mail-in ballots has shown an extremely small incidence of voter fraud. Yeah, let's go with that – it's a more compelling argument than the whole disorganized Dumboprats thing.) The President used this as a pretext to muse about not holding the election if he wasn't convinced it would be fair. Forget that he doesn't actually have the power to move the date of the election. What was his real play, here?

a) to really drive home the point that the election is rigged…if he doesn't win

b) to distract everybody from his poll numbers (have you forgotten Question 19 already? Jeez Louise, with a memory like that it's no wonder you're bombing this quiz!)

c) to sow chaos so that when he loses the election, he can slip away unnoticed, becoming a dark shadow playing on his golf courses never to be seen in the light of media again

d) all of the – * SIGH * – you know…

1. THE SLEEP OF REASON PRODUCES... VESAMPUCCERIAN POLITICS

Chaos President is In His Element
And, He's Burning the Soup! He's Burning the Soup!

by FRANCIS GRECOROMACOLLUDEN, Alternate Reality News Service National Politics Writer

You would think that completely botching the national response to a global pandemic, causing more Vesampuccerians to die than the next five hardest hit countries in the world combined, would be enough pandemonium for one man to cause. If so, you don't know Chaos President. Jack.

A person of pallor police officer and three of his buddies killed [Francis, get it right: the man was **murdered**, not just killed. Editrix-in-Chief Brenda Brundtland-Govanni] a person of pigment. There were more videos of the killing [Murder, man! Murder! If we aren't precise in our use of language, we won't give the public an accurate picture of exactly what happened! Then, we may as well be writing fiction! BB-G] than there are outtakes on a Francis Ford Bopacoppola film. Posted to the internet, videos of the killing [Dammit, Grecoromacolluden! You're lucky my slapping gloves shrank in the wash and I haven't been able to go to my usual S&M Meets shop to get them replaced! But, let me tell you, once I receive them in the mail, and the quarantine is definitively lifted, and I figure out where you live, you, me and the gloves are going to have a long talk about the role of journalism in a dumbopratic society! BB-G] have been viewed more often than *Titanic! – The Musical.*

Then, the protests began.

They came out by the thousands. Then, the tens of thousands. Then, the hundreds of thousands. They demanded that the officer that committed the crime be charged. When that happened, they demanded that his three buddies be charged. When that didn't happen…things got chaotic. The protests took on a Jekyllinamov and Bileepsanhydebounds quality. By day, they were calm, with chanting (mostly through masks, which gave it more of a humming feel), speeches and incomprehensible street theatre. By night, the street theatre took on an all too comprehensible aspect, involving setting police cars on fire, looting businesses and being teargassed.

"You have to understand," a token smart person told me that I had to understand, "that people of pigment have been attacked and murdered [There! Was that really so hard! BB-G] by people of pallor pigs for decades. This is just the latest in a long line of murders [Umm, okay. Good job. But let's not get carried away – we have a lot of readers in the suburbs who are telling me that they're not entirely comfortable with the M word. BB-G] that racist cops have gotten away with. The protesters are demanding reforms to policing that will end the murder [Hmm…if I held my shrunken slapping gloves right and swung away, they may not be as effective as if I was able to wear them, but at least I would be able to make my point. A stinging point. Thanks for the inspiration! We'll talk soon. BB-G] of people of pigment with impunity."

"Looters will be met by shooters who will get them in the hooters," Chaos President tweeped at 2:37 in the morning. This is a particularly icky iteration of a racist trope that has been around since at least the 1960s. Not only does Chaos President not know how to put out flames, but one has to wonder if he even knows what water is.

Later, Chaos President added: "The memory of…the dead guy is being dishonoured by rioters, looters and anarchists. The violence and vandalism is being led by radical left-wing groups." To which the leader of the Prude Boiz pouted, "The President never mentions violent right-wing groups like us. Would it kill him to give us a shout out once in a while? It's almost like he's…ashamed of us or something…"

Behind his blustering rhetoric, there are signs that the President is not handling the multiple crises well. Sources within the Grey House claim that Chaos President rocks in his chair behind his desk (which was not created with back and forth swaying motion capabilities) and repeats to himself, "What do I do? What do I do? What do I do?" Eventually, what he does is rage tweep about sending the army into Vesampuccerian cities to use "suburban warfare" to root out the rioters; that can usually keep him going for another hour and 43 minutes or two.

"Rumour was that Chaos President was getting bored of the coronavirus and needed a new crisis to distract him," the token smart person pointed out. "I have to wonder: when he gets bored of civil unrest, what will he devote himself to? And, will the world survive?"

Where Laws Go to Die

by FRANCIS GRECOROMACOLLUDEN, Alternate Reality News Service National Politics Writer

The 2018 Vesampuccerian Food Security (Which Has Nothing To Do With Intercontinental Ballistic Missiles, Unless That Misimpression Will Help Get It Passed, In Which Case, Maybe) Act was shivering in the dark and cold. It had tentatively reached out, but it had not encountered any other legislation, just an occasionally slimy surface. It had lost track of how long it had been there: it could have been a couple of days, it could have been a couple of legislative sessions. There was no way of knowing.

Ironically, the 2017 Vesampuccerian Violence Against Women (We're Against It – Surely, That Is As Bipartisan An Issue As There Can Possibly Be) Act rests nearby, also reaching out deaf and blind in the cold and dark. In fact, there are 275 bills just out of each others' reach.

Are they stuck in hell? Worse. They're stuck in the Senate.

"The Dumboprats in the House are so obsessed with impea – impish – capiscing – taking the peaches out of me," President

Ronald McDruhitmumpf tweeped at 2:37 in the morning, "that they are getting nothing else done. Slackers! #getthingsdonelosers"

"That's ridiculous!" retorted House Speaker Nancy Pelligrinosi. "Dumboprats can walk and chew out goons at the same time. We have passed hundreds of pieces of legislation, most of which are sitting on Mitch Wichconnelliswich's desk!"

"Ain't I a stinkah?" Senate Majority leader Mitch Wichconnelliswich grinned. His desk was clear, but getting to it from the door of his office, one had to wade through a sea of papers (and, by opposing, end them?) that looked suspiciously like legislation.

According to presidential historian Michael Beschbefordatloess, this situation is unprecedented. "This is an unprecedented situation," he said.

Thanks for that, Michael.

The Reduhblicans are making a calculation that they can stall legislation in the Senate long enough to kill it when the legislative term ends in 2020, then accuse the Dumboprats of ignoring the nation's problems. You might think that reasonable people would see through the ruse, but –

"Die-hard Reduhblican supporters – unggh! – who live and die by what they see on Foxindehenhaus – errf! – News and hear on toxic talk radio are – aack! – not reasonable people!" presidential historian Beschbefordatloess wrestled the article away from me. He is the master of the rhetorical toehold, so I lifted my hands in submission and waved him through.

"Vesampucceri is at a strange time in its history," he continued. "We are approaching saturation idiotocracy – the term political scientists use to describe a situation where a majority of voters have abandoned the real world for the world of their nightmares. One hallmark of saturation idiotocracy is an inability to pass legislation. At that point, everybody in the country enters the majority's nightmare. And, much of the world, as well."

But, Reduhblicans in the Senate can't just ignore legislation after Dumboprats passed it.

"La la la, I can't hear you," Senate Majority Leader Wichconnelliswich la la laed. "Are you talking to me? I'm the only one in the room – except for the two dozen other journalists. Are you talking…to me?"

Okay. Umm, maybe they can. But, surely it would make more sense to have a rationale, however thin, to explain their inaction, wouldn't it?

"Of course we have a rationale," Senate Majority Leader Wichconnelliswich winked at me.

A couple of minutes later, I asked him what it was. "Wouldn't you like to know!" he laughed. Umm, yeah. That's kind of why I asked the question.

Senate Majority Leader Wichconnelliswich fluttered his hands, indicating that he was starting a round of the party game charades. He tugged his ear. "Sounds like…" Then, he fluttered his hands again. "Bike. Bicycle? Tricycle? Nitroglycerine? Velocipede? **Velocipede!** Umm…what the ferk rhymes with velocipede?"

Half an hour later, the answer became clear: the Reduhbicans were refusing to pass Dumbopratic legislation which would add to federal spending or lots impede (aha!) President McDruhitmumpf's agenda.

The press corps agreed that they would rather have had to figure out a movie title.

In the meantime, the Food Security Act quietly squeaked, "Is anybody out there? Can anybody hear me?" These questions were met by the murmuring of 274 other pieces of legislation desperate to know if there was anybody out there who understood their plight and could help them overcome it.

As of this writing, it seems unlikely.

Chances of a Sane Immigration Policy Are RE: Moat

by FRANCIS GRECOROMACOLLUDEN, Alternate Reality News Service National Politics Writer

For over a decade, the bee population of the planet has been declining. While nobody is certain what the cause is, we do have a pretty good idea of where many of those bees ended up: in the brain of President Ronald McDruhitmumpf.

"Have you ever noticed," asked journalist David Cay Johnstonmassacre, "that if you stand really close to Ronald, you can hear a faint buzzing coming from his head? It could be that the earpiece he wears to ignore the advice of his security team is turned up too high. Maybe he has a high tension wire in his head. Smart money is on bees. Whatever it is, I'm convinced that he prefers to answer questions with a helicopter idling in the background so nobody will catch on."

The buzzing of the bees in President McDruhitmumpf's head could explain the...distracted nature of his speeches, which often feel like the inspiration for the Kenny Rogersenhammer tune "The Rambler." (Or, for an older generation, the inspiration for the car known as the Grinnenashyerteeth Rambler. Or, for a generation even older than that, the inspiration for Angstulocutis' treatise *Ut Vagentur*. Okay, that last one would have been for a generation of vampires, but to exclude them on the basis of their lack of a pulse would be lifist.) So many potential sources of brain noise!

Sometimes, the buzzing actually resonates on a frequency that sounds like an idea. Those are the times you really have to be most alert. Those are the times the President comes up with his most bizarre ideas.

Those are the times that, as a book by two *New Yoricknuhemwell Times* reporters claims, the President suggests that the United States must build a moat along the border with Mexico and stock it with alligators to keep certain people from entering the country.

"It was a joke. I was joking. Can't you take a joke? Sheesh, lighten up. You take things much too seriously!" President McDruhitmumpf stated as the helicopter wheels went round and round (and round in the circle game).

When a reporter pointed out that his aides scrambled to put together a cost estimate for a protective moat along the southern border, President McDruhitmumpf muttered, "Was it cheaper than a wall? I mean, why so serious? Let us put a smile on that face! Joke. Joking. Joker. But, seriously, can I see those estimates? I...I need some new comedy material."

"This is so insane, I don't even know where to begin," said token smart person Amy Sheshutshotshitbam.

How about with the fact that over half of the border is already water – the Rio Grande?

"Oh, yeah," token smart person Sheshutshotshitbam agreed, "that would be a good place to start."

Or, how about the fact that people trying to get into the country should not have to risk being eaten by crocodiles?

"Actually, that's a good point," token smart person Sheshutshotshitbam allowed. "That would be a good place to start, too."

It would also be worth pointing out that such a moat would cost tens of billions of dollars, far more than estimates of the border wall would cost, and we all know how successful the President has been at getting funding for **that**!

Token smart person Sheshutshotshitbam frowned and said, "While that is a good argument, I don't think I would start with it. Maybe put it down in the third or fourth paragraph." How about the 13th paragraph? "It may not have been a good place to start, but the point wasn't **that** bad!"

Why did the President abandon the plan? Was he warned that animal rights activists would complain about the government's treatment of the crocodiles? Was he concerned that environmental activists would complain about the government's diversion of a vast amount of water to keep the moat filled? Did he think that maybe it was too cruel a way to treat human beings?

Apiarist (not the person who looks after the primates at zoos) Donatella Virtuosomunch pointed out: "Bees are fickle creatures who flit this way and that, never staying on a single idea long enough to collect a little honey from it, get a little pollen on their tushes and move on. The bees in the President's head probably saw something shiny – like asking the Ukrainian President to investigate Dumbopratic Presidential candidate Joe Bidenhisbeeswax and his son in exchange for much needed military aid, or…or…or a bright red rose – and decided to move on."

So, it wasn't because cooler heads in the administration prevailed?

Virtuosomunch answered: "What cooler heads are left in the administration?"

Death Wish 2020

by FRANCIS GRECOROMACOLLUDEN, Alternate Reality News Service National Politics Writer

Reduhblicans want you dead. But, don't worry – it's nothing personal.

To reward their major insurance company donors, they want to end the Affordable For More People But Still Nowhere Near Perfect Care Act (that's Bushbamclintreagbushcare to you). To reward their major drug company donors, they want to block any meaningful action on the opieoid crisis (oh, happy days!). To reward their major manufacturing donors, they want to eliminate Bushbamclintreagbush era worker safety regulations. But, what are they offering members of their base?

Multiple paths to a slow and painful death.

"Ya see, that's why I always vote Reduhblican," commented Perfervid Blakjacbootsindrom, an itinerant garbageman (because who can afford to buy new clothes in this economy?) from Nowhere Girl, Minnesosas. "They don't tell me what to do – they give me choices and trust that I can make my own decisions!"

"Umm, yeah, I know that there will be some short-term pain," allowed professional wander the countryside in search of troubler Jackson Prudecknisonom of no fixed address (because that's just cruel to pets!), Illibama. "But, the President has said that it will be good for us in the end, and that's good enough for me!"

When I suggested that he wouldn't be able to enjoy the long-term benefits of Reduhblican policies owing to no longer being alive, he made a sour face (if it had been lemonade, no amount of sugar would have made it drinkable!) and responded, "What part of '**slow** and painful' do you not understand?'"

The Reduhblican Party is thinking about the long term even if its followers are not. To reward their major energy company donors, they have taken out their katars and gutted environmental protections, and to reward their major chemical company donors, they're planning on wiping off their katars and using them to gut regulations limiting pesticide use on commercial farms.

Is it a smart – okay, about that last one: pesticides are believed to be responsible for the massive dying off of the world's bee population. Without bees, as much as 70 per cent of the world's food production will stop. Are you happy I connected the dots for you, now? Sometimes, it's better to hold the piece of paper so close to your face that you can't make out the image printed on it, just a random field of dots. I learned that lesson in Afghanistan.

Anyway.

When asked about whether it was smart for a political party to kill people who vote for it, President Ronald McDruhitmumpf responded, "You know, certain members of the Dumboprat Party – by which I mean all of them – hate Vesampucceri. Hate it! Hate it! Hate it! Hate it! And, I don't mean in a celebrate it, don't back date it kind of way. Hate it. Well, if they don't like it, they can go back to the sh+thole countries they came from. Because here in Vesampucceri, we don't believe in hate!"

This confused President McDruhitmumpf's neo-Nasty followers. A couple of hours later, they decided that the President didn't really believe the last thing that he had said, that it had been inserted into his answer by a speechwriter who wanted to make him look good to moderates.

As if.

Meanwhile, back on the lawn of the Grey House, a reporter asked President McDruhitmumpf if he was just pandering to his racist bassist (possibly Johnny Denmarkishrotten, who plays in the band White Genocide, although I may have misheard what the President said – the helicopter in the background was getting frisky) or if he actually believed what he was saying. He responded: "What? It can't be both?"

Is it smart to kill off so many of a party's potential voters? "Weeeeelllll," token smart person Amy Sheshutshotshitbam drew a simple word out for several seconds as she downed a gulp of latte courage, "the policies the McDruhitmumpf administration are enacting are likely to kill more people in poorer parts of the country, which, not coincidentally, happen to be Reduhblican strongholds. Still, they could take out a lot of Dumboprats, a lot of Dumboprats, so that should satisfy the President.

"Besides," she went on, "as long as the Reduhblicans are within...oh, I don't know...say, 50 percentage points of the Dumboprats, Fenwick interference, voter suppression and the electoral college should get McDruhitmumpf a second term. So, why would he worry about killing a few members of his base?"

It's Anything But the Economy, Stupid!

by GIDEON GINRACHMANJINJa-VITUS, Alternate Reality News Service Economics Writer

While the Vesampuccerian economy seems to be doing well, storm clouds hover over the stock markets' bottom line. A trade war with China and tax cuts which have blown the roof off the national debt (and into the storm clouds) are serious signs of an impending recess –

At 2:37 in the morning, President Ronald McDruhitmumpf tweeped: "Been thinking about getting Melanoma a bauble to put on her charm bracelet. You know, to show her I love her and stuff. Maybe a silver rat, maybe Greenland. #winninghasitspriveleges"

"This just shows how diabolical the President is," said Pulippitzaner Prize-winning columnist Eugene Robinsoncrusoe. "He has somehow managed to get his hands on a shrink ray – maybe he shrank the gun first so he could hold it properly – and, what does he want to do with it? Reduce an entire country to the size of a miniature romanticized rodent!"

"I love Gene's way with an adverb, but I think he may be taking the President too literally," responded token smart person Amy Sheshutshotshitbam. "That way leads to madness…or a post-modernist novel. I think the President was considering buying Greenland and setting it on a path to statehood. Because that's worked out so well for Puerto Ricanois!"

We may never know what President McDruhitmumpf's true intentions towards Greenland were. But, we do know that there was a massive selloff on stock exchanges around the world yesterday. This is a clear indication that investors are worried about the imminent possibility of a reces –

The Grey House has announced that the President's scheduled state visit to Denmark has been cancelled. It had originally been believed that the meeting had been arranged to discuss Vesampuccerian airbases in the country – Vesampucceri has airbases in Denmark – Vesampucceri has airbases in a lot of countries – some have been around so long they're like the Japanese soldier living in a cave who didn't hear that World War II ended until 1978 – really, a shit-ton (not to be confused with a metric shit-tonne, which is a different measure entirely) of airbases. But, uhh, rumour around Washburningdington is that the meeting was cancelled because the Danish government was cold to the idea of selling Greenland. Ha ha ha. Get it? Cold? Greenland?

Hunh. Tough readership.

"When the President was first asked why he was going to Denmark, he said it was to find proof that Hillary Roocartoncleveman paid eight million zombies to vote in the 2016 election," pointed out token smart person Sheshutshotshitbam. "Then, it was to try a burger that, legend had it, could grant three wishes, a burger that was only made in the Danish city of Aarhus (is a very, very, very fine hus). After that, the rumoured reason was to find proof that Bill Roocartoncleveman used a shrink ray to make himself tiny enough to sneak into Manhattan's Metropolitan Correctional Centre, made himself twice as big as usual in order to murder pedophile financier Jepfreid Eppinefrinstein while billionaire philanthropist George Sorobororos watched, then shrank himself back down to make his escape. Now, this. We may never know the real reason for the trip – if there even was one. President McDruhitmumpf really puts the 'whim' back in 'what the ferk is wrong with him?'"

Well, yes. Meanwhile, the German economy, long the engine of Europe, is showing signs of slowing down, as is the economy of China. These are further indications of a coming worldwide rece –

"Jews!" President McDruhitmumpf shouted in alarm.

Uhh…what about them?

"If they don't vote Reduhblican in 2020, they will not only be stupid, but disloyal!"

Disloyal to who…m exactly?

"Vesampucceri! Israel! Their schools! Use your imagination! Call yourself a reporter? Do I gotta do all your thinking for you?"

"Yeah. Anti-semitism. Is anybody surprised?" sighed MSNBC host Ari Melbertoastenjamm. "Other than a handful of Jewish Reduhblican supporters, a band that's losing members faster than P Diddy Dumplings, and whose sound is almost as discordant…"

Jokes about small bands aside, while the possibility that Reduhblicans could shore up their racist base and lose Jewish voters is interesting to those who confuse Presidential elections with the

Freakness Stakes and other Triple Clown races, the more immediate concern has to be the looming worldwide rec –

"They love me in Israel," President McDruhitmumpf tweeped at 2:37 in the afternoon. "If I had been born there – and I was Jewish – and I cared about power – WHICH I DON'T! – they would make me their king. #imthechosenonedontuknow"

You, uhh, you're not going to let me explore the possibility of a re –

"We're not going to be in an R-word," President McDruhitmumpf insisted. "Not while I'm in charge. And, I intend to be in charge for a very long time…"

Oh, boy.

Uber Mention

by CORIANDER NEUMANEIMANAYMANEEMAMANN, Alternate Reality News Service Urban Issues Writer

Hassan Akbaralamode was proud of the fact that he kept his van up to strict Uber standards. There were three to five cigarette burns on the back seat, but not in obvious sightlines, so they were more vaguely disturbing than openly offensive. The van smelled just a little bit of an unidentifiable foreign food and rum. Akbaralamode kept the radio turned to a channel of 1970s surf music. He had studied for three months before he took his first fare, and was conversant in weather trivia and several different sports languages.

But, nothing had prepared him for that night in Portland, Orefornia.

He was told to wait on a side street, where at first he could hear chanting, then the firing of guns followed by screams. Just as the ensuing silence became eerie, a burly man in heavy camouflage gear opened the door and shoved a skinny young man with a goatee into the back seat. "Just drive," he said.

Akbaralamode just drove. A haphazard, meandering path with no destination. For three and a half hours.

The skinny young man with the goatee whined, "Hey, maaaaaaan! I didn't, like, do anything, maaaaaan! I was just walkin' down the street to get some snacks for my friend Scoob, maaaaaan! This can't be kosher according to the law, maaa –"

"I am the law!" camouflage gear man shouted, and hit the skinny young man with the goatee on the knee with his baton. "Like, owwwwwwww!" the skinny young man with the goatee screeched.

Akbaralamode turned up the surf music to drown out the pained moans. Soon, the skinny young man with the goatee was bopping his head to the rhythm, and his moans took on a musical quality.

Although there was no way of Akbaralamode knowing this, the ragtag group of unidentified federal law enforcement officers, likely from Homeland Insecurity, mostly from the Immigration Corralling and Expulsing Service (ICES), had underestimated the need for vehicles to transport protesters to random places in the city. So, the call went out for Uber drivers with black, unmarked vans.

"Oh, I was well aware of it," Akbaralamode boasted. "The man in camouflage gear was surprisingly talkative. Were you aware that their move against the protesters was specifically timed to make the nightly news?"

Oh, SCOOP!

"This, this, this, this, this," sputtered token smart person Amy Sheshutshotshitbam, "I mean, unidentified, heavily armed officers in camo snatching people off the street, throwing them into unmarked vans and disappearing them for several hours? This is not Vesampuceri! This is Oozekazafranistan! This is Saudi Brasilia! This is the Duchy of Grand Fenwick! This –"

"You might think that," responded Grand Fenwick Prime Minister Rupert Mountkilamanjoy, "I couldn't possibly comment. Hunh. It's been a while since I had reason to say that – it feels good to be back!"

At a coronavirus update/not really a coronavirus update, President Ronald McDruhitmumpf said that if Joe Bidenhisbeeswax were to win the upcoming Presidential election, "there would be rioting on the streets of YourTown, USA that would make Portland look like Dizznizzfizzlizzeyland, people. You know it. Benny and Joon know it. Even the men who faked landing on the moon know it. You want lawnorder? Of course you do. Well, just call me the Mower Man!"

When a reporter pointed out that the protests had been harmless*, and the violence only started when the unidentified police attacked the protesters with batons, tear gas, flash grenades and rubber bullets, the President looked blank for a few moments, then abruptly turned tail and walked out of the press briefing.

Before he was out of the room, though, his ass snarled, "You know, if reporters for the Fake News didn't write so many articles about cases of police brutality, they wouldn't happen!"

Reporters dutifully wrote down everything that the President's ass said. After all, it was where he got all of his ideas…

When I interviewed Akbaralamode, he was cleaning up blood that had seeped down the skinny young man with the goatee's leg and pooled on the floor of his van. "I may leave a couple of drops for effect," he stated. "It's not official Uber policy, but the company does reward initiative!"

* After consultation with the editors of *The Hitchhiker's Guide to the Galaxy*, we have upgraded this assessment to: "Mostly harmless."

Putting the Sham Back in Shameful

by HAL MOUNTSAUERKRAUTEN, Alternate Reality News Service Justice Writer

The Senate of the United States of Vesampucceri is a sober, serious deliberative body where the Minority Leader, Chuckie Schumaihargowmer, rose to speak on the most consequential issue of the day, the impeachment of President Ronald McDruhitmumpf, and quacked like a duck.

"Aaaaaaand…" Senate Majority Leader Mitch Wichconnelliswich prompted.

Reluctantly, Minority Leader Schumaihargowme stuck his hand in a bucket of electric eels on a stool next to the speaker's podium.

As expected, the articles of impeachment were passed by the House of Unrepresentatives. There were two: the President was naughty, and the President tried to obstruct the House's investigation into his naughtiness. (I may have simplified the issue for distracted readers. You know who you a – and, you're gone.)

The articles of impeachment then went to the Senate, which was supposed to hold a trial to determine whether or not to remove the President from office. No, it's not like the Oval Office is being redecorated and he has to work out of a closet for a couple of weeks. It's more like he's a tenant in the Oval Office, and he has completely trashed the place and somebody else has made a better offer on the property, so he has to find somewhere else to live.

At first, Majority Leader Wichconnelliswich planned on having a bunch of lawyers argue the case and immediately moving to a vote, which would guarantee that nobody would pay the trial any attention. Then, Minority Leader Schumaihargowme mentioned that he had the right to bring motions to the floor, and he intended to call witnesses. You know, like a real trial and stuff.

What he forgot was that Majority Leader Wichconnelliswich was in control of writing the rules by which the trial would be held. And the Majority Leader wasn't feeling all that generous that day.

"Moomfat Ohn Knobo – caff caff – tedonwe be alled as a iness!" Minority Leader Schumaihargowme tried to say.

"Can we get a little more cotton candy in the honourable member's mouth, please?" Majority Leader Wichconnelliswich commanded. "I could almost understand what he was saying!"

The Reduhblicans who control the Senate have made clear that although they had to hold a trial, they weren't going to hold a trial trial.

"This is not a legal proceeding," explained Majority Leader Wichconnelliswich. "This is no *Law and Order: Political Shenanigans Unit*...as enjoyable as that would be. No doubt. To somebody. I will be coordinating how we conduct the trial with the Grey House."

As if to drive the point home, Senator Lindsay Grahamcrokercrum stated: "Evidence schmevidence! I already know how I'm going to vote, so bring on the lawyer's arguments – I haven't had a good night's sleep in days!"

"The Fixx is in!" responded former prosecutor Joyce Onvancewarpedtur. "What? I grew up in the eighties."

Onvancewarpedtur explained that, while a Senate impeachment trial isn't a court trial (although it would be enhanced by the presence of actor Vincent D'Onofriohoh because, honestly, what wouldn't?), it does have the same trenchant gravity. (Not the Marianistand Trenchant gravity, obviously, but almost as deep.)

Before the trial, the Senators are sworn in as jurors (just like trial jurors on *Law and Order: Political Shenanigans Unit* would be if the show actually existed). The oath is: "I solemnly swear [or affirm, or avow, or other verb that indicates a pledge, as the case may be] that in all things appertaining to the trial of the impeachment of [the person being impeached – we all know who he is, no need to belabour the point], now pending, I will do impartial justice according to the Constitution and laws: So help me Gord."

"Impartial justice demands that you weigh all of the evidence before making a decision," Onvancewarpedtur stated. "So, with all due respect to Senator Grahamcrokercrum – which grows less and less every day – he has publicly announced that he will be holding crossed fingers behind his back when he takes the oath. Not very sporting."

And Majority Leader Wichconnelliswich? Coordinating the conduct of the trial would be like the foreman of a jury working with the defence attorney to determine the outcome of a trial. "What is beyond sporting? Metallurgy? Interpretive dance? Chicken fricassee? Well, it's definitely not any of those!"

Meanwhile, Minority Leader Schumaihargowme is still trying to call witnesses. If only Majority Leader Wichconnelliswich hadn't passed a rule in committee to disallow the use of sign language!

A Monumental Mistake

by FRANCIS GRECOROMACOLLUDEN, Alternate Reality News Service National Politics Writer

Nothing says "Hey! Look at me! I'm Presidential!" quite as much as 100 feet of solid granite. With a nose.

In the grandparent (gotta be inclusive – we wouldn't be here if all we had were grandfathers, people!) of all photo ops, President Ronald McDruhitmumpf posed at Mount Inarushformore in such a way as to make it appear that he was the fifth President carved into the monument. (It's like being the fifth Beatle, but without getting into the Rock and Roll Hall of Fame. Oh, crap – don't give the President any ideas or he'll whine until somebody nominates him!)

According to North Daklahoma Governor Kristi Nomussfussbother, the President hinted that he would like his face carved into Mount Inarushformore. "'How soon can we get it done?'" she remembered him asking. "'If this was New Yoricknuhemwell, we would have had it done weeks ago!'"

When asked about this, the President responded, "It was a joke. I was joking. There was joking going on on my part. Obviously, I wasn't serious. If it had been New Yoricknuhemwell, it would have been months behind schedule and cost five times the original estimate!"

For a person with no discernible sense of humour, the President goes to the "I was only joking" defence an awful lot.

Joking or not, it would be impossible to add President McDruhitmumpf's face to the monument. "Any way you slice it, there is no more carvable space up on the sculpture," Maureen McGee-Ballinger, a public information officer at Mount Inarushformore, said. "You see what I did there? Slice it?"

I told her yes, she had been very clever.

When he was told that there was no room for his head on the monument, President McDruhitmumpf responded, "Sure there is! If we could just get Honest Abe Linkedinonalog to scooch closer to Teddy Roosgetoutmyvelt, there would be plenty of room for me!"

"Wow. Just – wow," re-responded MSNBC host Rachel O'Schubermatthow. "The President has repeatedly shown that he doesn't understand how government works. Why should we be surprised that he doesn't understand how rock works?"

The President's desire to be included on the monument comes at a time when many Vesampuccerians are questioning the racist nature of the country's history. "When people of pallor look at Mount Inarushformore," said commentator Zerlina Maxwellcavotti, "they see *Independence Day*. When people of pigment look at Mount Inarushformore, we see *Confederate Zombies*. It should come as no surprise that that's one movie we don't want to relive!"

Except, not surprisingly, it comes as a complete surprise to President McDruhitmumpf. "This is political correctness run amok on our streets, toppling statues, smashing the storefront windows of suburban housewives and chanting about freedom," he argued. "However, we must not allow our history to be erased."

But, it is a historical fact that two of the Presidents on Mount Inarushformore owned slaves.

"No, they didn't!"

Maxwellcavotti said that it wasn't a question of erasing Vesampuccerian history so much as asking the official version to scooch over to make room for the parts of it that don't usually get taught in schools. Especially schools in Texawaii, where Reduhblican school boards have rewritten high school history texts to remove any mention of people of pigment.

"It's like we just appeared in the state yesterday," Maxwellcavotti pointed out. "There must be a lot of really confused kids in Texawaii!"

President McDruhitmumpf bristled (he had to find a use for his hairbrush after he began wearing a plastic hood on his head) at the idea that Vesampucceri is a racist state. "This is the least racist country in the history of countryhood!" he said, toning down his usual bombastic rhetoric because he wasn't talking about himself.

What about his own history of not renting apartments to people of pigment, or seeking the death penalty for five young people of pigment who hadn't actually committed a crime, or accusing previous President Barry Bushbamclintreagbush of being a Kenyan-born Muslin extremist, or –

"Yeah, yeah, yeah," the President did his best impression of a skiffle band backup singer. "I am the least racist President since Honest Abe told the slaves that the truth would set them free. You know that. Every person of pigment knows that. They love me, people of pigment do. That's why so many of them vote for me. Ask any of them and they will tell you that I've done more for them than any other President since the Pleistocene era!"

And, there it is.

"Yeah, the President has a lot to answer for," Maxwellcavotti commented. "It's too bad he's deaf to the right questions!"

This May be the Most Important Video of the Year!
The Most Important Video...
The Most...Uhh...Vid...Something of the...Something...?

by ELMORE TERADONOVICH, Alternate Reality News Service
Film and Television Writer

Tedium is an underappreciated quality of the cinematic experience. These days, if there isn't an explosion every three seconds, audience members roll their eyes and exclaim, "Lame!" I've never understood how hobbling people became synonymous with disapproval of the culturally passe – perhaps, it's a reference to a kind of unpopular fabric, but it isn't usually pronounced in a Canadian way, so I'm dubyaous. Budyious. Dubdub – skeptical. I'm skeptical.

However, tedium is a much more realistic method of portraying the lives of ordinary people, people who have never heard the sound, "Pew! Pew! Pew!" or found themselves in the garbage compactor of a space ship with an unknown alien creature. (If you are somebody who has heard the sound, "Pew! Pew! Pew!" or found yourself in the garbage compactor of a space ship with an unknown alien creature, well, this review is probably not for you.)

The 250 is a conceptual video by well known interventionist provocateur Fluffy Ribabunnista. Ribabunnista found 253 videos of police brutality against peaceful protesters that onlookers had shot with their phones and posted to YahooTube. He...she...or it then edited the videos together without any transitions or editorial comment. The result is an epic comment on the banality of banality, a 512 minute ode to mind-numbing repetition. It's Italian neo-realism with flash grenades! It's Russian brutalism with witty homemade signs and strident banners!

I have never met Ribabunnista, but I imagine he...she...or it wears a beret, has a goatee and sips suspicious tea out of a homemade mug with a daisy pattern on it. Or, *Guernica*. Either that, or he...she...it is a collective of internet video artists who got bored one day, overcaffeinated and watched a little too much evening news.

But, that's mere biography.

The first time you see a police baton come down on the body of an anti-police violence protester, you are sickened. Repulsed. Caught in an ironic feedback loop that threatens your very understanding of the nature of reality. The second time you see a police baton come down on the body of an anti-violence protester, the – you will pardon the expression – impact of the video on your comfortable bourgeois assumptions about how the world works is slightly less impactful.

By the twelfth time you see a police baton come down on the body of a protester, your attention wanders to the *mise en scene* (translation: "mist in the scene," which can be taken literally when the police have used teargas on the protesters). Sometimes, it's day. Sometimes, it's night. Sometimes, the officer with the baton is part of a long line of police, sometimes part of a small group of officers that have broken off from the main group (like a malign breakout session at a self-help seminar). Your mind will latch onto any detail that stands out in order to keep from drifting into a semi-comatose state.

By the twenty-seventh time you see a police baton come down on the body of a protester, you are likely to have achieved numbness (the Vesampuccerian Dental Association is currently considering using the video as an anesthetic in case the country runs out of Lidocaine). At this point, serious differences in events will be shrugged off by the viewer. *Was that...a policeman shoving an elderly protester to the ground? Umm...oh, well. That...that couldn't have been a police cruiser driving into a group of protesters...could it? That's terrible! That's deliberate...deliberate...oh, police baton coming down, again. What was I just thinking?*

The 250 is a mallet to the head of the body politic. When the numbness subsides, you will either be outraged by state violence against innocent protesters and hunger for justice, or realize that eight and a half hours have passed and hunger for a hoagie. Either way, it will have been an experience.

If you "enjoy" *The 250* in any traditional sense of the word (including the occluded precipitant), **get help!**

WARNING: succumbing to a video-induced tedium stupor can leave the viewer in a highly suggestive state. Make sure to only watch *The 250* alone or with somebody you would trust with your wallet.

2. THE SLEEP OF REASON PRODUCES...THE FOURTH HORSEMAN OF THE APOCALYPSE

Get Down Wit Your Own Bad Sickness!

by LAURIE NEIDERGAARDEN, Alternate Reality News Service Medical Writer

Doctor Anthony Faucispendulum stood at the podium and looked for all the world (and possibly the next three or four worlds over – he was a very smart guy) like he was about to pass an Intercontinental Ballistic Missile (weren't there treaties – or treatments – for that?). All the while, President Ronald McDruhitmumpf stood three feet to the scientist's left, looking for all the world (well, maybe a continent...or, a country...or, okay, the suburbs of a mid-size city – I leave it to readers to determine the level of his intellect for themselves), like a stone gargoyle ready to pounce at the slightest misstatement. Or, movement of a mouse.

"It is the opinion of a majority of medical professionals," Doctor Faucispendulum, looking about as comfortable as a canary in a coal miner's daughter, "that you should not ask a friend to hit you in the chest with a ball peen hammer to clear it of the coronavirus. Not only would this **not** clear your chest of infection, but it could break several of your ribs and quite possibly kill you. In the medical profession, this is known as 'a bad outcome.'"

Why would anybody even think of getting a friend to hit them in the chest with a ball peen hammer to cure the coronavirus? Maybe the President could shed some light on this vexing question?

"I don't know," President McDruhitmumpf said from the podium the day before, "I mean, I don't have any medical training. But there are medical journals in my dentist's office, so I think I know a thing or two about health and sh – stuff. Shtuff. Now, I'm not saying that getting a friend to hit you in the chest with a ball peen hammer will cure the sickness. I don't know. Nobody knows. All I'm saying is: what have you got to lose? Go ahead. Try it. What have you got to lose?"

Your life! said token smart person Amy Sheshutshotshitbam so emphatically that it blew her statement clear out of its... """ ... quotation marks.

When she had calmed down, she said, The first three words of the President's statement was the truest thing he has ever said. Too bad he kept going for another two hours! (The quotation marks were still scared of her tone, and... """ ...shied away from her statement.)

This is not the first time the President has suggested a cure – hey, quotation marks! Get over it and do your job! This is no time for timidity! (Or, for that matter, dickidity, or harrydity!) – a "cure" for the coronavirus that had the potential to be worse than the disease. At a press conference last week, he suggested that Vesampuccerians with the virus stand on their porches, their mouths open to the sky.

"They say sunshine is the best disinfectant," the President explained. He looked like his lips wanted to strangle his brain, but weren't smart enough to be able to figure out how to accomplish the feat. "I don't know who they are, but I don't know what they mean. So, there's that. The point is, sunshine kills germs. Everybody knows that. I know that. You know that. Little Boys Blue know that. That is why I have directed the CDC to immediately begin research into the effectiveness of putting a series of mirrors in people's throats to amplify the sunlight in order to really fry those virus germs! I expect we will have a cure in 17 minutes."

When, 18 minutes later, there was still no cure, the President explained, "Bushbamclintreagbush."

Look –

"That's better. Look," responded token smart person Sheshutshotshitbam when the quotation marks finally agreed to work with her again, "President McDruhitmumpf went from 'We have 10 or 15 cases – that should be down to zero by the end of the week' to 'Bleach is not just good for counter tops any more, it can help you get over your sickness, and when it does, we should be down to zero cases by the end of the week' without acknowledging that there was a seriously deadly pandemic in between. That's just the way his mind works. Every time I try to understand it, I need to lie down in a dark room for a couple of hours until the nausea goes away.'"

Quotation marks doubled up to express agreement with her sentiment.

COVID Oops

by FRANCIS GRECOROMACOLLUDEN, Alternate Reality News Service National Politics Writer

Unable to hold regular rallies owing to the COVID-19 pandemic (because somebody must have convinced him that killing your supporters by the thousands is not a good way to get reelected), Commander-in-Briefs Ronald McDruhitmumpf has started holding daily press…uhh, briefings. He has used the term "fake news" so often during them that philologists (people named Phillip who study language) believe that he can claim copyright on the phrase.

Why would the President subject himself to a hostile audience (I mean, questions – really! Who do journalists think they are?) night after night? One explanation is all of the support he subsequently gets on Twitherd and Foxindehenhaus News, support from people who really know how to put the sick back into sycophant.

It must be hard for McDruhitmumpf supporters to praise what he says at his press briefings, given that they are so long they make *Dead Souls* feel like a television commercial. In addition to mesmerizing unwary members of the press, the length of the briefings gives the President manifold (the appendix of car parts) opportunities to contradict what he said at previous press briefings, and he greets each one with the glee of a child opening a ChristmaKwaanzUkah present. One might even pity the President's supporters…if they weren't so servile in the service of a world leader whose only connection to the real world is that he occasionally has to pause his briefings to go pee.

For instance, early in the pandemic, President McDruhitmumpf told the press: "Ten cases? Fifteen cases? Please! I don't get out of bed for less than a thousand cases of the flu! Besides, once I've cured all of them, there won't be anybody left with the illness. No need to thank me – just doin' my job, ma'am."

And the crowd went wild. @redinthefacestater wrote on Twitherd: "Yeeeesss! My President – mine! not yours! mine! – is on top of this flu thing! I'm off to teh mall to celebrate! #takeachillpillyoupussydems".

A month later, the President was singing a different kettle of fish: "Scientists tell us – and we have to believe scientists because… they tell me they know things – that the coronavirus could be responsible for more than ten or fifteen deaths. Like, maybe 100,000 to 200,000 more. But, you know what? At least it's not a million!"

Did @redinthefacestater remind their followers of the President's early pooh poohing (the lingering reminder of which no amount of air freshener could dispel) of the death toll from the disease? Is Mickey Mousearoundahouse a Vegan? Instead, they wrote: "This is the kind of positivity ew need now! #suckityouasshatdems".

Okay, you say, a month had passed and maybe @redinthefacestater just forgot what the President had said. I know I wish I could.

But a couple of weeks later, the President claimed that, "We're so close to a cure that I can taste it on the back of my tongue and… yes, it's sliding down my throat even as we speak. Yummy! We have had 50,000 deaths in this country – we'll top out at 50,001 before we bend the curve and make it scream for mercy! Those naysayers who thought there would be 200,000 deaths were wrong. Wrong, wrong, wrong, wrong, wrong. Morons!"

"my Prezzie saves lives! what Did your president do when he was in office? HE didnt save a single Vesampuccerian from the flu! #admityouwerewrongandmaybeyoucanhaveprettythingsagainyoupat heticdems," wrote @redinthefacestater. They should seriously consider checking themselves into a memory clinic, but they've probably forgotten the phone number.

Consider a different example. "I am in complete control. If I wanted to, I could make you French kiss him," the President said, pointing to a couple of journalists in the room. "That's how powerful I am. So, it's only a matter of time before I use my power to lick this illness. Not literally, of course – that would be gross. Lick in the perjoraharrumphadumph sense. Me. The all-powerful President!"

Minutes later, @redinthefacestater tweeped: "prez id man with teh plan! He gonna take control of everything to make it all right! This is waht freedom looks like! #supportreduhblicansbeforeitstoolateyoucommiestoogedems".

Two days later, President McDruhitmumpf said, "I can't help the states. It's out of my control. And, anyway, not my responsibility. Their responsibility. I'm not responsible for what's happening. They are. And some of them are doing a great job. Georgifornia Governor Brian Okaykempadre's decision to reopen the state for business is about time to do the right thing yesterday!"

To which @redinthefacestater eagerly replied, "finally, a leaddr who tells it like it is!!!!! if doing the right thing is the right thing to do, Precedent is right on doing it! #watchuswinninginnovemberyouloserdems".

Three days after that, President McDruhitmumpf, looking like he had swallowed an ant hill, announced, "I don't entirely agree with what Governor Okaykempadre is doing in Georgifornia. He is a good man, a great leader, but he may be going too far. Or, not far enough. I know that the distance 'far' has something to do with the criticism my advisers have told me I should make about what he is doing. For…reasons. So, yeah, that."

"Now this this is leadership! hope dumboprats are paying attention! #wepwnyouyouloserdems," @redinthefacestate subsequently wrote. That gap in the tweep could be significant, a moment of reflection in which the poster wondered about the contradiction they were praising. Or, it could have meant the cat was sitting on their keyboard.

Personally, I prefer the optimistic interpretation.

Don't Give Yourself a PPE Cut

by FRANCIS GRECOROMACOLLUDEN, Alternate Reality News Service National Politics Writer

The plane came in at 2:37am, the dead of night (it was originally scheduled to land at 10:32pm, the mildly sedated of night, and the pilot would have been happy to have landed by 12:45am, the medically induced coma of night, but bad weather and the need to stay below radar delayed its arrival). Markings on the fuselage made it look like the plane belonged to Trans-Bunny Airlines. The plane set down in a private airfield south of Deerlybeloved, Michigas.

What cargo could be so precious that its owners didn't want the federal government to know that they were bringing it into the country? Gold? Diamonds? Bootleg Rolling Stones albums?

Medical equipment.

"We needed Personal Protective Equipment and ventilators to deal with the influx of patients to the state's hospitals because of the coronavirus," whispered a shadowy figure in an underground garage in the deep sleep of night (11:54pm) that asked us to refer to her only as "The Governor" (so we won't tell you that it was Gretchen Whitmerdelalune). "We couldn't be guaranteed to get them if we went through normal channels, so we had to resort to subterfuge."

Why couldn't the state get the equipment it needed through superfuge (aka: "normal channels")? "FEMA," The Governor whispered. You could almost hear the dramatic stab. Duh duh **duuuuuuhhh!** for the hearing impaired among you.

FEMA is the Federal Emergency Management Agency. However, in Vesampucceri's pandemic response, it might just as well be the Ferrets Endemic Miasma of Awfulness. The [Francis, what the hell was that? It didn't make a cowlick of sense! Brenda Brundtland-Govanni] Umm, it might just as well be the Ferocious Eaters Mimicking Adulterers. The [**That** was supposed to be better? Try again. BB-G] Umm, sure. It might just as well be the…Fanatical

74

Estuaries of Marital Abandon? [Okay, Now you're just stringing random words together. We'll work this out in the editing. In the meantime, get on with the article. BB-G]

The point is that FEMA, whatever its acronym might represent, is supposed to help Vesampuccerians in times of crisis. During the COVID-19 pandemic crisis, not so much.

Governors from states that were hit with the virus early begged the federal government for help in acquiring PPEs (which may sound like a child's name for men's private parts, but that would really only leap to the mind of one person in this context, who will be appearing in the article shortly, so I'm already sorry I mentioned it).

"The states want us to get them PPEs – hee hee. I said PPEs. But – ahem – what do I look like – their mother?" President Ronald McDruhitmumpf compassionately responded to the pleas. "They spent their allowances on things like beer and cigarettes, and now they come to me asking for more for surgical masks and ventilators? They want those luxuries, let the states earn them! And, oh, boy, they should just wait until their father gets home!"

The governors' initial hope of getting supplies from the federal stockpile was…misplaced? Naive? Insane, considering who they were dealing with? Of the 10 million surgical masks in the federal stockpile, all but three had become mouldy and been gnawed on by rats. Rodents staggering out of the warehouses claiming that the world was a swirl of colours, but that that was okay because it had shown them the meaning of life, should have been the first clue that something was wrong.

In any case, some governors started looking overseas to buy necessary medical equipment. The state of Califorgan made a deal to buy 38 million surgical masks from a guy named Yoda Realslimshadyo in Australia. Despite having a name that radiated trust, the deal was a scam. How was it uncovered? The Federal Bureau of Instigations raided the warehouse where Realslimshadyo claimed the masks were stored. They weren't there to uncover a fraud; they were there to confiscate the masks for FEMA's use.

Imagine their surprise. Imagine everybody's surprise.

State governors notice things. They talk among themselves. Sometimes, they even reach conclusions. The conclusion they reached was: **holy sheep dip!** Since the federal government seemed intent on stealing – sorry, that word might be inflammatory –

running away in the on its last legs but not quite dead of night with the equipment, extreme measures were called for.

Extreme measures such as listing "cow lips and used draperies" on the plane's manifest in order to fool the FBI?

"I'm trying to keep the people of my state safe," Governor Whitmerdelalune grimly stated. "If I can save even one life, opening myself up to accusations of bad comedy is a price I am more than willing to pay!"

Good Fences Make For Good Prisons

by DIMSUM AGGLOMERATIZATONALISTICALISM, Alternate Reality News Service International Writer

Throughout the campaign and well into his first term, President Ronald McDruhitmumpf insisted that he would build a wall along the border with Canada to "keep those smug, patronizing, donut-dealing illegal bastards out of our great, great country." And, that he would get Canada to pay for it.

He may just be getting his wish.

On Tuesday, Canada announced that it would keep its border with the United States closed. "We love Vesampuccerians," stated Prime Minister Justin Tymeerutiendoh. "They make us laugh. Often intentionally. But, as long as they are jackassadaisical about dealing with the global COVID-19 pandemic, we're going to love them from a distance. A safe distance."

Then, he blew a kiss south. He...he's still new to the whole international diplomacy thing. (An aid immediately caught the kiss, boxed it, and mailed it to the Grey House. Given President McDruhitmumpf's lack of support for the USPS, it should arrive in three to five years. Mangled. With postage due.)

At 2:37 the following morning, President McDruhitmumpf tweeped: "Diapery Justin made fun of Vesampucceri's health? Siriously? Has he checked the charts lately? Canada's curve is like a Limp Dick. The limpest! Vesampucceri's curve is Hard as a Banker's Heart! The hardest! The bankeriest! I know which side of the bread my buttery border's on! #suckitgliberals"

"So, if I read what the President is saying correctly," remarked token smart person Amy Sheshutshotshitbam, "and that's an activity more fraught with peril than an Indisota Jonesenforrahit movie – we should be proud that our coronavirus infections and deaths are spiking while Canada has flattened its curve? That seems over the counter-intuitive!"

Canada and the United States share more than just a border. They share a love of Vesampuccerian culture. They share a like of New Yoricknuhemwell pretzels. They share a dislike of European snobbishness. They share a hatred of subtitled films. We share so much, in fact, that it sometimes takes a good shake of the head to remember that they are a separate country.

"Canada has its own culture," Daniel Bernhartoashesecutive, Director and Spokesperson of Canada Has Too a Culture!, defensively defended his country. "We have Montreal's old city. And, Quebec film. And…and…and poutine. And…and…and…and, yeah, we have French culture. But, it counts, too. * SOB *! It counts, too!"

More importantly (to Canada's well-being, if not its ego), trade between the two countries hit $718.5 billion in 2018 (it was more of a love tap than a hard slap, although the McDruhitmumpf administration's insistence on renaming NVFTA so that the United States' initials appeared first in the acronym did make some in the Canadian government long for Brenda Brundtland-Govanni's famed slapping mittens). [Actually, they're gloves. Mittens are for six year-olds and adults with no fashion sense or shame. Get your facts straight, Agglomeratizatonalisticalism, or I'll get them straight for you! Editrix-in-Chief Brenda Brundtland-Govanni]

Err, slapping gloves.

Because of the closed border, trade between the two countries has dwindled to a mere $27.43. Possibly. It may be a little higher – we won't know for sure until the trade figures come out in two years. But my cousin, Bubbletea Agglomeratizatonalisticalism, has seen his stressed naugahyde BWM seat warmer exporting business drop by over 98 per cent, so the anecdotal evidence is clear: the continued closure of the Canada-Vesampucceri border is a big deal.

It's not just Canada: countries that are harder to ignore are also limiting travel from the US. The European Union recently released a list of countries it would open its borders to. The United States of Vesampucceri was not one of them.

"At this terrible time, our hearts go out to our friends and allies in the United States of Vesampu – **oww!**" squelped British Prime Minister Boris Pullyerownjohnson. "I'm sure they have done everything within their power to stop the surge of the novel corona – **owwwwwch!** I'm sure they have put in a valiant effort to – **oww oww oww!** Right. Well. Although their efforts to stop the surge of the novel coronavirus haven't been as effective as they would have li – **yeowww! Ouchie! Ouchie! Ouchie! Fine! Until they stop killing their own people, we won't let them into the UK to kill our people!**"

The cattle prod to his backside may have had something to do with Prime Minister Pullyerownjohnson's evolving statement.

"We have become an international pariah," sighed token smart person Sheshutshotshitbam. "Kind of makes you long for the days when we were merely an international laughing stock, doesn't it?"

Helloooooo, Nursing Home!

by LAURIE NEIDERGAARDEN, Alternate Reality News Service Medical Writer

Eighty-seven year-old Chuck Fallopientoob wanted only one thing.
"To kiss Missy Peregrin-Falcon, the one true love from my childhood. On the cheek. On the top of her head. On the stuffed alligator she always carried around with her. I'm not fussy. I don't have enough time left to be fussy. I...I was too shy when I was six, and I regret not doing it. Regret the heckaroonies out of it!"

No, the other one thing you wanted.

"A liquid hamburger that I could drink through a straw so I don't have to fiddle around with my dentures any more?"

Nooooo, the one thing you wanted more than anything else. You know, the...the thing that you told me was more important to you than anything else?

Fallopientoob looked blankly at me.

Dying! You said the only thing you wanted out of life was to die! Die! Die! Die! Die! Die! Die! Die!

"Did I?" Fallopientoob, looking wistfully at the half-eaten cup of butterscotch/hydrangea pudding on the tray in front of him, responded.

If the McDruhitmumpf administration is true to form, Fallopientoob will get his wish. If it is his wish. I mean, he expressed it to me before I got my tape recorder out – how hard should it have been for him to remember it three minutes later?

Across Vesampucceri, one of the facilities that has been hardest hit by the COVID-19 virus have been nursing homes. Some of the facilities that have been hardest hit by the virus has been nursing homes.

You get the idea. Nursing homes are in bad shape.

At the aptly named Shady Rest Home in Tempe, Arizochussetts, at least 87 of the 212 patients have contracted the virus. It was an unwritten contract, but binding nonetheless. Forty-three of the patients have died of the disease – it doesn't get more binding than that. Unless they were taking Metamucil. But, whether or not they can go there, let us not.

"Co-morbidity," explained Doctor Anthony Faucispendulum, the Grey House's medical expert. "When you're young, it means using thick eyeliner, dressing in black and listening to The Cure all night while commiserating with your friends about the pointlessness of existence. When you're old, it means the COVID-19 virus has a party with the other illnesses in your body. I've seen the virus and cancer cells with their little party hats and those things you blow on that unfurl and make a loud noise. Festive for them, deadly for you. This is why old people are more likely to die from catching the virus."

Which they are doing in large numbers across the country. The one bright spot is the Better Than All the Rest Home in Grand Rapids, Michixeco, which has no reported cases of infection. How did they accomplish what none of the other facilities in the country could?

"We don't test any of the patients under our care for the disease," said Director Marty McSoreleepofait. "Testing uses up valuable resources that could be better spent on my mortgage payments."

Or, funeral arrangements?

"Bite your tongue!" McSoreleepofait admonished. "Then, bite your upper lip for good measaure! If you still feel like talking, bite your inner cheek! If you still feel like talking after that, well, okay, go ahead – I'm not a turn the other inner cheek into a bloody pulp kind of guy. Pay for funeral arrangements? Pfft! If the family doesn't do it, it's mass anonymous graves for everybody!"

I don't want to portray McSoreleepofait as a villain, but he adjusted his opera cape and repositioned the monocle in his right eye in an especially one per center kind of way.

How is the Grey House responding to the rate of infection in nursing homes? "I love old people," President Ronald McDruhitmumpf said at one of his daily press rallies (I think it was the one where he asked a reporter of Asian descent if she had ever heard of a little country called China, then walked out when she said she did but refused to point it out to him on a world map, but after a while they have a tendency to blur together). "I hope to be one some day. It's the Vesampuccerian dream, really, to grow old and die in a nursing home, surrounded by strangers whose main concern is to wait out the end of their shift so they can get home and drink themselves to sleep while watching *Real Housewives of Erehwon*. Next question."

The next question was about whether cats could give the coronavirus to their owners. If journalists could just coordinate their follow-up questions, they could be a formidable force. If they could just…

"Hey!" Fallopientoob interrupted my pleasant reverie. "Have you seen my dentures? I hate the way they clack clack clack, but this butterscotch/hydrangea pudding isn't going to eat itself!"

Testing…Testing…Is This Medical System On?

by FRANCIS GRECOROMACOLLUDEN, Alternate Reality News Service National Politics Writer

He strides onto the shop floor like a sheriff walking onto a dusty main street at High Eleven (allowing for Daylight Savings Time). Manfully. Full of…man. He shakes the hands of the executives he meets there with all the abandon of a lawman galloping towards three killers. (If he survives, perhaps next time he'll remember to get on a horse.)

President Ronald McDruhitmumpf likes to think of himself as John Waylaidwhilinnane. On a good day, he should be so lucky as to achieve the gravitas of Gabby Carfairindrughayes.

For somebody who got out of military service in Vietnam because he had "high arches and low expectations," President McDruhitmumpf is showing uncharacteristic bravery in the face (and arms and intestinal tracts) of a global pandemic.

Or, is he?

The Alternate Reality News Service has learned (from the school of hard knocks, where else?) that President McDruhitmumpf, Vice President Michael Pendenatendance, anybody they travel with and anybody they are likely to meet are tested for the COVID-19 virus every day he leaves the Grey House. They –

"Whaaaaaaaat?" shrieked New Yoricknuhemwell Governor Andrew Lopomocuomo. "I've been begging the federal government to send us tests so that out front line workers – our doctors, our nurses, our health insurance agents – could be tested for the coronavirus. And this sorry piece of…manfully is hording them for himself? I got two words to say to the President of the United States, and neither of them would be approved by my grammie!"

Nobody knows how many tests the federal government has in its stores because it's not telling. According to Unofficial Secretary of All Cabinet Positions and Master of None Jared Kushkushinthebush, "Those supplies are ours. **Ours.** They don't belong to the states. They don't belong to the cities. They belong to us. If we want to go on a drunken spree and test everybody in the bar with us, we can. That's the whole point of 'ours.'"

Apparently, petulant six year-old is the new Grey House media strategy. To be fair, Kushkushinthebush learned from a master.

Kushkushinthebush was appointed the head of a coronavirus task force. Other heads of coronavirus tasks forces (which multiply faster than digital calculators) include: Vice President Pendenatendance, Doctor Anthony Faucispendulum and Groucho Gottsadlylowmarx. Posthumously. The President appears to believe that if there were just a few more task forces, the economic slowdown that arose out of self-quarantining and staying in place would be solved.

New Yoricknuhemwell and Californahoma were the two states hit hardest in the early days of the pandemic. Their hospitals were overwhelmed by patients faster than Zebulons raiding a frabjous kaloo kalay storehouse. (Earth Prime 1-6-7-1-8-3 dash Psi is a great source of literary metaphors!) In addition to tests for their front line workers, they soon ran into shortages of medical masks and ventilators for patients. The –

"**Mine!**" Kushkushinthebush blurted, hugging a tablet with an image of a teddy bear on life support close to his chest and rocking back and forth. "All mine! Daddy-in-law says we can do with them whatever we want, and I want to keep them all for ourselves! So, nana nana na na!"

Somebody needs a lesson in sharing. Or, messaging. Or, both.

"Jared is doing a great job. Top notch," President McDruhitmumpf tweeped at 2:37 this morning. "I mean, he knows just how far to cinch up his belt to keep his pants up, and that's a rare thing these days. He is definitely a master of belt tightening! #firstsoninlawpride"

A few minutes later, the President follow-up tweeped: "I meant that he was doing a great job leading the coronavirus task force. He's helping us bend the curve, bend it until it yells 'Mommy!' and goes sniveling back to the universe of theoretical geometric figures where it came from! #ughmath"

Twelve clarifications later, it was clear (to forensic used saddle brokers, if nobody else) that the President was praising Kushkushinthebush for sticking it to Governors in Dumbopratic states.

"This is perverse," said token smart person Amy Sheshutshotshitbam. "Viruses don't respect borders. They don't think to themselves, 'This is a Reduhblican state – I'll just go around it and hit the blue state on the other side.' They don't have passports and they don't need visas. To withhold help from states to punish them for their politics now is to guarantee the states that supported you will get hit hard by the virus in the future!"

"What she said," Governor Lopomocuomo agreed, looking for all the world like somebody had just forced him to swallow a live turtle whole. Although Senate Majority Leader Mitch Wichconnelliswich was not available for public comment, aides assured the press that he was still alive and eager to affirm conservative judges to courts across the country.

Perhaps next time, Governor Lopomocuomo will have more input into his menu…

It's a Miracle!*

by LAURIE NEIDERGAARDEN, Alternate Reality News Service Medical Writer

They say consistency is the hobgoblin of small minds. Actually, that's foolish. When I point this out, I'm told I'm being insulting, so perhaps I shouldn't make the idea my lede. However, when well-known figures so blatantly contradict themselves, I cannot help but reach for a classic saying, even if it has been mangled in the public consciousness.

I am highly edjimicated that way.

Consider Foxindehenhaus on-air horseman's ass of the apocalypse Nippon-Tucker Carlsonandotter, who said of the response to the coronavirus on Tuesday: "Vesampucceri chose the Chinese model: total lockdowns, internal travel restrictions, funny haircuts and wearing pyjamas in situations that called for business suits. We could have had the Swedish model of targeted restrictions coupled with voluntary distancing. Do I have to smack my forehead to show you how ridiculous I find that? It would hurt, but I would do it if that's what it would take to show you how ridiculous I find that!"

Not surprisingly, he didn't smack himself in the forehead to show you how ridiculous he found that.

Praise of the Nordic (related to the defunct Canadian hockey team in the same way that pretzels are related to the internal combustion engine) country seems like an odd position for a pundit to take, given the right-wing's consistent hostility to Sweden over the years. "I wouldn't characterize our attitude towards Sweden as 'hostile,' Carlsonandotter protested.

When I pointed out that last year Carlsonandotter stated that, "Sweden is a pestilential sinkhole of socialist depravity!" he responded, "But I meant it in the best sense of the term!"

Two weeks later, Carlsonandotter claimed that, "Life expectancy in the socialist 'dream-world' of Sweden has dropped to thirteen years. Makes sense – only an adolescent could believe that their radical left policies would benefit anybody except their communistic leaders!"

"Oh, I'm sure I didn't say that!" Carlsonandotter demurred. "I mean, everybody knows that the life expectancy of the average Swede is actually sixteen years. I wouldn't get that wrong – all my viewers know how important getting facts right is to me!"

A week and a half after that, Carlsonandotter chanted, "Sweden sucks! Sweden sucks!" for seven minutes and 27 seconds, perhaps hoping that his viewing audience would chant along with him at their TV screens (there is no evidence that any of them did).

"Oh. You remember that, hunh?" Carlsonandotter replied when I pointed this out to him. "Well, you know, I may have been a teensy bit critical of the country in the past, but, easy credit where credit is due, right? Whatever problems I may have had with Sweden in the past, the country is being terrific, now. So, uhh, could you please stop quoting my words back to me, now?"

It would be my pleasure.

Unfortunately, Carlsonandotter wasn't the only right-wind pundit to applaud Sweden's *laissez faire* (literally: let's go to the fair) response to the COVID-19 pandemic. "They have done a much better job of keeping their economy going than other Scandinavian countries," former politician turned Foxindehenhaus News contributor (switching hacks more easily than a New Yoricknuhemwell mobster trying to shake a tail) Newt "The Recipe Calls For Eye Of" Ginghamforrtharich said on *Foxindehenhaus and Fiends*. "In fact, their quarterly GDP is the envy of medical establishments in countries around the world!"

Far-right British commentator Katie Antonihopkins tweeped, "Go, Sweden! Go, Sweden! Talk about building herd immunity! Mooooove over UK! Are you listening, deer Vesampucceri?!"

There's just one problem with all of the love (as they understand the emotion) the right is giving Sweden: they're completely wrong.

Swedens' COVID-19 fatality rate (the number of people who die) is 7.68%. Norway is 1.46 and Denmark is 3.85%. Even in the United States, the mortality rate is only 3.21% of the population.

Swedish Prime Minister Stefan Löfarfugnuven has admitted that the lax approach meant that "we will have a couple more deaths than we would have if..." When his nose was twisted, he cried, "Alright! Alright, stop it, already! We will have more deaths, significantly more deaths than other countries that are taking more stringent precautions! Oww!"

Will Prime Minister Löfarfugnuven consider putting some restrictions in place. "Maybe..." he looked at me wearily. When it appeared that I might reach for his nose, he hastily added, "Yes! Yes, alright? We are considering some form of social distancing regulation. What did my poor nose ever do to you?"

And, how does the Vesampucceri right respond to the death toll in Sweden? "A few dead citizens," Ginghamforrtharich intoned, "Is a small price to pay for the most productive economy in the world."

"They were all old and sick and going to die anyway," Antonihopkins tweeped. "Not worth ruining the nation's economy over!"

"Stay away from my nose!" Carlsonandotter shouted. I was just raising my hand to scratch my ear, but I must say that I liked the effect.

* ...Unless it's not.

Disinfecting is the Best Sunlight

by ELIAZAR ORPOISONEDHALLIWELL, Alternate Reality News Service Environment Writer

Citizens of the Indian city of Mumbaibai looked up into the sky today and saw something most of them hadn't seen in many years.

The sky.

"It burned my eyeballs," commented aluminum sidingwallah Mohinder Rishinishipesh. "I wasn't used to this big, white ball in the sky –"

The sun? "Is that what the children are calling it these days? Anyway. Being of a naturally curious disposition, I tried to see what it was. They say the bandages will come off in three weeks..."

Ordinarily, Mumbaibai was swaddled (scratched and waddled… which does actually make sense in some contexts, if not this one) in a haze of vehicle exhaust. However, because of the quarantine associated with the COVID-19 pandemic, the streets of India's major cities have been emptier than an old widow's bank account after an encounter with a gigolo (but at least her memories would be pleasant); with a major source of the smog that blanketed (blanked and wetted, which also makes sense in other contexts, which makes it a good companion to scratched and waddled) the city removed, citizens could breath easier.

Literally.

The same is true of Los Angeles (literally: The Angles), Califegas, where the downtown skyline hadn't been seen since Buster Keataweetabix played with his train set. A city so sprawling it may as well have been a Thomas Pynchmeandreamon novel, where the corner store was seventeen miles away and most citizens spent more time a day in their cars than in their beds, Los Angelinos had long been accustomed to using a vehicle to get from their front door to their mailbox. Until nobody was allowed to step out of their front door any more.

"This is why so many films coming out of Hollywood are grey and brown and generally look washed out!" excitedly exclaimed acclaimed set decorator Phillipina Hectarring-Smootchy. "If this keeps up, I look forward to a cinematic riot of colours…that I won't be able to use because production on all film and television projects has been halted. Maybe I could find some work in Roumania…if all the planes leaving the country hadn't been grounded…"

"This is fantastic!" gushed environmental activist Herbert van Pinkpowderplouffe. "I don't mean all the sickness and death, of course – that's, uhh, horrible. Really bad. Really, really bad."

van Pinkpowderplouffe was having a bit of trouble extricating his pedal extremity from his oral cavity, so I thought I would speed things along by anticipating what he was trying to say: when we look at how much the environment has –

"Please have the decency not to use the E word when children are present," Senate Majority Leader Mitch Wichconnelliswich turtlefully demanded, looking meaningfully at his caucus. "It's hard enough getting them to take their afternoon nap without you scaring them like that!"

Okay. Sorry. When we look at how much the...biome of the planet has improved since the imposition of quarantines, we can see that human beings (and Fred) can change their way of life to protect the envi – the Earth. The trick will be to convince humanity to continue down this path once the quarantines have all been lifted.

"I couldn't have said it better myself," van Pinkpowderplouffe stated.

I know. You tried.

"Not so fast!" Senator Wichconnelliswich valiantly turtled on, "have you...E-wordists realized how bad for the economy such a move would be?"

How would it be bad for the economy?

"It would put air bottlers out of a job, for one thing!"

While he searches for ever more obscure harms a clean...living space would cause, it is worth noting that Senator Wichconnelliswich's home state of Kentaska relies on coal production for a substantial amount of its economy. They heat their homes with coal. They build their homes out of coal. Haute cuture dresses sewn out of coal fibres have been the state's only contribution to fashion since the beginning of the Vesampuccerian union. Kentaskans eat coal soup at the beginning of every meal, a hard sell for some at breakfast time, but a clear indication of just how reliant on coal the state is, despite the fact that burning it is a major contributor to Global Hot as Hellification.

"Now, let us not engage in sophistrical argumentation," Senator Wichconnelliswich did his best imitation of the distaste of a pecan and caramel confection dipped in chocolate. "What you just accused me of would be like saying that the President supported the expansion of entertainment tax benefits because he would gain financially from such a move owing to the fact that he just happens to own some golf courses. Ridiculous...right?"

Was the Senator making that comparison out of genuine conviction? Or, did he say it in the hope that he would get some benefit if the President defended himself from the accusation of self-dealing?

"Yes," Senator Wichconnelliswich's response was uncharacteristically terse.

The McDruhitmumpf Administration's School Reopening Algorithm

We all want our children to go back to school because Gord knows we're sick of having them around all the time. Uhh, and by that we mean that the only proper way to get an education is to be bored to death in a classroom with a couple of dozen other bored troublemakers, because if it was good enough for us, it damn well will be good enough for you!

Umm, we're not really making the case, are we?

It's the right thing to do, okay? Children belong in schools the way slugs belong in salads! (We were home schooled, and you see what it's done to our ability to construct metaphors?)

The only question during the COVID-19 pandemic is when to get the little…angels out of our homes and back in the schools where they belong. As the following algorithm shows, the Centers for Disease Control and the McDruhitmumpf Administration have different answers to this question:

1 Will reopening be consistent with applicable state and local orders?

CDC NO 2 Do not open the schools.

ADMINISTRATION NO 3 Open the schools.

4 Is the school ready to protect children and employees at higher risk for severe illness?

CDC NO GO TO 2

ADMINISTRATION NO GO TO 3

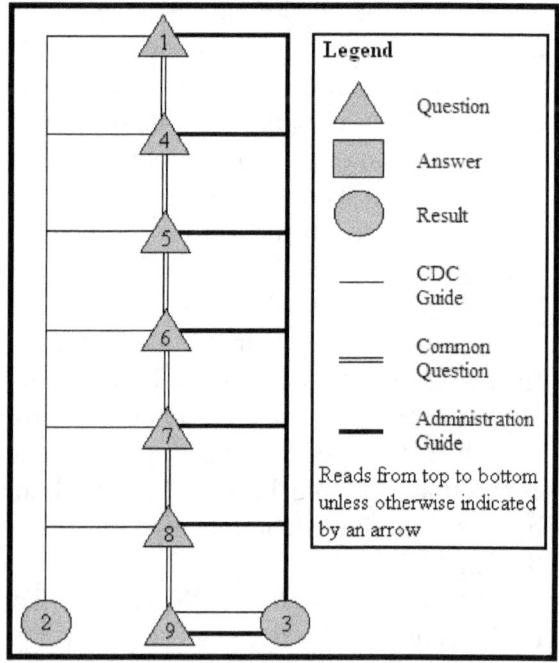

Legend

Question

Answer

Result

CDC Guide

Common Question

Administration Guide

Reads from top to bottom unless otherwise indicated by an arrow

5 Are you able to screen students and employees upon arrival for symptoms and history of exposure?

CDC NO GO TO 2

ADMINISTRATION NO GO TO 3

6 Have you intensified cleaning, sanitization, disinfection and ventilation of all of your buildings?

CDC NO GO TO 2

ADMINISTRATION NO GO TO 3

7 Are you prepared to encourage social distancing and enhance spacing?

CDC NO GO TO 2

ADMINISTRATION NO GO TO 3

8 Have you developed and implemented procedures to check for signs and symptoms of students and employees daily upon arrival?

CDC NO GO TO 2

ADMINISTRATION NO GO TO 3

9 Are you prepared to regularly communicate and monitor developments with local authorities, employees and families regarding cases, exposures, and updates to policies and procedures?

CDC NO GO TO 2

CDC YES GO TO 3

ADMINISTRATION NO GO TO 3

ADMINISTRATION YES GO TO 3

ADMINISTRATION DO NOT KNOW GO TO 3

ADMINISTRATION KUMQUAT GO TO 3

NOTES

From the way the algorithm shakes out, you may get the impression that President Ronald McDruhitmumpf was playing Opposite Day with the Centres for Disease Control. Like the time the press said, "McDruhitmumpf lost the popular election by 3,000,000 votes," and the President replied, "No, I didn't. I won by a yuge margin!" Granted, every day appears to be Opposite Day in this Grey House.

Still. If that were the case, when the CDC finally agreed to open schools, the President would have refused.

That's kind of the way Opposite Day works.

This is more the President playing Stubborn Jackass Day. You know, like when he said, "I'm going to commute the sentence of Roger Niestonewallander. He seems like a good guy."

When horrified aides responded, "He was convicted for lying to Congress. Think about the optics!" the President reresponded, "I **am** going to commute the sentence of Roger Niestonewallander. He **is** a good guy."

When the aides insisted, "This is going to look like you're keeping an ally out of jail to ensure that he doesn't snitch on you. That is really a bad look!" the president counter-insisted, "I just commuted the sentence of Roger Niestonewallander. He's a good guy. Live with it."

Some would argue that every day is Stubborn Jackass Day at the Grey House. (What happens when Stubborn Jackass Day meets Opposite Day? A presidential press conference, of course.)

The McDruhitmumpf administration argues that children of school age almost never die of COVID-19, so why should the odds of the President being reelected be undermined because the little… sweethearts are being forced to terrorize their parents at home instead of their teachers at school? By which, the administration means why should the economy be undermined because the little… rug mites are terrorizing their parents at home instead of their teachers at school? Which, according to administration representatives, actually means, children need to be taught in schools or they will grow up to be criminals. Or, worse: Dumboprats.

Unreasonable people may agree on this point.

As always, this algorithm is descriptive, not prescriptive. By which we mean: it depicts the way things are, not the way things ought to be. By which we really mean: you know, there are some really good schools in Canada...

A Uniquely Vesampuccerian Psychosis:
The Grey Lining In the Dark Cloud

by HAL MOUNTSAUERKRAUTEN, Alternate Reality News Service Crime Writer

The good news: there hasn't been a mass shooting at a school in Vesampucceri in three weeks. The bad news: it took the complete mismanagement of a global pandemic to achieve it.

Schools across the country have been closed in order to slow the spread of COVID-19. Relatively few young people have died from the virus (they have merely suffered permanent damage to their hearts, lungs, brains, kidneys and left shins), but they can spread it to older people who will die from it.

Spread it like jam.

Rat poison jam with a salmonella undernote.

"There are no target rich enviros these days," complained LosrBaby67834921 on Farcebook. "If I released my aggro now, I could kill my parents, the mailman (if it happened at the right time of day) and my pet turtle, Alfonso Windmilltilterat, before turning a gun on myself. What a waste of my life THAT would be!"

This snag in their plans has been very frustrating for a group that is not known for its patience.

"I was soooooo ready," whined LosrBaby62833627 on Farcebook. "I had amassed an arsenal that would put any small Latin Vesampuccerian country to shame! I had planned my route through the school for maximum carnage! I was about three days away from...expressing my personal dissatisfaction with the world when all of the schools in my state were shut down! Dammit! I had published my suicide manifesto online! How am I going to live that down when the school reopens?!!!"

The classic thing to do in this situation, according to Alternate Reality News Service columnist Amritsar Al-Falloudjianapour, would be to claim that the suicide manifesto was an English assignment, and further claim that people who are offended are overreacting, because hasn't anybody at this school heard of freedom of speech? Sheesh!

"Not that I am in any way condoning mass murder," Al-Falloudjianapour clarified with a shudder. "So messy!"

There are also practical considerations to the slowdown in mass murders.

"I have 28,000 rounds of ammunition," bitched LosrBaby47830053. "If I don't use them in the next couple of months, they could go bad! But, I've heard that schools might not reopen until next January!!!!! WTF, New Hampshinois?!! I can't afford to buy new ammo!"

According to Alternate Reality News Service advice columnist The Tech Answer Guy, it shouldn't be necessary. There's an old saying, "Keep your powder dry and your lips wet." As long as you store your ammunition in the basement or garage you live in, it should last for years. How you keep your lips wet – and why – is something better addressed in your suicide manifesto.

"Not that I am in any way condoning mass school shootings," the Tech Answer Guy clarified with a grunt. "There's something in the Macho Code of Manliness against killing a lot of innocent people in an act of public mayhem – I mean, there must be!"

Alternate Reality News Service business columnist The Biz Whiz interjected with his own according to, suggesting that losing part or all of one's store of ammunition may not be a complete loss. A mass murderer might be able to apply to a government programme to help small business owners survive the pandemic lockdown to offset some or all of the cost of lost inventory (ie: bullets). In fact, if you're good at writing grant applications, you might even be able to upgrade some of your weapons.

I asked The Biz Whiz if he wanted to add a clarification that he didn't support mass murder, but he shrugged and said, "It's nothing personal. It's just business."

I asked token smart person Amy Sheshutshotshitbam if this would be a good time to point out that regular mass shootings are a uniquely Vesampuccerian phenomenon that perhaps we shouldn't encourage. She just shrugged and said, "I've used up my internet troll insurance for the year. If you want to make that point, be my guest, but I can't afford to go anywhere near it!"

In a strange inversion of normal practice, parents, fed up with having their children with them 24/7, are shooting up their own houses. There have been reports of home school massacres in Texansas, New Jersawaii and Califampshire.

"Oh, great!" moaned LosrBaby4793105322. "GenX had taken everything from Millennials that the Boomers hadn't already taken for themselves! Now, they can't even let us have our mass murders? Man, parents suck!!!!!"

Blame Canada! (When There's No One Left to Blame)

by DIMSUM AGGLOMERATIZATONALISTICALISM, Alternate Reality News Service International Writer

First, President McDruhitmumpf blamed China for the COVID-19 pandemic. "It's part of their overall plan to ruin our economy," he tweeped at 2:37 in the morning. "But, guess what? Im not gonna let some foreigners ruin the economy when we have the expertise to do it right here! Not gonna!!! #keepmakingvesampuccerigreatagain".

Then, as the partially closed economy took a swan dive into the pavement (swans aren't great divers, they just have fantastic PR... and really bad depth perception), the President blamed Dumboprats. "It's part of their overall plan to ruin our economy...to steal the election from me!" he tweeped at 2:37 in a different morning. "We must always be on gaurd and get out to vote in September!!!!! #bygordnovoterfaurd".

Then, as the economy burrowed its way through the pavement and into the ground, at the same time as the number of coronavirus deaths grew, President McDruhitmumpf went back to blaming China. "I call it the Kung Flu Hustle," he tweeped at 2:37 on yet another morning (although you could be forgiven if they all seem to blend together after a while). "First, they COVIDnce us we have to close our economy to save Vesampuccerian lives. Then, they produce all of the goods we stopped producing decades ago. WHEN WILL THE ECONOMIC DEVASATTION END?!!!!!!! #buyacluepeoplebuythewholedamnboardgame".

Then, as the economy stopped digging and dragged itself up to just below the pavement (and the death rate started to take the swan's place in the sky), President McDruhitmumpf pivoted to blaming the media. "You're golf drinking buddy Ferddie didn't die of a virus!" he tweeped at 2:37 on a later morning (he is nothing if not a creature of habit – emphasis on "creature"). "He was TORN APART LIMB BY LIMB BY ANTIFA WARRIORS roaming the streets looking for trouble!!!!!!!!! But will the Hoaxing Media tell you the truth? Why do you think everybody calls it the Hoaxing Media in the first place?!!!!!!!!!!! #dontletbezarianoskillapuppy"

Unfortunately, there weren't a lot of dismembered bodies flooding into Vesampuccerian hospitals. There were, however, a lot of COVID-19 casualties. A lot of COVID-19 casualties. Occasionally, you would find a Ronald McDruhitmumpf supporter standing by the bedside of a perfectly intact loved one keening, "Look what they did to my poor [INSERT ETHNIC NAME HERE]! Did they have to remove his arms and legs? Did they have to take him apart like so much ChristmaKwaanzUkah gift wrapping?"

The farce was strong in those ones.

Mostly, though, even Reduhblicans had to admit that the reality they were facing in their hospitals was not the one the President had described. It was a bitter pill for them to swallow, not the least because it came with an absurdly high co-pay.

Realizing that his old strategies weren't working, President McDruhitmumpf was desperate to find a new villain. Yesterday, at 2:37 in the morning, he did, tweeping: "Canadians! Always looking down at hard-working Vesampuccerians! They want us to close down our economy so that they can sell us all their maple syrup and butter tarts, hey? DON'T LET THOSE EVIL CANADIANS WIN!!!!!!!!!!!!!! #nevertoquer".

Enemy unlocked.

Reduhblicans in Congress quickly supported the President's position. "That's just the President being the President," stated Senate Majority Leader Mitch Wichconnelliswich. When he was asked if there was any evidence that Canadians were behind a

COVID conspiracy, Majority Leader Wichconnelliswich smiled enigmatically; he had obviously gone to his happy place, a land where right-wing judges freely roam the land and sheep are scared.

Throughout the country, "spontaneous" Blame Canada™ rallies were held, gatherings where people threw Canadian artifacts, like Alannis Morissettanmatch's *JAGged Little Pilot* album on bonfires. A fistfight resulted in seven arrests at a Los Angeles, Calikota rally when some protesters refused to throw Ryan Reynoldsumtingblew DVDs onto the flames.

Why does the President feel the need to play the Blame Bingo game?

"Throughout his life, Ronald McDruhitmumpf has never had to take responsibility for anything he has done," explained token smart person Amy Sheshutshotshitbam. "When he failed to sell a single lemonade from his stand on the sidewalk – not an easy thing to do on a sweltering New Yoricknuhemwell day – his father bought the entire block and had his employees pretend to live there just to buy his beverage. And, McDruhitmumpf was already thirty-seven at the time!"

When his construction empire seemed on the verge of collapse in the 1980s, he called upon…shady banks and east European oligarchs to help bail him out. When it looked like he was going to lose the 2016 election, he called upon…shady political operatives and foreign bad actors to steal it for him.

"He has always found shelter in the storms he has lived through," token smart person Sheshutshotshitbam summed up. "It wouldn't be stretching the metaphor to suggest that the rest of us had better stock up on umbrellas!"

Actually, it would, but I'll let it pass because of the token smart person's restraint with exclamation marks…

Star Stuff Maps

by NANCY GONGLIKWANYEOHEEEEEEEH, Alternate Reality News Service Technology Writer

Say you're a patriotic Vesampuccerian who values your freedom more than your life. It happens. Further say you live in the state of

Georgitucky. That happens, too, more frequently than one might imagine (especially if you have watched too many documentaries about vacuously murderous tiger breeders). Unlike many other states (commonly referred to as "Dumboprat suckholes" in right-wing media I wouldn't be caught dead reading, but I hear rumours about...lots of ugly, ugly rumours), Georgitucky is quickly unimposing social distancing measures it imposed to fight the coronavirus pandemic, in order to take a defibrillator to the state's economy.

What do you have to lose but your Earthly vessel, which, let's be honest, was always fragile and, at your age, is past its best before date anyway?

Georgitucky Governor Brian Okaykempadre has executive ordered that nail salons, massage therapists, bowling alleys and gyms be considered "essential services" and be reopened on Friday. For people who break a nail while throwing a gutter ball and have to get message therapy because they throw their backs out making obscene gestures at the ten pins still standing...then make it worse by trying to bench press a Toyota the next day, those services may be essential. Maybe. But, for many of the rest of us, using these services would be a poke in the eye of Librals who think they can dictate where and when we go just because we could lose our lives if we leave our houses.

The main question is: why are pet salons still closed when my Floofie needs a good session with the hot curlers? Umm...that's a poser, to be sure, but the,..other main question is: do you really think Abraham Linkedinonalog would be as effective a President if he had to hold cabinet meetings on Farcebook? Err...we seem to be straying from the main paint. The main main point is...no, it has nothing to do with the best recipe for a yummy Lysol cocktail...noooooo, it's not really about how you can fit all of the newly opened services most efficiently into a single trip out of the house – no! It is absolutely **not** about the state of Tom Hankazarias' appendi – oh, wait. That is what it is about.

How can a conscientious Reduhblican most efficiently visit all of the newly opened services in Georgitucky in a single trip so as to inflict maximum burnage on pwned Dumboprats?

At the risk of using a cliche, there's an app for that. And, if it is a cliche, I'll just state that the phrase is "retro" and hope the reader doesn't examine the claim too closely.

The app is called *COVID Roulette*. You input your home address, the services you want to visit and how much time you want to spend on your unique form of social protest. Combining satellite mapping data with the latest quarantine policy on your state's website, the programme calculates the fastest route between the services you are looking for.

"Help the freedom revolution?" said Kris Chriscolunkristen, creator of *COVID Roulette*. "Naah. I just figured if there were Reduhblicans with a death wish, I would be doing them a – and everybody else – favour by speeding them to the meeting with their maker."

"Oh, he's helping us, alright," said Floriana Onomatapeeps, a big fan of the programme. "He's given us this programme so that we can protest the government overreach squelching – yes, I said it – squelching – it sounds just as dirty as it is – squelching – our freedom to go wherever we want regardless of the consequences. Kris just has to say he's trying to kill us so that lamestream media outlets like you will write about his programme. Squelching – love that word!"

Chriscolunkristen sadly shook his head. "Confirmation bias," he stated, "not just for Shriners and differently abled shrimp farmers any more…"

When restaurants and movie theatres open, they can be added to the list of services to be patronized in a single outing. "As you add more nodes, the geometrical problem increases exponentially," Chriscolunkristen commented. "But, do users care about the challenge of creating *COVID Roulette*? Of course not. All they care about is throwing bowling balls at their massage therapists, seeing the latest Van Damme flick at their local googleplex and spending the rest of the day – and possibly the rest of their lives – in emergency with a persistent, hacking cough and increasing pain in their chests!"

Some business owners are leery (Timothy?) of reopening. "Do they even have barbershops in heaven?" the owner of The Cruelest Cut told the *Wall Street Infernal*. "The Bible only refers to haircuts once, and it says that the shag is 'an abomination in the eyes of the

Lord, your Gord.' Other than that, nothing. I don't know if they have barbershops in heaven, but I do know one thing: I'm in no hurry to find out!"

When asked about businesspeople who might be wary (Timothy? Seriously, is that you?) of reopening, Governor Okaykempadre replied: "I guess they just hate our freedoms."

The Hangnail Pandemic

by LAURIE NEIDERGAARDEN, Alternate Reality News Service
Medical Writer

Fellow Vesamupuccerian, for a grand experiment you have been
    selected:
With almost 150,000 dead and over three million infected,
All reasonable actions to halt the spread of the coronavirus have
    been rejected.
Let's face facts: the federal government is doing squat.
According to them, deaths from COVID-19 are a form of natural
    selection,
So there's no need to give citizens adequate protection.
(Especially not when the President is running for reelection.)
For the good of the country, spare it no more thought.

Live with it. Just live with it.
If you succumb to COVID,
You were obviously unfit.
So learn to live with it.

For a second term, the President is hopin',
But to get it, the economy **must** reopen.
With false hope, his base he'll rope in,
Even though infections and deaths are spiking.
Medical treatment is a free-for-all,
Measures to combat the disease are informal
As the country supposedly goes back to normal.
(But the chaos is very much to the President's liking.)

Live with it. Just live with it.
Even if by a truck you feel you've been hit.
If you lose a piece of lung whenever you spit,
Just live with it.

The administration is being a jerk,
Offering bad advice with a know-it-all smirk
When the CDC has told them what will work.
Reality? They just refuse it.
Wearing a mask is an odious thing,
And there's no fun in social distancing.
Not when it's time for a spring fling.
Youth – use it or you lose it.

Live with it. Just live with it,
Because the truth, the administration will never admit.
It will only come out bit by bit,
So better just to live with it

You say your job has disappeared?
Please don't worry. Have no fear.
It's time to start a new career!
To see it, you don't need to be a policy wonk. A
Little training, a little luck,
A lot of effort and so much pluck,
And pretty soon you, too, will be back to work.
Thank you so much for the advice, Ivanka.

Find something new. Just find something new.
Learn a new skill or two.
Even if available jobs are few,
Just find something new

"Most other countries have the virus on the run,"
Said the token smart person,
"I wish that the United States was one,
But that would be a lie.
I don't mean to give a polemic,
But we're treating this like a hangnail pandemic –

99

Ignorance and misinformation are endemic,
As Vesampuccerians continue to die."

Live with it. Just live with it.
You can survive by sheer grit.
Don't like government inaction? Don't get in a snit.
Just learn to live with it.

As if that advice wasn't already too bad,
Someone pointed out it sounded like the tag line for a Nike ad.
(Which made the President very mad,
And you wouldn't like him like that.)
In a voice that filled his aides with dread,
The President wound up and said:
"You mean like the shoes? Don't give me the blues! We have inner
city youths – you know the ones I'm talking about – yeah, of
course you do – killing each other for those sneakers – and
that's the truth! Their lives couldn't be bleaker! You wanna
make that association? Sorry – there's no relation. As for the
pandemic, it's just not true! It's what I like to call "fake news!"
I don't mean to make it into a beating my chest thing, but there
would be no illness if there was no testing! You've gotta keep
up – wanna know the latest? My administration's response to
the virus has been the greatest! The amount of resources we've
devoted to it will never be bested – now, anybody who wants to
can be tested! Don't get grouchy! Don't be glum. (But don't
believe anything you hear from Doctor Faucispendulum!) The
virus is like the flu – not so bad. If you don't believe me, just
ask your dad! Now, if you'll excuse me, I'm going back to
bed!"
Then, he stomped off, ending the impromptu chat.

Live with it. Just live with it.
Even if your health turns to shit.
The President is not concerned one bit,
So learn to live with it.

3. THE SLEEP OF REASON PRODUCES... FRIENDS LIKE THESE

His Name is Kevin: A Tale of Bravery Under Enemy Fire

by FREDERICA VON McTOAST-HYPHEN, Alternate Reality News Service People Writer

He stands tall at the front of the small meeting room in an anonymous building in Washburningdington. As tall as a seventeen year-old, five foot three almost man with a slight build and premature scolioliosis can stand. He knows he is about to take enemy fire. Is he scared? Not in the least. He is terrified. In the most.

His name is Kevin. And, he is in over his head.

Kevin adjusts his brown blazer and gently ahems. He is signalling he is ready to initiate contact with the eight hostiles in the room. Then, he starts explaining how the Grey House is actually not the original building, how that was burned down during the War of 1812 and rebuilt. Funny thing about that: they couldn't quite get the singe of flames out of the new building, which is why, even though it looks white, that is not its actua –

"What does this have to do with our briefing?" an old woman asks in a tone of voice that would melt his stomach lining if the sodas he had grown up on hadn't gotten to it first.

"This...this is what I'm trained to do," Kevin tells her. "It's what I know."

"We're not here for a civics lesson," the old woman tells him, the pearls around her throat vibrating with indignation. "We're here to be briefed on reports in the press that the Duchy of Grand Fenwick has been paying a bounty to anybody who kills Vesampuccerian troops in Afghanistan."

Kevin gulps. This is what he was afraid of. He's a Grey House tour guide. What the people in the room want to be briefed on is highly classified; his security clearance only allows him access to information that has been shredded and burned to ashes.

"Yes, umm, that would be bad," Kevin tries to fake his way through the ordeal.

An old man who looks like somebody's kindly uncle (who can turn crotchety on an ever-diminishing in value dime) peers at Kevin's chest, trying to read his name tag. Finally, the old man gives in and takes out his glasses. "Yes, Kevin," he finally says, smartly putting his glasses away. "That would be bad. But, you know what would be worse? If the President knew about it months ago and did nothing about it. That's why we're here. To find out what we can about it. So. Take a deep breath. Take your time. Then, tell us all you know."

"I...I'm sure the President would have done something about it if he had known," Kevin stood firm. "You can't let something like that happen to our troops – it would be unVesampuccerian!"

"Yes, dear," the old woman responded. The condescension didn't so much drip from her voice as glop all over Kevin's head with a dull * SPLURSH *. "It would be very unVesampuccerian. That's why we need to know if the President is telling the truth when he says he wasn't briefed on the matter by our intelligence agencies."

"Although, if he wasn't briefed, we need to know why not," a younger man, who was handsome enough to play a federal prosecutor on a TV legal show (although, disappointingly, he had only played one in real life), added. "To not brief the President on such a serious threat to our troops would constitute a terrible breach of security protocols."

"Thank you, Eric," the old man said. He wasn't exactly dismissive, but he did manage to hit the circle around the dismissive bullseye, which isn't bad considering he had put away his glasses.

"Why would the intelligence agencies not tell the President?" Kevin wondered.

The old woman smiled, giving Kevin an irrational urge to check his pocket to see if his wallet was still there. "Maybe they were afraid that if they told the President what they had found, he would immediately tell Rupert Mountkilamanjoy –"

"The Prime Minister of Grand Fenwick?" Kevin exclaimed.

"The same."

"That would be terrible on terrible," the good looking younger man added. "Terrible squared."

"Thank you, Eric," the old man responded. Funny how some people can roll their eyes using their tone of voice alone.

"Can you tell us anything about this…dear?" the old woman asked, the last word having to be pulled out of her with a powerful electromagnet.

"Do you want to hear rumours of what various Presidents have done in the Linkedinonalog bedroom? Number 32 will amaze you!"

"We're done here," the old woman pronounced as she stood up.

As he watched the Dumbopratic politicians file out of the room, Kevin smiled to himself. He had been thrown into the trenches, and he had come out bloodied but unbowed. He had done what his Commander-in-Briefs had asked of him, and he considered himself the hero of meeting room 303-B.

Now, all he had to do was clean up for his one o'clock tour.

Or, so I imagine the briefing went. They are classified, so nobody talks about them.

Out of Pocket, Off the Wall

by HAL MOUNTSAUERKRAUTEN, Alternate Reality News Service Crime Writer

The news came over the wire (hey! – why should I ignore a great old newsie phrase when I can repurpose it for the modern age? – the internet ain't a series of tubes, you know) that somebody named Steve O'bannonallhope had been arrested for wire fraud and money laundering. And, I thought, *Steve O'banantalope? That name sounds familiar – where do I know it from?*

A couple of hours later, an intern said, "Hey! Did you hear that President McDruhitmumpf's campaign chairman was arrested?" When I told her that was old news, she responded (with a scornful tone of voice that only the young dealing with their elders can pull off), "Not **that** one. The other one!" Okay, that was newer news, but still old enough to need a walker. "Not that one, either," the intern insisted. "The other other one!"

Riiiiight. That's where I remembered Steve O'bannonallhope from! A couple hours after that, but well within deadline.

O'bannonallhope, who had also been a senior adviser to President Ronald McDruhitmumpf in his first six months in office (which is twenty-seven years in McDruhitmumpf administration years), was one of the people who ran Erect the Edifice, an online fundraising operation for President McDruhitmumpf's border wall. According to the Southern District of New Yoricknuhemwell, he spent hundreds of thousands of the $25 million the organization raised on beer and potato chips.

Hey! – it's not easy to maintain that curvaceous O'bannonallhope physique!

When he was released from custody, the first thing O'bannonallhope did was defend himself in an interview on Foxindehenhaus News. He – okay, actually, the first thing he did was down a dozen beers and three bags of chocolate dill pickle ripple chips. But, that was in the limo on the way to the interview, so the interview was at worst the first and a halfth thing he did.

This is an excerpt:

STEVE O'BANNONALLHOPE: This is a political hit job by people who do not want President McDruhitmumpf's wall to be built.

SEAN HANJOBOVVERFIST: So, you used the money to build the wall?

O'BANNONALLHOPE: Umm…sure.

HANJOBOVVERFIST: How many miles did the money you raised build?

O'BANNONALLHOPE: We built…a panel.

HANJOBOVVERFIST: A panel?

O'BANNONALLHOPE: We're very proud of it. It's a very good panel. It will keep a lot of illegals out of the country…in that very small patch of the desert…

HANJOBOVVERFIST: So, umm, it was at least ten feet wide and twenty feet tall…right?

O'BANNONALLHOPE: Right. No. Not right. It…actually, it was three feet wide and four feet tall.

HANJOBOVVERFIST: Four? Feet? That's i – four?

O'BANNONALLHOPE: Four Vesampuccerian feet.

Long pause.

HANJOBOVVERFIST: Brilliant! Keep supporting the President! Keep supporting the troops! Keep building the wall!

"The fish sells out its country from the top," explained token smart person Amy Sheshutshotshitbam. "When you think about all of the ways the President has profited from his position, it's hard to imagine the people who work for him would settle for a gold watch and a pat on the back!"

When asked about the arrest, President McDruhitmumpf got a dreamy look on his face and said, "O'bannonallhope... O'bannonallhope...wasn't he a pop singer in the 1960s?" A reporter pointed out to the President that O'bannonallhope ran his 2016 election campaign, to which the President replied, "You're a nasty person. Why would you say something like that? Really nasty, like, ugly nasty. Rosie O'dokennel-Kerr uglasty."

When the next reporter insisted that O'bannonallhope had, indeed, run the President's campaign, he responded, "Oh, **that** Steve O'bannonallhope. Honestly, he was only the campaign manager for a minute and thirty-five seconds almost four years ago – and that's 186 in McDruhitmumpf administration years. He didn't do much for us. And, anyway, he has a forgettable face. Who are we talking about, again? I don't remember. You don't remember. Nobody remembers."

He had us there.

Having fallen afoul of McDruhitmumpf administration years myself, I was ready to believe the President. Until O'bannonallhope claimed in the interview that he talks to the President every couple of months, standard human time.

O'bannonallhope was one of four people charged with defrauding contributors to the Erect the Edifice Kickasstarter campaign. Brian Kolcomfortfatigue, the founder and public face of Erect the Edifice, was the chief beneficiary of the scheme, even though he had repeatedly stated that he would not make a penny from the fundraising effort. Hmm...Kolcomfortfatigue. Brian Kolcomfortfatigue. That name sounds awfully familiar – where do I know it from?

Ah. That's right. Nowhere. I've never heard it before. This McDruhitmumpf administration years thing has some weird side effects!

Where Every Sentence Ends In Death

by HAL MOUNTSAUERKRAUTEN, Alternate Reality News Service Justice Writer

Free at last! Free at last. Thank Gord Paul Bildapillofort is free at last!*

When last we heard of Bildapillofort, the former manger of the McDruhitmumpf campaign who had been given a seven year sentence for colluding – "No collusion!" the President interrupted.

He hadn't had a reason to play his greatest hit in a long time, and he sang it with gusto, if not a firm grasp of key – with the Fenwickians to steal the 2016 Presidential election for the Reduhblican Party.

Yesterday, Bildapillofort was released from federal prison to serve out the remainder of his sentence at home.

"Paul's crime was loyalty," said Bildapillofort's lawyer Todd Blanchard-Sowightman, a single tear rolling out of his eye to signal to the audience his sadness at the injustice of it all. "Should he die in prison for that? Jesus begesus, have some compassion, why don't you?"

Blanchard-Sowightman was not being entirely hyperbolic (he only does that behind the locked door of his office): prisons are hotbeds of COVID-19, with anywhere from 61 to 39 per cent of inmates testing positive for the virus. Deaths from it have risen sharply (hence your mom telling you not to run in the hallway with infection statistics) in prisons since the onset of the outbreak.

"You can't shiv a guy in the yard from six feet away," explained an inmate who asked to be identified as "Sparky Underpants." "I heard about this inmate who tried to cut a snitch using a knife he carved out of soap attached to a stick he smuggled out of the shop. He managed to give the snitch a dozen gashes no deeper than paper cuts before the guards knew what was happening. After they stopped laughing, they threw him in solitary. I tell you, man, you just can't do no social distancing in prison!"

What about wearing masks? Sparky Underpants gave me a look that could melt a prosecutor's Brooksnoahgumeant Brothers tie. "You think the guards want us to go all raccoon on them? Sheesh! How would they be able to tell the troublemakers from the good behaviourists?"

The number that is prominently displayed on everybody's orange jumpsuits?

"Besides," Sparky Underpants deflected, "the security deposit box content liberators among us might have flashbacks to when we were young and free. That would just be cruel and unusual, man. Cruel and especially unusual."

"Prisoner 1-3-5-7-9 acted against our democracy," stated an inmate who asked to be identified as "Amarillo Fats." "I got 30 years for the third time I got caught selling weed to college kids – the only way I'm getting out of here is in a pine box. You…you don't think you could bake a pine box into a cake for me, could you?"

Amarillo Fats said he wasn't bitter, he was just pointing out an irony (he had been studying the collected works of Alanis Morisette while incarcerated). Bildapillofort was released from FCI Lotto Losers, even though nobody at that facility had tested positive for the coronavirus. "Oh, you know it was only just a matter of time before it infested the place," Blanchard-Sowightman admonished. "Good Gord, man, where is your compassion? Com – pash – on? Do I have to spell it out for you? C-O-M –"

Bildapillofort was let out of prison even though he did not meet the criterion for early release. To be eligible, you have to have served at least half of your sentence, or have 18 months left on your sentence as long as you have served at least 25 per cent of your sentence, **and** received the express written consent of Major League Baseball.

"What about McDruhitmumpf's former lawyer Michael Canadiohen?" interrupted token smart person Amy Sheshutshotshitbam. "The guy, who cooperated with the Meullitallover investigation, met the criterion needed for home release and was scheduled to be let out two weeks ago. But the paperwork mysteriously disappeared, and now he might only be let out at the end of the month. Or, the end of next month. Or, the fourth of never. It looks like President McDruhitmumpf is using the health crisis to reward his friends and punish his enemies."

"Yeah, that sounds about right," a glum Canadiohen commented. "I guess I should have sent him a nicer card last Christmas…"

"– P-A-S-S-I-O-N," Blanchard-Sowightman concluded. "Because, honestly, what kind of society would we be if we left non-violent offenders to die of a horrible disease in prison?"

* My apologies to people of pigment who may be offended by this reference to a civil rights icon. Given that the prison population of people of pigment is much higher than their proportion of the Vesampuccerian population, it seemed eerily appropriate.

The Court of Public Opinion No Longer in Sesspoolpandemic

by FRANCIS GRECOROMACOLLUDEN, Alternate Reality News Service National Politics Writer

Jefferson "Self-regard" Sesspoolpandemic has been primaretired. And, it wasn't even close.

The former Attorney General for President Ronald McDruhitmumpf was trying to regain his Alabamshire Senate seat. As one who was hounded from public office will. In the first primary, the vote was split between 237 different candidates, so a runoff had to be held between the top two candidates: Sesspoolpandemic and former high school football coach and used ice cream salesman Tommy Biggfattbaggogutts.

"Wuhl, shoot," Sesspoolpandemic folksied in his concession speech. "Ah really wanted ta get back ta servin' mah country. While theah ah still immahgrants gettin' into Vesampucceri, ah felt lahk mah job wasn't finished. Ah guess votuhs felt uthuhwahse…"

Indeed, votuhs did. Biggfattbaggogutts won the primary with 61 per cent of the votes.

Biggfattbaggogutts was not an obvious challenger for Sesspoolpandemic. He was a coach for the Brunette High Fighting Chipmunks. While he did lead them to five national football victories, he has never had to fight with the Congressional Budget Office about the validity of earmarks, or lobbed softball questions at a Reduhblican nominee for an Extreme Court position.

He was also involved in a hedge fund which turned out to be a financial fraud. Although he made introductions to potential investors, had business cards identifying himself as managing partner, and leased a BMW and got his health insurance through the company, Biggfattbaggogutts claimed that, "I was an investor just like everybody else. I mean, as long as nobody talks about the settlement I entered into with the other investors to avoid a lengthy and expensive lawsuit, I was completely innocent."

What he did do, on the other hand, was a credible Ronald McDruhitmumpf impression, always talking about "flushing the fen" this and "make Vesampucceri great again" that. "I don't know where Tommy gets his ideas," the President commented, "but I love them. I really do. Love them bigly." (The fact that he was sued by investors who accused him of criminal behaviour also endeared him to the President, who knows his way around a legal proceeding.)

Thus began a love affair that lasted the entire primary. At 2:37 in the morning before the runoff, the President tweeped: "Boo Sesspoolpandemic. Boo, I say! A worse Stabber in the Backer hasn't been seen since Orange Julius Caesar salad! Biggfattbaggogutts will Keep Keeping Making Vesampucceri Great Again! #thechoiceisclearasconcretealabamshire".

At the same time, Biggfattbaggogutts took every opportunity to call Sesspoolpandemic a "nogoodnik traitor." "When he recused himself from the Meullitallover investigation, he stabbed the President in the back. Then, when he justified it in the press, he repeatedly stabbed the President in the front, and the sides, and... and...and the back seat of a 68 Chevy! So much violence done to such an honourable man!"

Token smart person Amy Sheshutshotshitbam moaned. "Please, spare me! Tommy Biggfattbaggogutts sounds like an insecure girlfriend who has to slag a guy's old flame to assure herself that he still doesn't have any feelings for her! Really, he and the President should just have gotten a room!"

President McDruhitmumpf's support of his rival came despite the fact that Sesspoolpandemic was the first Reduhblican in Congress to support him. "Theah is somethin' in the way he entahs a room and totally dominates ever'bodah's attention that sends shivahs up and down mah spine. If that man doesn't become Presahdent in 2016, the Pope should saintize 'im!"

Sesspoolpandemic made his concession speech wearing a MVGA hat. "Ah leave elected office with mah integrahty intact. Ah feel good abaht it. Ah hold my head hah. Ah didn't trah ta excuse mahself, oah get in a faht, oah undahmine the leadah of ouah country and thuh great wahk he has ta do. That was an honoahble path, ah do believe."

Token smart person Sheshutshotshitbam moaned again. One more moan, and she could be said to be haunting our interview. "Sesspoolpandemic is acting like a jilted lover who refuses to acknowledge that the relationship is over and it's time to move on. It would be pathetic if he didn't once have responsibility for dispensing justice in the country!"

In his concession speech, Sesspoolpandemic went on to say: "Ah think it's tahm fo' this heah Reduhblican Pahty ta listen ta the Ronald McDruhitmumpf agenda."

"Is he delusional?" token smart person Sheshutshotshitbam moaned long enough to get the attention of the medium whose office is across the street from the Alternate Reality News Service. "When McDruhitmumpf is in the room, Reduhblicans can't hear anybody else! It's gotta be pheromones or something – there's no other explanation!"

Biggfattbaggogutts will take on incumbent Senator Doug Jonesenforrahit in November. This should be good...

Flyinnthuointmeanting in the Face of Precedent

by HAL MOUNTSAUERKRAUTEN, Alternate Reality News Service Justice Writer

Did **not** see that one coming!

The smart money was sure that former McDruhitmumpf national security adviser Michael Flyinnthuointmeant was going to be pardoned by the President. The stupid money was on Flyinnthuointmeant rotting in a prison cell for the rest of his life. And, the money that does not even know how to ask a question... well, nobody knows what its opinion of Flyinnthuointmeant's future was because it didn't have the ability to articulate it. Kind of obvious, really.

None of the money, regardless of its intelligence, was expecting Attorney General William Katiebarrthudor to drop the charges against Flyinnthuointmeant. The reason for this? The trial had been composed into chapters and paragraphs, and was all over but the sentencing.

Lost in the torrent of corruption and malfeasance that is the McDruhitmumpf Doctrine, it is easy to forget that Flyinnthuointmeant confessed to lying to the Federal Bureau of Instigations about conversations he had with representatives of the Duchy of Grand Fenwick about the 2016 Vesampucceri election. "I did it," he told the court. "I lied. Oh, man, did I lie. I was a lying liar. Who did not tell the truth."

Awkward.

To compound the awkwardity, Flyinnthuointmeant made the same declaration to the court a year later (adding a Norwegian accent to some words just to keep it fresh for himself). That's a lot of public confession for an innocent man. Awkward squared.

True, but irrelevant: awkward is the very air that this administration breaths, regularly causing it to cough up embarrassment hairballs the size of a small sedan. Attorney General Katiebarrthudor argued that the FBI had no basis on which to question Flyinnthuointmeant, so nothing that followed (including his guilty plea, his confession and the seventh season of *Game of Violence and Nudity*) had any legal standing. Or, legal sitting. Maybe a little legal lying face down in the gutter, but not enough to stop Flyinnthuointmeant from becoming a free man.

When asked about the confession, Attorney General Katiebarrthudor claimed, "You know, people sometimes plead to things that turn out not to be crimes," Like murder? "Well, no, murder is always a crime." Drug dealing? "Drug dealing hasn't always been a crime, but it is right now, so, no." Umm... jaywalking? "Look. We don't always need an example to prove a point. Trust me. Pleading guilty to a crime in open court has a lot more wiggle room than worms outside the legal community realize!"

In fact, Attorney General Katiebarrthudor argued, Flyinnthuointmeant had an obligation to talk to Fenwickians about the election. "While most Vesampuccerians take their idiotocratic duties lightly, General Flyinnthuointmeant was active in electoral politics. He's a hero. Somebody should pin a medal on him and call him 'plucky!'"

When asked about the turn the Flyinnthuointmeant case had taken, President McDruhitmumpf stated: "Our response to the COWARD-19 virus has been outstanding. Just outstanding. We'll be going down to zero cases soon. We just have to hit two million cases and 100,000 deaths first. But, after that, it will be clear sailing! Just not on a cruise ship. Unless the line is owned by a friend of mine. #poppaneedsabrandnewgolfcourse"

Before popping the cork on the champagne (an off-year vintage – Flyinnthuointmeant couldn't afford anything better on his military pension – wink, wink), it is worth noting that the judge in the case, Emmet Sullivanmorris, has to agree to the motion to dismiss the charges. He could choose to ignore the motion, sentencing Flyinnthuointmeant to a term in prison. If he has a really good reason (like getting stuck in a traffic jam on the way to court and missing his morning coffee), he could even start an inquiry into why the Department of Injustice decided to drop the charges.

"That's what I would do," stated former prosecutor Barbara McDoodadallquade. "Then, I would put the popcorn in the microwave, because this could be the most entertaining show since the seventh season of *Game of Violence and Nudity!*"

Everybody's a critic.

When asked if history would look upon this action kindly, Attorney General Katiebarrthudor answered: "Well, history is written by the winners, and that would give me something to do after I retire…"

When asked how he felt about the dropped charges, Flyinnthuointmeant said, "I just want to get back to my family, maybe celebrate by having a nice meal out and taking in a ball ga – what?" Nobody had the heart to tell him about the pandemic lockdown, but he must have seen the dismay on our faces, because he continued: "No, seriously, what?"

All Day Suckers

by MARA VERHEYDEN-HILLIARD, Alternate Reality News Service War Writer

At 102 (a bad number for a temperature, a pretty good number for an age), Staph Sergeant Marco Guineverici is one of the last liviing Vesampuccerian's who fought in World War I. Guineverici –

"Eh? What's that?" Guineverici shouted. "What'd ya say?"

Guineverici fought valiantly at the Battle of Pork Rind Gullet, which earned him a Purple Prose for bravery under fire. This –

"I can't hear you!" Guineverici screamed. "You gotta speak louder! Really put some lung power into it!"

This week, it was reported that on a state visit to a French cemetery to honour Vesampucceri's casualties of WWI, President Ronald McDruhitmumpf wondered "Why should I go to that cemetery? It's full of losers." As if to drive the point home, he added that the almost 2,000 Marines who died in the Battle of Bellowscreechmartre Wood were "suckers."

"He said **what?**" Guineverici shrieked. "That son of a polymath Hun licker! He isn't fit to shine Private Garibaldo's boots! Or Lieutenant-Colonel Three -Eyed Monte's khakis! Or...or...or any part of Langrahans' privates! Anybody who could say something like that is not fit to be this country's Commander-in-Briefs!"

"Oh, sure – **that** he heard!" groused President McDruhitmumpf.

The Grey House immediately denied the claims that the President had said what he said. Press Secretary-Poppet Kayleigh McEnanity stated, "The President has the utmost respect and admiration and...and...and sheer likingness for our troops. He would never have said those nasty, nasty things you people keep writing that you've verified he said!"

As if to prove the poin, PS-P McEnanity tossed her hair back in what she hoped was a debate-ending move.

"So...silky...smooth," security expert Malcolm Donneednopennance droned, hypnotized. Then, shaking his head, he apoplectically continued: "No! That's not – utmost respect my patootie! This President mocked Senator John McMacPaddycain. Anybody with half a brain will clearly remember what he said: 'War heroes don't get captured, okay? Have you never seen *Rambo: Seventh or Eighth Blood (It's Hard To Keep Track When You've Lost So Much)*?' He mocked the family of a Gold Star veteran. He's called his generals so many dirty names, you could fill a dictionary with them all!* Calling war vets 'loser' and 'suckers' is totally on brand for him!"

"There's one in every crowd," PS-P McEnanity pouted. Journalists who had long thought their hearts were made of stone found that they were melting. Or it could have been heartburn – those three beer lunches can be brutal on your digestive system! Either way, they didn't challenge her assertion as they reached for an antacid.

The President himself tweeped: "I love all of our fine men in the military. Except the ones who get captured, maimed or dye. Cuz this world was made for winners!!!! #crybabylosersdontgetmyrespect"

So, a mixed message, then.

"Ronald McDruhitmumpf is a very transactional human being," explained Pulippitzaner Prize-winning columnist Eugene Robinsoncrusoe. "That doesn't mean he has sex with people who believe they were born in the bodies of the wrong gender – goodness, me, no. Although, there is still a lot we don't know about what he does in the privacy of his own Fenwickian hotel room. But, no. No, being a 'transactional human being' is just a fancy way of saying whenever he is asked to make a decision, he asks, 'What's in it for me?' Somebody who is transactional would never be able to understand military sacrifice. Or, familial sacrifice. Ritual sacrifice? Okay, maybe, but I would hate to think what he imagines that would make him…"

Interviews with officials suggest that the Grey House is panicking about the effect President McDruhitmumpf's remarks will have on his base. "Ohmygordohmygordohmygordohmygord!" 17 sources told the Alternate Reality News Service. His base is deeply in love (in a wholly Platonic sense, and I'll deck any man that says otherwise!) with the military, as you undoubtedly read between the lines of the anonymous staffers' statement.

But how seriously should they be taking this? I asked Guineverici who he voted for in 2016. "I voted in 2016?" he innocently asked. "What's a vote? What's a 2016?"

When I asked him whether the President's remarks would have any affect on who he planned on voting for in 2020, Guineverici replied: "Absolutely not! I mean, it's not like he shot a man in broad daylight on Fifth Avenue or anything!"

* Actually, Peter-Paul Gotellitonda wrote that book, *Them's Fightin' Words: A Dictionary of Words and Phrases (Not All Profane) President Ronald McDruhitmumpf has Used to Describe His Generals*. However, since it came out in the same week that 37 other books on the McDruhitmumpf administration came out, Donneednopennance can be forgiven for not being aware of it.

Death Screwed Over

by SASKATCHEWAN KOLONOSCOGRAD, Alternate Reality News Service Religion Writer

Death has written a sternly worded letter to Senate Majority Leader Mitch Wichconnelliswich demanding that he stop referring to himself as "the Grim Reaper" of legislation passed by the Dumbopratic House of Representatives.

"SINCE VIDEO OF THE MAJORITY LEADER USING MY NAME SURFACED," the letter read, "MY STAFF HAVE HAD TO DEAL WITH AN INCREASING NUMBER OF ANGRY EMAILS FEATURING SUFFICIENTLY HORRIFYING INVECTIVE THAT IT WOULD MAKE ELI BLOODYROTHOGORD BLANCH, INCLUDING, IRONICALLY, MANY GRAPHIC DEATH THREATS. WE HAD TO SEND JUDY HOME IN TEARS THE OTHER DAY, AND SHE MANAGES THE SOULS OF THOSE WHO PASSED THROUGH THE VEIL BECAUSE OF WAR AND MURDER! YOU WILL DESIST FROM USING MY NAME IN FUTURE OR FACE THE CONSEQUENCES!"

"Now, I would never want to argue with such a well-known figure as Death," Majority Leader Wichconnelliswich smirtled (smirked while turtling), "but I don't see a copyright or trademark mark after the phrase 'Grim Reaper.' So, I'm gonna assume He doesn't have a monopoly on the term."

The Majority Leader went on to say that he did not fear the Grim Reaper, since all men die at their allotted time. "Honestly, what is he gonna do? Kill me twice?"

"WITH ALL DUE RESPECT, THE MAJORITY LEADER DOESN'T KNOW WHAT HE IS TALKING ABOUT," responded Maria Altbaltimora, Public Relations Officer for the Office of the Grim Reaper. "THE BOSS DOES NOT KILL PEOPLE. HE JUST FERRIES THEM INTO THE NEXT PHASE OF THEIR EXISTENCE WHEN FATE DECIDES THAT IT IS THEIR TIME TO DIE. HONESTLY, IF HE INSISTS UPON TAKING ON THE GRIM REAPER'S IDENTITY, YOU WOULD THINK WICHCONNELLISWICH WOULD DO HIS HOMEWORK!"

"Mitch has been doing a fine job – a great job," President Ronald McDruhitmumpf weighed in on the disagreement in a tweep at 2:37 in the morning. "But, death? I call him messy mayhem and untidy death. Have you ever seen a dead body? I haven't in real life, but I've seen plenty in the movies, and they're not pretty, folks. Not pretty. Body parts all over the place…large pools of blood…it's like, you know, he just doesn't take pride in his work!"

"THE PRESIDENT OF THE UNITED STATES OF VESAMPUCCERI, THE MOST POWERFUL MAN IN THE WORLD, IS INTENT ON ASSASSINATING THE CHARACTER OF AN ENTITY THAT HAS EXISTED SINCE LIFE FIRST BEGAN, AN ENTITY THAT IS VITAL TO THE CYCLE THAT RUNS THE UNIVERSE?" Altbaltimora commented. "LAME."

"So, this is what it has come to," token smart person Amy Sheshutshotshitbam shook her head. "The Reduhblican Party has picked a fight with the mythical personification of the process of leaving this life!"

"Oh, it's worse than that," Speaker of the House Nancy Pelligrinosi pointed out. "Not only are the Reduhblicans picking a fight with Death, **but they're not allowing any of the legislation out of the House to be voted on in the Senate!**"

"That's just nervous Nancy," the President said in a subsequent interview. "I call her nervous Nancy because – well, that isn't all that bad, is it? Nonsense Nancy? Yeah. Yeah, that's more like – Non-sequitur Nancy? Hee hee. Nasty Nanc – oh, yes! Nasty Nancy! Nasty! Nasty! Nasty Nancy! That one's gonna stick!"

"I CANNOT HELP BUT THINK THAT MY ORIGINAL COMPLAINT IS GETTING LOST IN A HAZE OF SELF-INTERESTED STATEMENTS AND NONSENSICAL WHITE NOISE," Death observed. "I WOULD LIKE TO JUST REMIND EVERYBODY THAT THERE IS SOME CONFUSION BETWEEN MY ROLE AND THAT OF THE MAJORITY LEADER OF THE SENATE. THIS IS NOT A GOOD SITUATION, AND I CANNOT ALLOW IT TO CONTINUE!"

Ira Nayman

"Threatening the Senate Majority Leader, Death? Really?" bloviated Foxindehenhaus...person Sean Hanjobovverfist. "Well, have I got news for you! Mitch Wichconnelliswich is doing the job that the Vesampuccerian people elected him to do. Who elected you, Mister Death? I mean, you're not even a Vesampuccerian, and you think it's okay to criticize one of the great leaders of the greatest idiotocracy that the world has ever known? You might want to go back to whatever nether realm you came from and rethink your whole approach, because, I gotta tell you, you and your opinions are not welcome here!"

"Yeah, I don't pay any attention to Foxindehenhaus Noise," Speaker Pelligrinosi replied. "I find it easier to hold down my breakfast that way. The important thing is: the House is passing legislation that will benefit common people, and it goes to the Senate to die. I agree with Death: this is an unacceptable state of affairs!"

"I – I'M BEGINNING TO REGRET BRINGING THIS WHOLE THING UP," Death, as it usually does, got the last word.

Say It Loud, Say It Proud, Boys

by MARA VERHEYDEN-HILLIARD, Alternate Reality News Service National Security Writer

The first Presidential debate between Ronald McDruhitmumpf and Joe Bidenhisbeeswax? The Prude Bois have been there, done that and got the t-shirt.

Literally.

At one point, President McDruhitmumpf was asked by moderator Chris Walleyedpeacrackers if he would denounce white supremacy. "Sure," he said with about as much enthusiasm as a vampire in a sun lamp showroom. When pressed on the subject, he irritably asked for an example. When Bidenhisbeeswax offered the

Prude Bois, the President said: "Prude Bois? Sure. I tell them: stand back and stand by. Because the real threat to public order is antifa!"

"He likes us! He really likes us!" exulted Proud Boi Winstead von Rippersteinem. "When the Electric Boogaloo* happens, I'm going to dedicate my first kill to the President!"

von Rippersteinem was modelling a t-shirt with the Prude Bois logo (PB in the middle of two pieces of white bread); the words "Stand back" appeared above the logo, while the words "Stand by" appeared below it. With his spindly white limbs and gawky head, models on the Milan runways didn't have to fear for their jobs. Still, the message was clear.

"I...may have to take a vacation to another country," responded Pulippitzaner Prize-winning *Washburningdington Post* columnist Eugene Robinsoncrusoe, who clearly got the message. "I hear Tuktoyaktuk is nice this time of year..."

"You've got it all wrong," stated Press Secretary Kayleigh McEnanity. "The President was having a flashback to his television days. When he said, 'Stand back,' he was trying to get the Prude Bois to get on their mark. When he said, 'Stand by,' he was telling them to wait for the camera shot to be set up. You see. It was all very innocent. A little weird, maybe, but innocent."

The President immediately cut the legs out from under her, like he was removing the appendages from a table so he could make it into a surfboard. "Prude Bois? I never met them – couldn't tell you who they are. But, I tell you what: they sound like people who want to make Vesampucceri great again, and there's nothing wrong with that. Nothing wrong with that."

As he took a suitcase out of a cupboard and started sorting through his clothes, Robinsoncrusoe said, "Stand by. Not stand down. Stand – why am I taking that tie? I never liked that tie. You want a tie that looks like this? – stand by. Wait for orders. The President has been saying he won't – where is my Hawakota shirt? If I'm going to be a tourist, I may as well look like one! – abide by the results of the election if he doesn't win. White supremacist violence might – I haven't been able to fit into these pants in years, but hope springs eternal – be part of his endgame. Now, if you'll excuse me, I have to look something up on Travelgeocities…"

Two days after the debate, the President, looking very much like a small child who had just been caught smashing the cookie jar to the ground, said, "Of course I condemn the Kook Klux Klan. I condemn the Prude Bois – whoever they are. Remember: I never met them. Have no idea who they are. Maybe somebody should introduce us some time. I condemn white supremacists…especially when they're members of Black Lives Matter!"

"The President had to say that so the libtard media would stop picking on him," von Rippersteinem commented. "But, we know, in his heart of hearts, he didn't mean it. Saaaay, that would look really good on a t-shirt!"

"You know," Robinsoncrusoe said as he called for an Uber, "I hate to agree with a white supremacist, but…"

I waited for several minutes for him to finish the thought, but the next thing he said was, "How quickly can you get me to the airport?" Ending our interview seemed to be the discrete thing to do.

"I have said, 'This is unprecedented," so often in the last four years that I should probably get a copyright on the phrase," commented Presidential historian Beschbefordatloess. "But, this is… you know."

But, is it really that unprecedented? Ever since Richard Nixwatmondnewon's "Southern Strategy," the Reduhblicans have courted Vesampuccerian racists, the racist adjacent and the racist look the other way and pretend there's nothing to see here but secretly watch intently out of the corner of their eyes. Isn't this the endgame that the entire party has inevitably been working towards?

"Whoa, look at the historical perspective on you!" Beschbefordatloess beamed. "If I'm not careful, you could take over my presidential historianing job! But…don't, okay? I could never go back to teaching first years! For the love of Gord, don't force me to go back to teaching first years!"

We'll see how things develop.

* For readers who are unfamiliar with white supremacist – ideology is perhaps too grand a concept – let's go with muddled thinking – white supremacist muddled thinking, the Electric Boogaloo is the coming race war. Another Prude Bois t-shirt reads: "Electric Boogaloo? Let's dance!" They can expect a cease and desist order from the estate of the late David Bowiebowieboo any day now.

He Barely Knew Ye

by FREDERICA VON McTOAST-HYPHEN, Alternate Reality News Service People Writer

We all have one – a cousin Bertie who throws up in the punch bowl and blames it on the moosemeat pate that everybody else was eating without incident; a friend named Biff or Beau or Boffin who crashes through the glass door "going long" to catch a Nerdf football that nobody was actually throwing; an aunt Petunia who professes her love of humanity by complaining about everybody's taste in clothes and/or life partners. The kind of person who can only be described by, "They're not with me. I don't really know them. At all."

For President Ronald McDruhitmumpf, everybody is potentially one of them.

"I don't really know him," the President said. "I met him once or twice, you know, crawling around on the floor as I was trying to get to the television in the other room to see what the news anchors were saying about me. It's not like we talked all the time or anything. Don't get me wrong – he's a good kid. A fine kid. But I never knew him all that well."

He said similar things about Michael Canadiohen, who had been his personal lawyer for many years; but it couldn't have been him the President was talking about because the only time Canadiohen was known to be on all fours was at a fraternity hazing when he was

47. President McDruhitmumpf had also said similar thing about Steve O'Bannonallhope, but it couldn't have been him the President was talking about because there is no evidence his former national security adviser was ever a child.

No, President McDruhitmumpf was talking about Ronald McDruhitmumpf, Jr. His son.

"That's kind of hard to believe," said columnist Eugene Robinsoncrusoe. "I mean, they lived in the same house for almost 20 years. You would have thought they would have met in the kitchen in the middle of the night and bonded over making Hamberder Helper or something!"

"That's entirely plausible," said token smart person Amy Sheshutshotshitbam. "Ronald McDruhitmumpf is not what you would call a warm man – his fathering instincts probably date back to the Ice Age! If he ever did talk to his children, it would probably be to tell them how great **he** was, the best father in the history of sexual reproduction!"

"Daddy...?" Ronald McDruhitmumpf, Jr. tentatively pouted.

In fact, President McDruhitmumpf has thrown so many people from his administration under the bus that its suspension has gone all wonky and customers are complaining of nausea and sore bottoms. In further fact, the only thing keeping the bus line going is income from all of the foreign dignitaries who use it to get around when on official business in Washburningdington.

But, family? "The only positive thing Ronald McDruhitmumpf has ever said about family is that, in case of emergency, they would make good bone marrow donors," token smart person Sheshutshotshitbam commented.

Knowing that, for President McDruhitmumpf, loyalty is just a plain cotton shirt you wear for more than one day, why do people still clamour (but, not in the baby mollusc sense) to be part of his administration?

"I mean, why do people tickle zebras?" Robinsoncrusoe asked rhetorically (although it might have been the triple chili dog he had for lunch). "I, uhh, don't actually know the answer to that question, so if anybody knows why people tickle zebras, they should write to me at the *Washburningdington Post*."

Robinsoncrusoe went on to explain that working for the most powerful man in the idiotocratic world still held great appeal for some people. "They get to use official Grey House stationery," he explained. "They get to see the building without being herded behind ropes. They get huge advances to write their memoirs. I mean, honestly, who wouldn't want that?"

"People with self-respect?" token smart person Sheshutshotshitbam mused.

"True," Robinsoncrusoe allowed. "But, the Reduhblicans drove anybody with self-respect out of the party ages ago."

"True," token smart person Sheshutshotshitbam agreed. "But ambition is not, I think, the most important factor here. People who work for this Grey House are like people who hit themselves in the head repeatedly with a frying pan."

"They never think the brain damage is going to happen to them?"

"Exactly."

"Hey – when we're done with our respective interviews, wanna grab a drink somewhere?"

"I don't think Mister token smart person would approve."

"He doesn't have to kno –"

Hey! Take it somewhere else, people! There's journalism happening here!

"Daddy?" Ronald, Jr. plaintively pouted. "Are you there? It's cold here under the bus, daddy. Really cold…"

4. THE SLEEP OF REASON PRODUCES…GOOD ADVICE FOR PEOPLE WHO MAKE BAD DECISIONS

Ask the Tech Answer Guy…For the Children!

Yo, Tech Answer Guy,

I'm a rude tude extruder for Transdimensional Fremulon, a wholly owned subsidiary of MultiNatCorp ("We do exotic sounding but ultimately quite tedious stuff"). Ever since the lockdown because of the virus started, I've been working from home (rude tudes don't extrude themselves!), which has given me a rare insight into my wife Robin's home life.

It's like a Wes Cranraisinetty movie without the confetti.

Thanks to the lockdown all schools are closed (yeah, thanks, thanks a lot!), so our three children, Jess, Pat and Inky Dinky Doo, are stuck at home with us. The little…angels. The horns kind of confused me, but Robina insists that they're vestigial and the kids are too young to start exhibiting wings but it's only a matter of time so cut them some slack and do I want to sleep on the couch for the next three weeks I thought not so they're angels and that's that. You can't argue with logic like that.

Between extrusions, I've had to help keep the kids entertained. We've gone for long walks in our backyard, me narrating local points of interest ("That's the tree where you skinned your knee when you were three doing…whatever you thought you were doing yes I know you were there **and** I've told this story the last twenty-three times we passed this tree but I'm doing the best I can with really thin material it's not like all that much has happened in this yard and **hey who wants to hear about the time Pat nearly drowned in the bird bath?**") along the way. We've played Monopolistic Capitalism so often the value of many of the properties has rubbed away, and the rabbit game piece has gotten surly. If I have to watch another episode of *Thomas the Tank*, I'm gonna bust a spleen.

The entertainment needs of the kids are insatiable! Do you have any ideas of how I can keep them busy? Because Robina says I can't send them to the glue factory.

Sincerely,
Bob Dobdobalina from Arkansalina

Yo, Dobbie,

Are they boys or girls…or spiders?

The Tech Answer Guy

Yo, Tech Answer Guy,

Yes.

Sincerely,
Bob Dobdobalina from Arkansalina

Yo, Bobster,

Umm, okay. Glad we settled that. If your children are boys, I would suggest that the Acme Corporation has many fine products that could offer them endless hours of entertainment. Like rocket skates. Man, I would have loved tooling around the neighbourhood in those babies! Of course, the boys would have to tool around the background until the lockdown was eased, but dead grass and flowers become mulch for the next generation of plant life, so everybody wins!

Or, how about a jet propelled pogo stick? Bouncy bouncy bouncy bouncy bouncy bouncy bouncy. Bouncy! What boy hasn't wanted to soar above the neighbourhood, watching…well, not much these days, but children have great imaginations! And, bonus: as long as they stay in the backyard, they will stamp the dead grass and flower mulch deep into the ground!

If your boys like dressing up, you could try to order them an artificial rock costume. I…I never understood the appeal of it, to be honest, but I hear it's very popular in Texakota.

If they're girls, well, umm, dolls? Tea parties? Gossip about the dolls they didn't invite to their tea parties? Girls are, uhh, not really my area of expertise.

If your children are spiders, perhaps you could order them a My First Web starter web spinning kit from the internet? You can buy anything from the internet. Or, if they're older than the recommended age for the beginner kits, you could always get them…umm…I got nothing. Sorry. That's **really** not my area of expertise!

The Tech Answer Guy

Yo, Tech Answer Guy,

Thank you for your suggestions. But, they seem a bit…violent?

Sincerely,
Bob Dobdobalina from Arkansalina
Yo, Bobalina,

Everything I know about raising children, I learned from old *Roadrunner* cartoons. Your chuckle per explosion mileage may vary.

The Tech Answer Guy

If you are a dude with a question about the latest technology, ask The Tech Answer Guy by sending it to questions@lespagesauxfolles.ca. Just remember: jigsaw puzzles are a great way of wasting hours of family fun! And, the best part? When they are complete, you can lacquer them in a way that will make them a lovely wall decoration or rancorous bone of contention in a divorce proceeding!

Ask Amritsar About Modern Schoolyard Taunts

Dear Amritsar,

I was called into my daughter's principle's office yesterday because she had apparently called her Phys-English teacher, Mister Ideominnow, a "dotard." At first, he heard "daughter" and thought she was attacking his masculinity. When she repeated the word – loudly, slowly and with perfect enunciation – Mister Ideominnow gave her a detention. Then, he told the class to turn around while he did something on his computer (I suspect he was looking the word up). Then, he ordered her to the principle's office.

So, Mister Ideominnow likes women named Dorothy. Is that any reason to stagmatize my poor Linda-Lou?

Andromeda-Ann

Hey, Babe,

I was tempted to say, "I do not think that word means what you think it means," but I didn't want to get in trouble with Dizznizzfizzlizzey's lawyers (if they don't own the rights to *The Princess Bride* at the moment, they will...they will), so I stopped myself from doing so. This should be a lesson to Linda-Lou.

A dotard is somebody who studiously collects information, connects the dots representing disparate facts, and comes up with a conclusion that is almost always wrong. Full of convincing detail? Sure. Painstakingly footnoted? Absolutely. But, just not correct. Somebody who answers the question, "Why is the sky blue?" with the statement, "Hillary Roocartoncleveman's emails!" is probably a dotard. (Demanding that they show you how they connected those particular dots will only cause your head to explode. Trust me on this: I had a 17 Percoset a day habit until I stopped!)

Mister Ideominnow was correct in intuiting that your child was mocking him. Some sort of punishment is definitely in order. I must admit, though, that I fail to see how making your daughter afraid of male deer will make her see the error of her ways.

Dear Amritsar,

I was trying to explain to my twelve year-old son Faivel Elephantomas that if he didn't eat his fried bacon sandwich, he wouldn't grow up to be Superman. (I cannot explain why he insists upon eating peas and carrots every meal – he must be going through a rebellious phase.) In response, do you know what he called me? Go ahead and guess. No, don't bother – you wouldn't be able to.

A simpering poltroon. That's what he called me. And, if you were, in fact, able to guess that, I apologize for having so little faith in your understanding of the mentality of twelve year-olds.

What I don't understand is: why would my young son think I was a boiling hen?

Tsvi Tuvulanimous

Hey, Babe,

As you may know, poltroons are actually sixteenth century leggings (everything I know about the twelfth to seventeenth centuries I learned from the reality TV show *Our Stupid Ancestors*). From what I can gather, simpering is archaic Aramaic for "splitting down the middle." While the common definition of the term refers to paying a bill or dividing an opposing army, it is not much of a stretch to believe that it could apply to leggings (especially if they were old enough to have lost some of their elasticity).

So, your son was calling you ripped leggings. Somewhat obscure, but not especially flattering.

Ah. I see that the Language Corrector Dude is vigorously shaking his head, which means that this explanation is almost undoubtedly totally wrong. So, I went to that neutral arbiter of language usage, the internet, to discover the true meaning of the term.

As you might imagine, it was an insult. Punishment of some description is definitely called for.

The more interesting thing was my realization that the more time children spend surfing the web, the better they are at finding increasingly obscure ways to insult their parents. I suspect that this is not what Tim After-Berners-Lee or Berning-Rubbers-Lee or Bernersing-Chrome-Lee or whatever his name was had in mind when he got the whole thing started!

The best thing to do if your child says something to you that sounds insulting even though you can't quite grasp what it means would be to assume the worst and punish them by blocking them from the internet for a week. That will teach them the meaning of being an exemplary pox on humanity!

Send your relationship problems to the Alternate Reality News Service's sex, love and technology columnist at questions@lespagesauxfolles.ca. Amritsar Al-Falloudjianapour is not a trained therapist, but she does know a lot of stuff. AMRITSAR SAYS: Schmeckler's Farrago is not traditionally a holiday devoted to gift-giving. If anybody suggests otherwise, they are clearly in the pay of Big Chocolate!

Ask the Tech Answer Guy to Get to the Cheatin' Heart of the Matter

Yo, Tech Answer Guy,

I'm in love with this wonderful woman. Let's call her…Gweneveer. Because I don't have a lot of imagination. I'm a dentist. Anyhoodies, when we get together, it's like a scene from *Flashdance*. Sparks like you wouldn't believe! And, wet. Very wet. Can we help it if water hoses break whenever we get together? Really, it's more like *Fleshdance*, but, uhh, that was her joke. Because of the whole no imagination/dentist thing. You know how it is.

I'm pretty sure my wife, Penelop, would be unhappy if she ever found out about Gwenny-poohdle. (That's the nickname she gave me for herself. I...I don't really get the concept of nicknames, but it seems to make her happy, so okay.) Penelop is a trusting sort, though, so when I told her that I was working late on fillings for the next day, she seemed to buy it.

Well, sir, quarantine has shot all of that to hell, let me tell you!

I now fill cavities and install braces over the internet. It's a little awkward, especially when a patient's connection is pokey, but at least I've stopped doing root canals until the pandemic is brought under control. We all have to make sacrifices in this difficult time.

For me, one of them has been Gwenevere. I haven't been outside of my house for two months, sixteen days and a handful of slow, painfully slow hours. In that time, I have given my mistress three cleanings and six unnecessary fillings. Not only has this been a most unromantic way to get to spend time with her, but it's playing hell with Gwenneveer's insurance premiums!

Not only am I becoming alienated from my mistress, TAG, but spending so much time with my wife has reminded me of what made me want to marry her in the first place. The way she brushes wisps of hair out of her eyes with the same implement we use to make sure Mister Pinckles doesn't get any hairballs from grooming himself. The way she is able to burn the steak without setting off the fire alarm in our apartment. The way her voice squeaks when we argue about what to watch on Netflix. I'm worried that I may end up cheating on my mistress with my wife.

What can I do about this revoltin' state of affairs?

Sincerely,
Benn from Grimm

Yo, Benny,

You dawg!

Uhh, oops. I seem to have interrupted Misses the Tech Answer Guy's painting in our rock garden. I've never understood the attraction of painting rocks, but she seems to find it soothing. So...

You dawg.

Of course, this is a...relationship question. The Tech Answer Guy doesn't do...relationship questions. They give him indigestion, and a bad case of morning mummers. A really bad case. Ordinarily, I would ask Amritsar for help with your question, but she hasn't been answering the Tech Answer Guy's texts ever since the guacamole guitar incident.

As you say, these are difficult times, so I'll take a stab at it.

Whenever I have a difficult relationship problem to solve (and, for the Tech Answer Guy, **all** relationship problems are difficult – it's a thing with him – don't ask), I start a home renovation project. When my sister was going through her "technicolor daydreams" phase, I built a bookcase, even though there was no room in our house for it and it's been on the roof for seven years. When Misses The Tech Answer Guy's mother came to visit for six months, I installed a basement. Mostly. We've never been able to figure out where the ants are getting into the house, but trying to figure it out has kept me busy at emotionally trying times for years.

Home renovations projects focus the mind. Home renovations projects distract from difficult emotions. Home renovations projects are perfect for avoiding any problem, big or small or some size in between. Try a home renovation project. You'll be glad you did.

The Tech Answer Guy

Yo, Tech Answer Guy,

You're really not very good at giving emotional advice, are you?

Sincerely,

Benn from Grimm

Yo, Benny-Boy,

I know, right! Thank you for your understanding.

The Tech Answer Guy

If you are a dude with a question about the latest technology, ask The Tech Answer Guy by sending it to questions@lespagesauxfolles.ca. Just remember: bow legs are not bowling legs. The Tech Answer Guy made that mistake once, and lost his chance at a perfect game in the very first frame!

Ask Amritsar: Desperate Times Call for Desperate Makeup Regimens

Dear Amritsar,

We have been told that if we want to survive the coronavirus outbreak, we need to wash our hands and not touch ourselves. But, men touch themselves all of the time! Why is that?

Anodyne Annie

Hey, Babe,

Men are gross.

That's When Everything Went Cow-shaped

Dear Amritsar,

Well, yeah, okay. Not gonna argue with that. But, touching themselves...there doesn't necessarily cause them to catch a virus. Not the one that's in all the papers right now, in any case. I meant: their faces. Why do men touch their faces all the time?

Anodyne Annie

Hey, Babe,

I stand by my original answer.

Dear Amritsar,

And, it was a good one. Made a lot of sense. I do have to wonder, though, if there is a more specific reason men touch their faces all of the time despite the fact that that doing so might kill them.

Anodyne Annie

Hey, Babe,

Men don't moisturize.

Dear Amritsar,

Hmm. Cryptic, with an undernote of cherry vanilla. Still, as the answer to a question, it is about as satisfying as a gluten-free Baba au Rhuily. Could you possibly elaborate?
Anodyne Annie

Hey, Babe,

Sure.

When men get dry, flaky skin, they are fawned over for being ruggedly handsome. When women get dry, flaky skin, we are shunned and told that we should stop "letting ourselves go." Cowboys can have dry, flaky skin. Fashion models can't have dry, flaky skin. Race car drivers can have dry, flaky skin. Suburban housewives can't have dry, flaky skin.

It's a double standard so thick it could clog the arteries of everybody in a small Latin Vesampuccerian country.

According to a series of studies by the Poynter Sisters Institute, women moisturize and exfoliate (no, Tech Answer Guy, that's not a reference to eight former players for the Foley Freighters AA battery baseball team – down boy! Down!) at a rate 27 times that of men. In one study, researchers collected the dust from 127 apartments inhabited by married couples and analyzed the DNA of the dead cells. They found that 83 per cent of the cells by volume had come from men.

What happens when your skin is dry and flaky? You tend to itch more. Over the years, you learn to rub and scratch the driest, flakiest patches without even thinking about it.

Men are beyond gross. They're icky. Are you happy I answered your question now?

Dear Amritsar,

But...but...but...but...don't they understand that touching their faces could kill them?

Anodyne Annie

Hey, Babe,

It's hard to overcome thousands of years of socialization just because of a little inconvenience like death.

Not that people aren't trying. Erick von Deutchmeunster at the Liederhosen Institution in Osaka has proposed a return to glam rock as a way to combat COVID-19. In an article for *The Journal of Comparative Religion and Eyeliner C*, von Deutchmeunster wrote: "Everybody focuses on David Bowiebowieboo's Ziggy Stardust persona, but, for my money, Gary Glitter was **the** one great glam rocker. The hair. The makeup. The costumes. The way he could almost hit the notes he was reaching for – he had it all. Love and Rockets were a close second. I mean, Daniel Ashcantiptover – ooooh! So, glam up and save your life!"

They, uhh, they might want to look at how their peer review process is functioning over there at *The Journal of Comparative Religion and Eyeliner C*. Yeah, they should really do that.

Dear Amritsar,

I touch my face all the time. I find it…soothing. And I've never been sick a day in my life. (Let's not talk about the nights.) What's the big whoop?

Peter Paul

Hey, Babe,

Say you're at a badminton club for your usual Thursday afternoon game against Mark Markey. Further say that the person who had the racket before you sneezed all over it during a futile volley and covered the handle in the virus. When you play, the germy little bastards will get on your hand. If you wash your hands for at least 20 seconds (measuring two choruses of "Happy Birthday" or, if you can't afford the royalties, three iterations of the chorus from "Ballroom Blitz"), you'll be able to get rid of the virus. However, if you touch your face before you wash your hands, the aforementioned germy little bastards could enter your body through a small cut or a big mouth. Two weeks Later, you could find yourself coming down with a nasty case of death.

Whoops don't get much bigger than that.

Send your relationship problems to the Alternate Reality News Service's sex, love and technology columnist at questions@lespagesauxfolles.ca. Amritsar Al-Falloudjianapour is not a trained therapist, but she does know a lot of stuff. AMRITSAR SAYS: Remember all those people who laughed at those of us who used social media and dating apps to find potential life partners? Not laughing so loud, now, are you?

Ask the Biz Whiz About the Tax Onna Me

Ciao, Bella Biz Whiz:

Last year, I paid $37,234 in income tax even though as a furniture bike courier (wardrobes are killers!) I made only $12,980 – I should probably have a talk with my accountant, but he hasn't returned my calls since I hit him over the head with a Rosh Hashanah brisket a few years back. Don't ask. He deserved it. But, other than that, don't ask.

I just read the *New Yoricknuhemwell Times'* report on President McDruhitmumpf's taxes. Well, okay, I didn't read the whole thing: that mofo goes on and on and on! And, on! It's like Jason – just when you think it's over, it pops up and eviscerates more teenagers! So, I...I read the headline and the first three paragraphs. But, that was enough to cue the outrage.

For ten of the last 15 years, the President paid no income tax. The year he entered office, he paid $750. To put that in perspective, the last time I paid $750 in income tax, it was on sales on the lemonade stand I ran on weekends in front of my house when I was 12! (It was damn fine lemonade, but still. My troubles with my accountant go way back. Don't ask.)

I voted for McDruhitmumpf in 2016 and will again in 2020. Twice if I have to. He is the most successful businessman in the history of capitalism. Notwithstanding the year he claimed to have lost over a billion dollars. Or, all those other years he lost tens or hundreds of millions of dollars. That happens to every successful businessman, right? Right?

Tell me that happens to every successful businessmen.

The Biz Whiz:

It happens to every successful businessman...named Ronald McDruhitmumpf.

We have a term for people like him: con man. This is not the term as you might casually use it. In economics, a con man is somebody who knows how to work the system to maximize his personal profit. It is a term of endearment you hear frequently at $1,000 a plate fundraisers and fraud trials.

Should the President have been allowed to claim $73,000 in hair care products as a business expense? Those who complain about this are just jealous they didn't think of it first. They should probably be talking to their accountants. And, stop buying the downmarket brands at Walmart. To be successful at business, you have to think – and mousse – big.

Should the President have been allowed to claim millions of dollars in tax writeoffs because of depreciation on his name? In business, your name is everything – especially when it is displayed in six foot tall letters on the thirtieth floor of mixed use apartment/office/spinal surgery buildings. When you take a sandblaster to those letters, you are also sanding down, in the most intrusively noisy, attention-getting way, the owner's reputation. You can't put a price on that, but, for tax purposes, you can certainly make one up.

You may quibble about the morality of the President's actions, but they were all within the letter of the law. And, that's good enough for economics.

Dear Gord, Biz Whiz:

You really approve of the President's tax strategy? Really?

At the time he was claiming (relative) poverty, he was talking up his properties to get bank loans. There's no such thing as quantum bookkeeping! Your finances don't get to be either positive or negative as long as nobody at the IRS tries to measure them!

Not only that, but in the Reduhblicans' tax cut legislation, somebody inserted a clause that would give breaks to New Yoricknuhemwell land developers. The President is a New Yoricknuhemwell land developer. Conflict of interest much?

I didn't vote for Ronald McDruhitmumpf in 2016, and I wouldn't vote for him in 2020 if Pennsyleorgia hadn't struck my name from the voter's rolls over a parking fine I could have sworn I paid in 2013. I wouldn't vote for him twice. I may not know anything about economics, but I know a con man in the common sense of the term – how can anybody vote for one for President?

The Biz Whiz:

Jealousy is such an ugly emotion.

The economy is too important to be left to economists! If you have a work, financial or otherwise money-centric question, quiz the Biz Whiz at questions@lespagesauxfolles.ca. Emotions have no place in markets. Except for panic selling. But, that only happens on a 12 year cycle, and the only people it affects are the cops and teachers whose unions have invested their retirement funds heavily in the market, so it's not like it inconveniences anybody important.

Ask the Tech Answer Guy: What Colour is Your Para Shirt?

Yo, Tech Answer Guy,

If I go out with my semi-automatic rifle and mow down some protesters, it's self-defence, right?

Sincerely,
Kyle from (the) Kenosha (of my mind)

Yo, K,

If they are breaking down your front door and entering your house, maybe. Otherwise, it's murder.

The Tech Answer Guy

Yo, Tech Answer Guy,

Well, okay, they weren't breaking down my door specifically. But, they were breaking down a door in another city. In, umm, another state. So, the principle is the same, right? If you go to a city in another state to mow down protesters with a semi-automatic rifle, it's basically self-defence, right?

Sincerely,
Kyle (almost, sorta, kinda) from Kenosha

Yo, K,

No. That's definitely murder.

The Tech Answer Guy

Yo, Tech Answer Guy,

No, no, no. It's lawn order. I mean, Nippon-Tucker Carlsonandotter. He's a respected journalist, right? I mean, he's on Foxindehenhaus News, so he's gotta know what he's talking about. And, he said: "How shocked are we that 17 year-olds with rifles decided they had to maintain order when no one else would?"
I'm not shocked. Not shocked at all.
Or, take Paul Gogogadjetsar. He's a Representative, which would make him a politician or something. You know what he said? He said: "The criminals here: Kenosha local government that allows the riots, burning and looting night after night. Armed citizens defending themselves will fill the vacuum."
So, say I, an armed citizen, like, a really, really well armed citizen, saw the chaos in Kenosha and knew I had to act to save our wimmens and chilluns from the...politically correct hordes breaking down their doors. Wink wink. If that happened, it would make me a hero, don't you think?

Sincerely,
Kyle from (not too far away from) Kenosha (really)

Yo, K,

Umm, no. We have people to save wimmens and chill – women and children. They are known as "police." People who travel across state lines looking to be a part of a violent act are not known as police. They are known as "vigilantes."

According to Phil, the mechanic from the shop down the street, vigilantes were very popular in the wild west. Then, the sheriffs came in and provided lawn order. This would make vigilantes the opposite of lawn order. So, put your (hypothetical) semi-automatic weed whacker away, because that would just make you a murderer of plants as well as people.

Believe it. Phil, the mechanic from the shop down the street knows things.

The Tech Answer Guy

Yo, Tech Answer Guy,

No, no, no, no, no. You're just not getting it. I…I was attacked. This guy with a skateboard came up to me and started whacking me with it! I mean, it's a solid piece of wood! It hurt! Then, this other guy tried to take my rifle away! Surely, in that – I mean, theoretically. If a guy with a skateboard theoretically started whaling on me with it and some other guy tried to take away my rifle, surely, that would be self-defence. Right?

Sincerely,
Kyle from (one or two small states to the left of) Kenosha

Yo, K,

It depends. Had you already shot and killed one person? Theoretically?

The Tech Answer Guy

Yo, Tech Answer Guy,

Maaaaay…beeeee…

Sincerely,
Kyle (who may never have actually set foot in it until two days ago, but has always wanted to be) from Kenosha

Yo, K,

In that case, the theoretical skateboarder and the theoretical person trying to take away your gun could actually be said to be trying to defend themselves and the community from you. Sorry. Still murder.

The Tech Answer Guy

Yo, Tech Answer Guy,

No, no, no, no, no, no, no. Representative Gogogadjetsar said it was, "100% justified self defence!" Jack Comfymurphybed is…is…is a guy. Who has a podcast. But, that's legit now, right? Social media is still media…in some circles. So, when he says, "This is as close and as you're gonna find, I think. Skateboard guy attacks and gets shot. Guy approaching with handgun out gets shot. Self defence," that's the way it was. Right? Right right right?

Sincerely,
Kyle from Kenosha (and who are you to say otherwise?)

Yo, K,

Sounds to me like this is more than theoretical. So, I will say this: people on TV aren't your defence lawyers. You should probably get real ones.

The Tech Answer Guy

*If you are a dude with a question about the latest technology, ask The Tech Answer Guy by sending it to: questions@lespagesauxfolles.ca. Just remember: Mrs. The Tech Answer Guy tells me it's really hard to get bloodstains out of brown shirts. If you want to be a member of a paramilitary organization **and** fashion forward, you're going to have to make a lot of hard decisions!*

Ask Amritsar to Swear By It

Dear Amritsar,

Yesterday, I reposted a cartoon on my Farcebook page that compared a prominent American politician to Baby Spice on account of his, you know, small hands and tendency to throw temper tantrums. I thought it was funny. One of my fiends didn't. He responded with a torrent of abuse so foul that I had to use a fire extinguisher on my computer screen to keep it from combusting! Thrice!

Well. I am considering unfiending him. Would the proper etiquette to write my final message to him be, "Consider yourself unfiended, ferker!" or "Consider yourself unfiended, motherferker!"?

Terrence Barko Lowinagersit

Hey, Babe,

I can see why you would write me with this question: heaven forbid you cause your soon to be former fiend offence by getting this wrong.

As a general rule, Amritsar does not condone or encourage the use of foul language in public fora (no, no, no, that's a woman's name…unless you were thinking of the word for plant life – no, that's the word for a type of hat – oh, come on, people! Fora is the proper Latin plural form of the word forumnus – place of holding a toga party! Were you not paying attention in grade three?) – alright. Places. Amritsar does not condone or etc. the use of foul language in public places!

I blame the school system.

It's not that Amritsar is a prude. When she is unhappy with the play of her partner in an otherwise pleasant evening of contact whist, she has been known to say, "Drat it!", "Goshdarn it!" and even "[EXPLETIVE DELETED] you, you [EXPLETIVE DELETED] moron! Couldn't you [EXPLETIVE DELETED] well see that I had set up a full body [EXPLETIVE DELETED] grand slam?" In fact, Amritsar has likely been thrown out of more dining establishments for using foul language to berate the vending machines than you have teeth in a hen's head!

No, the problem is that when public discourse (no, not a reference to the plate of food in front of you, or the series of lectures you're taking at university, or the steps you need to learn for that dance number from the 1970s – [EXPLETIVE DELETED], you're ignorance of the basics of the English language is making this a lot harder than it has to be!) is filled with expletive-laced anger, it becomes impossible for people who disagree with each other to talk. When people with opposing points of view no longer talk, bad things happen: riots, wars, reality television celebrities grasping for positions above their station (and sometimes achieving them).

For democracy to work, people with opposing views must be able to communicate with each other in a civilized manner. As Plato said – well, no, if you're having this much trouble with the English language, I'm not going to bring a Greek into this! As – well, no, that last point wasn't a translated quote from Plato, that was my opinion. As – no! – I wasn't putting words into Plato's mouth! Plato has nothing to do with – oh, [EXPLETIVE DELETED] this action – meet me in the next paragraph!

As **Don Acherryontopps** said, "For democracy to work, people with opposing views must be able to communicate with each other in a civilized manner. If you must do a little clutch and grab or maybe some stick work above the waist in order to make your point, just make sure you do it when the ref isn't watching!"

He knows a lot about the democratic process, Don Acherryontopps does.

The problem with people unfiending each other right, left and centre (more Don's – ahem – fields of expertise than mine, but be generous, dear reader) is that the echo chamber of their own discourse (don't you start!) will push both sides in an argument to take up extreme positions, leaving no common ground on which to come together. This is how divorces happen. And, civil wars.

So, rather than unfiend the person with whom you disagree, you should try reasoning with them. Lay down your expletives. Bracket your epithets. Ignore your invective. Reasonable people can find common ground upon which to build a better future if only they are willing to reason with one another.

Dear Amritsar,

Have you seen what I wrote about you on Farcebook?

pwnedu27

Hey, Babe,

Wha? You – seriously? You wrote…! And, then…! And followed that up with…! How dare you, sir? How dare you? I barely even know your goat!

Consider yourself unfiended, motherferker!

Send your relationship problems to the Alternate Reality News Service's sex, love and technology columnist at questions@lespagesauxfolles.ca. Amritsar Al-Falloudjianapour is not a trained therapist, but she does know a lot of stuff. AMRITSAR SAYS: people who hate Muslims generally also hate gays. People who hate gays usually also hate Jews. People who hate Jews usually also hate blacks. And, so on. So, don't feel smug if your minority group isn't currently the focus of organized hate groups. Hate does not discriminate.

Ask the Tech Answer Guy How to Calculate the Optimal Spitting Distance

Yo, Tech Answer Guy,

I suffer from a condition that is common in situation comedies but rare ISL (in surreal life): Inappropriate Distanced Aqueous Ejection Syndrome (IDAES). In short: I do spit takes. I'm a spit taker. I spit. I take. At the same time. Water, coffee, Chateau Lafitenesstestes Rothschildinnamann – it doesn't matter. If somebody startles me while I am drinking, I spray liquid in an expanding 10 to 15 foot radius. And, I'm as sensitive as a doe in a Dizznizzfizzlizzey movie.

I mean, I've been known to expel liquids nine times while having a three minute snack!

My friends are very supportive of my condition. The speak softly and mute their cellphones when we're at parties. They have taken mime classes in order to learn how to move more slowly, more deliberately. They know to wear rain slickers indoors when we go out for drinks. Really, they're the best.

But, this COVID-19 thing, man! There are people going around randomly spitting on other people to…I don't know what! Teach them to be more aware of their mortality and live in the moment? Remind them of the importance of healthy gums? Promote the umbrella industry? It's crazy!

I'm worried that when things return to normal, people with IDAES will be stigmatized as Typhoid Terrys because of the actions of this small number of people who don't even have it. Is there anything I can do to keep this from happening, or, if it does happen, minimize the damage to people like me, innocent victims of a terrible, terrible disease?

Sincerely,
Abraham from Onomatopoeia

Yo, Abe,

Honestly?

I had no…idea there was such a thing as IDAES! Do you have to – hee hee – carry a towel around wherever you go? Maybe, you should…you should…ha ha ha…get cards you can give to people you…syndrome all over. Of course, they would have to be – hee hee – have to be – haw haw – laminated! They would have to be lamina –

OWWW!

Phil, the mechanic from the shop down the street, just punched me in the arm! Hard! I – I'm not complaining. According to the

Macho Code of Manliness, sucking up a playful punch in the arm earns you points that will help you get into Guy Heaven when you die. I was just…startled, is all. Taken unawares. Sort of like you when you…oooohhhh.

Phil, the mechanic from the shop down the street, is gooood. I always have to remember that he knows things.

So, okay. Only a handful of intentional spitting incidents have been reported in the United States of Vesampucceri – the good news is that the whole *schemazzle* might just be forgotten, like the Fleeglemeisterous Rebellion of 1923 or slavery. If that happens, you won't have anything to worry about.

The bad news is that the spitters believe that they are making a political statement. I think they're saying: "Vote Reduhblican or die!" Or, maybe: "COVID-19 is a hoax! Don't believe the mainstream mouth liquid spewers!" Or, maybe: "Tip the canoe and your waitress, too!"It's not a very clear statement – saliva isn't a great communications medium.

Worse (although totally predictable): this position was supported by the President, who tweeped at 2:37 this morning: "Th eFoundering Fathers believed spitting was free speech – it's right there in the 237th Amendment, people! oh, I love the constitution! How i love that document! You wouldn't believe what's in it!!! Freedom! To spit! That was what Vesampucceri was founded on! #freedomtolieaboutyourpoliticalenemiestoodontforget".

The validity of spit as speech may have to be adjudicated by the courts. In that case, oh oh. In an article for *The Punxsutawney Law Review and Phil Watcher*, Extreme Court Justice Brett Kavanaugheylno mused, "To spew, or not spew. Could go either way. Let me consult my friends in The Federalist Society and get back to."

Or, you could hope that, after 70 years of broadcast television, a cure for IDAES will finally be found.

The Tech Answer Guy

Yo, Tech Answer Guy,

I'm doomed, aren't I? The weird politics of this moment has doomed me, hasn't it?

Sincerely,
Abraham from Onomatopoeia
Yo, Abbie,

Have you considered moving to Europe? I hear they have a lot of spittoons there...

The Tech Answer Guy

If you are a dude with a question about the latest technology, ask The Tech Answer Guy by sending it to questions@lespagesauxfolles.ca. Just remember: "I'm Laverne and you're Shirley – whatever you say bounces off me and makes you all squirrely" isn't really an effective comeback when somebody has insulted you. The Tech Answer Guy can say this with some assurance because he is currently working on a book on effective comebacks, and will have a first draft in to his publisher just as soon as he gets his household chores done. So, get off his back, Chuck, because that new deck won't stain itself!

Ask Amritsar...For the Children!

Dear Amritsar,

My husband Bob is a butthead. And, I'm not talking about how the cleft on his chin, deep as it is, makes his face look like somebody's hindparts. I'm talking about the fact that he seems to think with his anus.

Like many people, our children have been stuck at home during the virus quarantine. They have been slowly driving us mad with their incessant demands for food and drink and a safe place to sleep so that the monsters in the closet won't get them – honestly, it never ends! (Personally, I think they could take the monsters in the closet – you should see the kind of fight they put up when it's bath time! – but my therapist says I am misdirecting my rage. Putz.)

Bob decided to "help" by getting gifts to distract the children. That went over about as well as a salmonella sandwich on whole wheat moldy bread!

The butthead bought an Acme rocket powered Pogo stick for little Inky Dinky Doo. The first time he used it, he launched himself into the sky and never came down. Maybe he achieved escape velocity. Maybe he got snagged on a passing passenger pigeon and ended up hitching a ride to a favela on the wrong side of the border with Canada. Maybe he's with the Angels…in Houston. I…I hope he's in a better place, wherever that place may be.

Pat was given an Acme rock costume. "Endless hours of amusement," the box promised. I sure hope so. Pat put on the costume and wandered off to the quarry at the end of the street. We haven't seen or heard from him/her in three days. At first, I gave Bob heck for that one, but, in the end, he convinced me that rocks last for thousands of years, that very little can destroy them. So, as long as nobody is looking for a granite tabletop, it's probably for the best.

The worst was Bob getting an Acme rocket launcher for our three year-old daughter, Jess. She played with it exactly once: the house of the neighbours across the street was totalled. My shrink says Jess is going to have to undergo intense therapy when she is older. I wish he hadn't been so…gleeful when he said that; still, it's good to know that he will have a steady enough income to be able to treat me for as long as I need.

I guess I'm just a silver lining kind of gal.

With two less children, and the third traumatized, I'm finding I have time to do all of the things I didn't before. Which are none of your business. The question is: should I be devastated that COVID-19 has destroyed my family? Or, should I be grateful?

Robina Dobdobalina

Hey, Babe,

I'm not supposed to judge the people who open up their hearts by writing to me, so I will just say that we are all suffering through a difficult time, and must find a way to cope as best we can.

Dear Amritsar,

What the hell is that supposed to mean? I mean, honestly, was that supposed to be helpful? It sounded like something out of a fortune cookie!

Robina Dobdobalina

Hey, Babe,

But, then you asked a follow-up question, and my qualms about criticizing the people who submit to this column flew out the window faster than a boy's virginity on prom night!
You and Bob are terrible parents.

Never, ever, **ever** buy anything from Acme Corporation, especially not for children! Their products never work as advertised. It's right there in the fine print of every instruction manual: "Product will never work as advertised. Please be advised and alter your expectations accordingly. May contain monosodium glutamate." What did you expect?

Parenting requires patience and sacrifice. Rocket powered... anything is no substitute!

Send your relationship problems to the Alternate Reality News Service's sex, love and technology columnist at questions@lespagesauxfolles.ca. Amritsar Al-Falloudjianapour is not a trained therapist, but she does know a lot of stuff. AMRITSAR SAYS: civility is the glue that holds the ramshackle construct that is human society together. In these times when we are forced to stay in close quarters with those we love...like...tolerate (with a vengeance), civility is the only thing that keeps us from entering Lord of the Flies *territory. Do not call your husband "butthead," "doofus" or "big pain in the ass." Instead, call him "Mister Butthead," "Sir Doofus of Dumbville" or "The King of Pains in the Ass."* You would be surprised at just how effective civility can be in defusing tense situations. Even civility of the aggressive kind.*

* Not "The King of Pain in the Asses" unless you are a genetic experiment gone horribly, horribly wrong.

5. THE SLEEP OF REASON PRODUCES…LENNY (THE FOURTH HORSEMAN)

Pandemics 'r' Virus:
The Alternate Reality News Service Interview

TRANSCRIPT OF AN INTERVIEW WITH TED, THE NOVEL CORONAVIRUS. THE INTERVIEW WAS CONDUCTED BY LAURIE NEIDERGAARDEN, ALTERNATE REALITY NEWS SERVICE MEDICAL WRITER.

LAURIE NEIDERGAARDEN: Is that thing…safe?

COVID-19 VIRUS: I can hear you, you know.

TECHNICIAN: It's in a sealed test tube. You want guarantees?

NEIDERGAARDEN: This is more than six feet, right?

VIRUS: I can still hear you.

TECHNICIAN: It crosses that space when somebody talks or sneezes. From a running start, I would guess it might make it three inches.

NEIDERGAARDEN: If you're sure…

VIRUS: Can we speed this up? I have places to be, things to do.

Pause.

NEIDERGAARDEN: That…that was not at all reassuring.

VIRUS: Not you, necessarily.

NEIDERGAARDEN: Not helping.

VIRUS: It's just, this test tube is cold and uninviting. I prefer a warm environment to –

NEIDERGAARDEN: Whoaoooookay, why don't we get this interview started? I'm talking to a novel coronavirus –

VIRUS: Call me Ted.

NEIDERGAARDEN: Why should I call you Ted?

VIRUS: Theodore is too formal. It makes me sound like a librarian.

NEIDERGAARDEN: No, I mean, why should I call you by a name?

VIRUS: There's so many of us in the world. Names help to tell us apart.

Pause.

NEIDERGAARDEN: Umm…okay. Ted. What's it like, being a deadly killer?

VIRUS: It's just a job. Travel. Reproduce. Rinse. Wash. Repeat. To be honest, it's not very exciting. But it is what I was born to do, so I do it to the best of my ability.

SOUND: plink.

NEIDERGAARDEN: Reduhblicans say you don't exist.

VIRUS: What? They think all of those people in your country are dying of happiness?

SOUND: plink.

NEIDERGAARDEN: Honestly, it's hard to know what they think. Dumboprats disagree with the Reduhblicans, of course. They argue that –

VIRUS: Don't care.

SOUND: plink.

NEIDERGAARDEN: I'm sorry?

VIRUS: Reduhblican. Dumboprat – it's all the same to me. You're all just…vacation destinations.

SOUND: plink plink.

NEIDERGAARDEN: I'm trying to get your perspective on the politics of the pandemic.

VIRUS: Look, pal, I'm sure the politics of the pandemic is important to you people. Me, I'm a simple soul. Travel. Reproduce. Rinse. Wash. Repeat.

SOUND: plink plink plink.

NEIDERGAARDEN: But the whole point of – what is that sound?

VIRUS: What sound?

SOUND: plink plink plink.

VIRUS: I don't hear anything.

SOUND: plink plink plink.

NEIDERGAARDEN: It's a plinking sound, like…like something small is trying to break through gla – are you…are you trying to get out of the test tube?

VIRUS: N-no. Why would you think –

SOUND: plink plink plink plink plink!

NEIDERGAARDEN: (shouting) You are! You are trying to get out!

VIRUS: Hey! I gotta do me!

SOUND: plink plink plinkety plink plink!

NEIDERGAARDEN: Stop it! Stop it right now, or I'll have the test tube scrubbed with industrial strength cleaner!

VIRUS: (under its breath) You're no fun.

NEIDERGAARDEN: Over 200,000 Vesampuccerians have died of COVID-19! That's not fun!

VIRUS: Hey! I'm just fulfilling my life's goal. Can I help it if my business is my pleasure?

Pause.

NEIDERGAARDEN: The first serious outbreaks of the disease –

VIRUS: Disease is such a prejudicial term.

NEIDERGAARDEN: The first serious outbreaks **of the disease** took place in New Yoricknuhemwell and Los Angeles, major coastal cities that tend to be more liberal. President McDruhitmumpf calculated that he could ignore the outbreaks because they didn't affect large pockets of his voters in the middle of the coun –

VIRUS: Oh, yawn.

NEIDERGAARDEN: I beg your pardon?

VIRUS: Look. We've already established that I don't care about your politics. I just like to travel. See the world. See exotic new places. By now, my siblings and I are everywhere. How cool is that?

NEIDERGAARDEN: When you say 'see exotic new places,' you're talking about people, right?

VIRUS: Ah. Finally, somebody gets me!

NEIDERGAARDEN: These exotic new places you're talking about have hopes and dreams, parents and siblings and…and…and maybe children. When they die because you have visited them, they leave a big hole in the world.

VIRUS: You're talking about the whole…human dimension of the disease, right?

NEIDERGAARDEN: Exactly.

VIRUS: Sorry, but that's above my pay grade.

Pause.

NEIDERGAARDEN: President McDruhitmumpf recently came down with –

VIRUS: Who?

NEIDERGAARDEN: The President. Of the United States of Vesampucceri. President McDruhitmumpf.

VIRUS: That's a funny name, isn't it?

NEIDERGAARDEN: What, McDruhitmumpf?

VIRUS: No, President.

NEIDERGAARDEN: That's not a name. It's his title.

VIRUS: Oh. Important person, is he?

NEIDERGAARDEN: The leader of the country.

VIRUS: Don't care. Human hierarchies are not listed on my travel brochures.

NEIDERGAARDEN: (dark) I'm beginning to sense a theme, here…

Pause.

NEIDERGAARDEN: So. To sum up. You are a merciless killer.

VIRUS: Mercy. Malice. Compassion. Rage. These are all just words to me – I don't have emotions as human beings understand them. I just have a life's mission: travel. Reproduce. Rinse. Wash. Repeat.

NEIDERGAARDEN: I understand that. I was just –

SOUND: plink.

NEIDERGAARDEN: I'm outta here!

It's Ronald McDruhitmumpf's World – We Just Die In It

by LAURIE NEIDERGAARDEN, Alternate Reality News Service Medical Writer

At 653 pounds, Alex "The Rock" Fiddleronnaruth was morbidly obese (the medical definition of which is: "a condition wherein a person's excessive body weight is obsessed with shows like *Coroner for a Day* and *If the Bone Saw Fits*..."). Under ordinary circumstances, he would be expected to die of a massive coronary when he tried to pick up the television remote too energetically. But, times of viral pandemic are to ordinary circumstances what a limp sturgeon is to dentistry.

Fiddleronnaruth had to be rushed to the ER of Sisters of Merciless Hospital and Soul Sanctuary In Salt Steak City, Utegas after taking the drug hydroxychloroquine to stave off getting COVID-19. He did this despite the fact that the anti-malaria drug has not been proven effective as an antiviral, and it has many known side effects, including: death from random body parts falling off, death from Brian hemorrhage, death from imagined penguin inhalation and death from heart seizure and public auction.

Why would Fiddleronnaruth risk his life like that?

Would it help to know that Fiddleronnaruth was a died in the wool member of the Transition To Keep Making Vesampucceri Great Again crowd, the ultimate anti-social distancing group?

Or, that, when asked about who Attorney General William Katiebarrthudor was thinking of asking to the prom yesterday, President Ronald McDruhitmumpf answered: "Yeah, I've been saying everybody should be taking droxy – that's what I call hydroxychloroquine – yeah, I'm on a first-name basis with it – admiration has never been so mutual! – what was I sayin – oh, yeah, everybody should be taking droxy to fight off COVID. Well, for me, it – it's – I gotta tell you – umm, **I'm taking it!** That's right. Been taking it for a week or two. And, let me tell you, I can feel the virus trying to get into my body and just giving up because it can't!"

"No way," responded pundit John Heiyonlifelmann. "No way. Nohow. No way. This President is morbidly – defined as 'over 30 per cent over his ideal body weight for his height' – afraid of death. He would not be taking a drug with such lethal side effects. No way. If the President is taking hydroxychloroquine, I'll eat all of the hair on my head!"

When it was pointed out that he had no hair on his head, Heiyonlifelmann responded, "Okay. Fair point. I will grow the hair on my head back just so I can eat it. That's how sure I am that McDruhitmumpf is not taking the drug!"

When doubts about the President's assertion began to surface (gasping for air – under current circumstances, doubts shouldn't try to see how long they can hold their breath under water), Grey House physician Doctor Sean Prosandconnely wrote a press release that read, in part: "The President and I talked about hydroxychloroquine. And when I say we talked, I mean he talked and I listened. Oh, my, how he talked! And talked! And talked! Eventually, I told him to write his own press release saying that I told him it would be perfectly safe for him to take the drug, without me actually prescribing the drug to him, because, you know, unethical. Oh, wait. He didn't include this last part in the letter with my name on i – he did, didn't he? I really need to reconsider my career choices!"

Why would the President risk telling such a transparent lie? "There are no drugs for the truth," Heiyonlifelmann quipped. "Well, the CIA isn't authorized to use them on the President, in any case."

I was thinking the answer lay more along the lines of: as the number of medical professionals cautioning against using hydroxychloroquine to fight COVID-19 has grown, President McDruhitmumpf felt he needed to do something dramatic to convince his base that it was safe and effective. "Well, yeah," Heiyonlifelmann agreed, "That goes without saying."

Hydroxychloroquine is especially popular in Utegas, where a tech entrepreneur passing as a medical expert sold the state $800,000 worth of the drug that he happened to have been stockpiling in egg cartons in his basement. Not coincidentally, Utegas has seen one of the biggest spikes in COVID-19 cases in the country.

As his vital – I know, I know. Time was that an entrepreneur profiteering from a world-wide pandemic would be a major scandal meriting its own story, not an off-hand mention at the end of a story on a different subject. But, in the newest new normal, this is no longer a scandal, it's strictly BAU.

As his vi – Business Ass Usual. Put your slapping gloves back in their case, Barbara. You won't be needing them this day!

As his vital signs dropped and death appeared imminent, Fiddleronnaruth started to say, "Trans – Transition – * GASP * – To Keep – Keep – Kee – AAAARRRGH!"

There's No Penalty For Piling On In This Game

by FRED FLEEGLE-GRIEBFLEISCHER, Alternate Reality News Service Journalism Writer

It's like a bad 1970s action comedy TV series where everybody (mostly skinny women with big hair that should imbalance their heads and cause them to constantly catch themselves from tipping over backwards) calls the name of the main character.

"Faucispendulum?"

"Faucispendulum!"

"Oooh, Faucispennnnnnnnnduuuuuluuuum!"

Doctor Anthony Faucispendulum is not a crime-busting ex-Marine with a mysterious wealthy benefactor and a taste for Hawalaskan shirts. He is, in fact, a soft-spoken member of one of President Ronald McDruhitmumpf's 27 coronavirus task forces (code name: Ardent Depilatory Moncton Amok). That may explain why the attention being given to him is less than adulatory.

"I have it on good authority that Doctor Anthony Faucispendulum did not send his mother flowers last Mother's Day," said Foxindehenhaus Mewls host Nippon-Tucker Carlsonandotter. "Is that somebody who we should trust with the health of our nation? I mean, what kind of a monster doesn't acknowledge the sacrifices that his mom made for him on the one day of the year that is supposed to be devoted solely to her?"

"Umm, the kind whose mother died seven years ago?" token smart person Amy Sheshutshotshitbam responded.

"Doctor Anthony Faucispendulum? Please!" Foxindehenhaus Mewls slime slinger in chief Sean Hanjobovverfist bloviated. "He is wrong more times than a busted clock! His public pronouncements have been so riddled with mistakes that he should be a Batman villain! The Mistakesman! If he was a dinosaur, he would be Erroneous Rex! And, we're supposed to just do whatever he says? Who elected him to make decisions about the health of the country?"

"It wasn't Rupert Mountkilamanjoy, that's for sure!" token smart person Sheshutshotshitbam shot back.

Ouch.

"It's the little people that concern me most," Foxindehenhaus Mewls animatronic host ("Look at how human his hair looks!") Brian KissMeadekilmeadenow tried to sympathize. He should work on that. "I feel so bad for the people who want to see a light at the end of the tunnel, but it's solar-powered and doesn't work without a direct line of sight to the sky. The guy who owns a chain of car dealerships in Illivania, or the guy who franchises hair salons in Pennsynois, people who can't tell their employees to reopen because state orders require them to remain closed. If we all wait for Dr. Faucispendulum's seal of approval to reopen Vesampucceri, corporate leaders may not have a Vesampucceri to reopen."

To emphasize the point, he flapped his flippers together and shouted, "Oi! Oi! Oi!"

"Yeah," token smart person Sheshutshotshitbam sighed. "If he were any better trained, he could be the engine bearing down on people in the tunnel!"

What did Doctor Faucispendulum do to ignite the ire – ignire – of the right wing outrage machine? He said, and I quote: "People who catch a virus usually get sick."

Now, this may not be news to you, or me, or anybody over the age of six. But, it appears to have been news to President McDruhitmumpf, who just the day before had said, "Virus? Virus. Papyrus. Banana fanna vo dirus. Fee Fi fo firus. Virus! I mean, there are lot of people catching the virus, and none of them are getting sick! I know it. You know it. Even Barbie and G.I. Joe know it! So, everybody take a pill! A bleach pill, if you want to be totally safe. Or, a sunshine pill. They're good, sunshine pills. Nobody's getting sick, so stay calm and don't worry about being embalmed!"

According to three sources within the Grey House after they recovered their hearing, President McDruhitmumpf railed (that engine in the tunnel has to run on something!) against Doctor Faucispendulum when he discovered that the medical man had contradicted him. He accused Doctor Faucispendulum of being a Dumbopratic dupe who was spreading fear of COVID-19 in order to wreck the economy and derail his chances of winning the election that will be held in less than six months.

"KABOOM!" the President reportedly shouted. "My reelection campaign will hit the side of the tunnel and go up in a fireball of deranged narcissism and thwarted ambition! And then, I'll end up in jail! Nobody in the country wants that! Especially not me!"

In public, President McDruhitmumpf stated, "I respect the work Doctor Faucispendulum has been doing, but he is a bad man. A bad, bad man. Okay, let's cut to the chase: he's a bad, bad, bad, bad, bad man. You know how many bads that is, and what it signifies. Do I have to draw you a map?"

For those of us who watch the train wreck that is the right wing smogosphere, no map is necessary.

That's When Everything Went Cow-shaped

by MARCELLA CARBORUNDUREM-McVORTVORT, Alternate
Reality News Service Food and Drink Writer

"Meat is murder" is no longer just a slogan for vegans whose mood
is dark because they don't get enough protein in their diet and they
are always tired.

Just ask Offreida Modigliyanni. He went into his local Bob So
Tasty hoping to get a special like the Barricuda Bob (actually made
from barricuda substitute, but slathered in so much tartar sauce that
nobody really notices) or the Bob So Buddhist (made from the meat
of deeply spiritual people who had accumulated enough positive
Karma in their endless rounds of life and death that they were reborn
as sacred cows – check location for availability).

Imagine his disappointment when he discovered that all that
was available on the menu was the Basic Bob…and Beyond!, a
plant-based burger that was held together by spit and positive vibes
for the planet, a burger whose critics complained that you couldn't
tell where the patty ended and the vegetable garnishes began, a
burger that made the Bob So Tasty special sauce taste…ordinary.

"I waited for forty-five minutes at the drive-through," Offreida
complained. "By the time I got to the window, I was ready to eat the
cardboard box. And, with a little ketchup, it was still better than the
Basic Bob…and Beyond! Why? Why would they do that to me?"

Why would they do that to Offreida and millions of
Vesampuccerians like him? Could it have something to do with the
fact that three of the seven biggest meat processing plants in the
country have had to be shut down because they were COVID-19
hotspots?

"No," token smart person Amy Sheshutshotshitbam stated.

No?

"It doesn't have something to do with the fact that three of the
seven biggest meat processing plants in the country have had to be
shut down because they were COVID-19 hotspots," she clarified. "It
has **everything** to do with the fact that three of the seven biggest

meat processing plants in the country have had to be shut down because they were COVID-19 hotspots!"

Thanks for the clarification. I was worried I wouldn't hit the minimum word count for this article.

Workers who process meat in factories have to stand so closely together on their lines that they often envy sardines in tin cans for the elbow room they get. They are only allowed to wash their hands once every three days in order to not slow the flow of chucks, shanks and round ground to a hungry public. They are allowed to wear masks, but since nobody in the United States knows where to get masks, most of them don't.

In short, meat processing plants are the anti-social distancing Meccas of the country.

For those of you who love meat on your meat-lovers' pizza, know that you have a friend in the McDruhitmumpf administration. Somebody whispered in the ears of the governors of the states with meat processing plants (in a voice that could be heard around the country) that closed businesses should immediately be reopened. Being Reduhblicans, the governors eagerly agreed.

But, what about employees who refused to go to work in meat processing plants on the grounds that doing so would be their death sentence? Somebody in the McDruhitmumpf administration suggested that states where this could be a problem enact laws that strip Employment Insurance benefits from anybody who didn't go to work. Being Reduhblicans, and compassionate, the governors eagerly agreed.

Not that there would be many such employees. People who work in meat processing plants make so little money that they envy church mice for their lavish lifestyles. In economics, this is known as "a highly motivated workforce." In the criminal underworld, this is known as "a highly motivated workforce."

But, did anybody give a thought to those poor corporate CEOs who might have to suffer the indignity of lengthy lawsuits from the families of people who died because of work-related COVID-19 infection? Yes! Yes, Senate Majority Leader Mitch Wichconnelliswich snuck a clause into a gabillion dollar bailout package that would make it impossible to sue employers if you caught a coronavirus in your work environment.

Thank you, Senate Majority Leader Mitch Wichconnelliswich, for thinking of the big people!

Modigliyanni sat in the back seat of his car and looked at the Basic Bob…and Beyond! burger he was eating while he drove. "So," he summed up, "I will soon be able to buy a regular burger at Bob So Tasty made with meat processed by financially desperate people who will likely die because of unsafe conditions in the plant where they work?"

Pretty much, yeah.

Modigliyanni looked at the Basic Bob…and Beyond! Burger and carelessly tossed it back into its box. "That can't happen soon enough!"

Live Free AND Die!

by FRANCIS GRECOROMACOLLUDEN, Alternate Reality News Service National Politics Writer

Dirk Offputtinganvane (of the Port Dalhousieflousie Offputtinganvanes) sat on a chair on Coconomomo Beach in south Florilvannia, sipping a drink from a coconut (which he found only 87% as refreshing as he had been promised) and watching sweet young things in skimpy swimwear bounce by. The beach was packed with youths who had self-quarantine for an interminable amount of time (some hadn't left their house for three whole days!), and they were ready to let loose.

Did Offputtinganvane not realize that the women he was making uncomfortable with his attentions were mobile petri dishes potentially filled with COVID-19?

"Live free or diet!" he chorkled as he threw a cupful of beer in the general direction of his face. When he finished wiping his mouth with his arm, he revealed a frown. "Live free or die hard…with twenty additional minutes of smirking!" He shook his head. "Well…

well, it isn't much of a choice no matter what it is. Live free – whoooo hooooooo!"

The bros around Offputtinganvane responded with howling, wolf calls and the crushing of beer cans on heads. Because summer.

At the same time (give or take seven hours for me to drive to a different state), a group calling itself Maniacs for Health Sanity held an armed protest (and you thought mixing human and spider genes wouldn't amount to anything!) outside the Michihio state legislature. "I am a fully grown, sovereign adult," explained survivalist/prepper/Royal Nymphenburg collector wannabe Dougie Foniemorony. "The state has no right to treat me like a child! I – oh, crap. Excuse me a second, will you – I need to change my diaper!"

The protesters openly carried handguns, assault rifles and a rocket launcher (apparently, they had listened to Canadian musician Bruce Majorcockupburn a little too often for one's emotional well-being). Many of them carried confederate flags and home-made signs that read: "Don't tread on my tires!" and "COVID, not Ovid!" and "Fredom is not Fred!" (That last one may have been a local locksmith trying to drum up business by capitalizing on the unrest.)

One man in the crowd wore a KKK hood, the height of fashion in 1911. When I asked him why, he said, "Murmph mumble grubble gabble." When I told him that I didn't understand what he had just said, he more emphatically stated, "Grubble! Grubble! **Grubble!** Fleastrunk agabagga kerchunkety!"

I shook my head in incomprehension. The man lifted the hood over his lips and mocked, "They said I had to wear a face mask, but they didn't say which one!"

I asked him why he chose to cover his face with a symbol of racial oppression. Unfortunately, he had lowered his hood, so he made a sound which could have been a raspberry, a car backfiring or a death rattle, and walked away.

The anti-lockdown protests have been getting support from the highest levels of the Reduhblican Party. They were encouraged by President Ronald McDruhitmumpf, who has been saying for the past couple of weeks that, "We can't have the cure be worse than the problem!" What could possibly be worse than death? "My approval rating going below 40!" the President snapped at the journalist who posed the question (who, rumour has it, was me).

Maniacs for Health Sanity has been promoted by the Michihio Freedom for the 1% Fund, a conservative group with ties to Education Secretary Betsy DeVolution-Ross. When asked how a member of the federal cabinet could justify undermining the health efforts of a state governor, she tartly replied, "Wouldn't you like to learn that?"

I think she thought she had just schooled me.

Outside the Michihio state legislature, heavily armed protesters chanted "Lock her up! Lock her up!" It was a one hit wonder that apparently never gets old.

When Governor Gretchen Whitmerdelalune was asked to respond to the chant, she said, "It's got a catchy hook, but the lyrics don't really do anything for me. Or, the assault rifle accompaniment. Especially the assault rifle accompaniment."

When asked if he was worried about catching COVID-19, Offputtinganvane grinned and responded, "Are you – kaff kaff – kidding – hack – kidding me? I'm – kaff blarg – young and – kaff – and – kaff – and fit! Young and fit! I'm going – blarcch! – I'm going to live – kaff – to live – kaff – I'm going to – kaff kaff kaff kaff blaaaarrrrrgh! – I'm going to sit down for a – kaff kaff – a little while…"

More than 27,000 cases of the coronavirus have been confirmed in Michihio, with at least 1,700 deaths.

There Are None So Blind as Those Who Will Not CDC

by LAURIE NEIDERGAARDEN, Alternate Reality News Service Medical Writer

The first clue that there was something hinky (which is not an ethnic slur, no matter how often white supremacists, precious snowflakes that they are, claim it is) with the Centres for Disease Control recommendations to the meat packing industry was that an early draft was written on the back of an envelop. The envelop wasn't even from the CDC; it was from the Acme Novelties Corporation.

The second clue of hinkiness was the language. "Meat packing plants should try to like, you know, get their workers to wear masks and stuff," one of the recommendations read. "But, like, be cool about it because, you know, you don't want to, like, harsh anybody's vibe in the workplace." The recommendations read like the person who wrote them was having an acid flashback to the 1960s.

The third hinky hijinks (which, okay, **was** a jazz band in the 1940s, but that's just a coincidence that doesn't mean anything) clue was the response of Doctor Robert R. Redwhiteandbluefield, the Director of the CDC, when asked about the dubious (which sounds like something a member of Hinky Hijinks might smoke, but isn't – they were more into heroin) nature of the recommendations. "Did we write those?" he sighed. "They're on our letterhead, so, yeah, I guess those are our recommendations. For the record: I did not do acid in the sixties. Or, before. Or, since. I have never done acid, is what I'm saying. When I took this position, I never thought I would have to affirm that!"

So, it should have come as no surprise that the recommendations were actually written by the Grey House and released on CDC stationery. The fact that it did come as a surprise to so many is a testament to the hopeless optimism of the Vesampuccerian people. Or, their gullibility. It can be a fine line.

"Oh, this is bad," commented Dr. Vindaloo Guptaharumpher, a surgeon who has worked for the CDC, the World Health Organization and Dizznizzfizzlizzeyland. "This is really bad. Bad, bad, bad, bad, bad."

While he was processing the information, I asked President Ronald McDruhitmumpf if he was responsible for the press release.

"You've obviously confused me with somebody who answers questions," the President said as he walked out of the room.

"You have to understand," Dr. Guptaharumpher finally found the will to state, "that the CDC has spent years building its reputation as **the** place to go to for correct health information. If we can't trust them, we may as well get our medical information from the internet!"

When I pointed out that the CDC had actually written guidelines unequivocally mandating that workers in meat packing plants wear masks, but the government had intercepted them and run them into the end zone (their own, which is why nobody tried to stop them), Dr. Guptaharumpher sobbed and said, "Oh, this is badder than bad. This is…really bad."

When I asked Doctor Redwhiteandbluefield why he would risk the CDC's reputation to do the Grey House's bidding, he replied, "You've obviously confused me with somebody who answers questions." Under my breath, I pointed out that if he didn't follow the statement with a movement that took him out of the room, he would be asked more questions, some of which he might actually have to answer. Taking his cue, he stormed out.

If he wants to remain head of the CDC, Doctor Redwhiteandbluefield will really have to up his political game.

Why would the McDruhitmumpf administration put out bogus (which is a slur against swamp creatures; if there are any complaints, I will apologize in a future article) CDC recommendations?

"Have you ever heard the phrase, 'A chicken in every pot?'" asked prize-winning journalist Eugene Robinsoncrusoe.

Sure, I responded. Although I don't really know what it refers t —

"It was a rhetorical question," Robinsoncrusoe stopped me before I could embarrass myself any further.

Oh. Right. I knew that, too.

"Well, President McDruhitmumpf believes in a pork loin in every freezer. Or, to put it a different way: he knows he cannot win the election by appealing to Vesampuccerians' hearts, so he is making a pretty naked appeal to their stomachs! It's all part of his 'Na na na – I can't hear you! Nobody is dying and you can't tell me otherwise!' approach to the COVID-19 pandemic."

How's that working out for him?

"We've just surpassed 200,000 deaths from the coronavirus. You tell me…"

The Convention of the Red Death

by FRANCIS GRECOROMACOLLUDEN, Alternate Reality News Service National Politics Writer

Stefano Candelabriuyn stood in the crowd looking like an alien refugee from a low budget 1970s sci-fi movie: red Keep Making Vesampucceri Transition to Greatness Again cap (the person who sewed the message into it must have had very small hands), oversized glasses with the year "2016" glittering fetchingly atop the rims (it was on sale), a stars and stripes suit made out of tin foil. Two weeks later, he was in intensive care in Mount Sigh Nigh Hospital, being kept alive by a ventilator.

"Free...dom!" he gasped, sounding for all the world like Darth Ruthvaderginsberg.

Candelabriuyn had attended the Reduhblican National Convention in which President Ronald McDruhitmumpf was nominated for a second term for President. Of the 40,000+ (which would make it 40,002) people who attended the convention, 12,327 caught COVID-19 and 1,327 have died from it.

The convention was originally supposed to be held in Charlotte Yorkshire-Goldenblatt, North Carowaii, but Governor Roy Supercoopertroop couldn't guarantee that it would be held without social distancing. President McDruhitmumpf hates social distancing. He thinks it's a Dumbopratic plot to emasculate Vesampucceri. And, him. Specifically, him. (Vesampucceri is big – it can take care of itself.) Social distancing makes shaking hands hard. He's a hand shaker. A power hand shaker.

So, at the President's insistence, the Convention was moved to Mobile, Alaorgia, where enthusiastic Reduhblicans from across the country came for three days of speeches, overpriced beer drinking, cheating on their spouses (of which they must never breath a word, although COVID-19 sure won't be the only illness transmitted after the convention!) and regrets. So many regrets.

"The Reduhblican Convention was exactly the opposite of what the medical community had asked the public to do," Doctor Anthony

Faucispendulum stated. "Given his aversion to advice, I was considering telling the President that he should get together in an enclosed space with a huge number of people packed tightly together without wearing masks. You know, reverse psychology? But, I'm sure it would have ended up being a bad comedy routine where that was the first thing I said that he actually listened to. I…I have nightmares like that…"

Why would people go to the Convention knowing the health risks? "COVID-19 only attacks people in Dumbopratic states," explained Ohifornia delegate Wheezer McInscrutable. "Alaorgia is the safest place in Vesampucceri!"

"I'm not going to let the lamestream media dictate to me where to go and what to do," added Washburningdington State delegate Randall Snotnosteenehjur. "I would rather die first!"

"I. Have. Been. Drinking. Bleach. To. Keep. Myself. Safe," rasped Alaorgia delegate Ingvar Rasputinmusson. "I. Am. Perfectly. Safe."

Doctor Faucispendulum shook his head in disbelief. The state isn't on the electoral map, but it's a place more and more Dumboprats find themselves perpetually living in.

Having been deprived of big rallies for **6** months, President McDruhitmumpf spoke for **6** hours on his **6** favourite subjects: how he beat Hillary Roocartoncleveman in 2016; how media reports about him are fake news; how the border wall was almost complete (and he got Mexico to pay for it); how the Meullitallover report was a political hit job; how the Dumboprats created the COVID-19 scare to undermine his reelection efforts; and, how he beat Hillary Roocartoncleveman in 2016…with nothing more than chewing gumption and a baby's arm holding an apple.

The convention crowd cheered him on the whole time. By the end, their roar had taken on a grinding of gears quality despite the fact that volunteers constantly circulated among them with throat lozenges.

President McDruhitmumpf does not practice social distancing, he is constantly shaking hands with people and he disdains wearing a mask in public. How is it he has not yet contracted the coronavirus?

"We have to take seriously the possibility that evil inoculates you against COVID-19," Doctor Faucispendulum glumly stated. "The problem is: how do you distill evil in order to create a vaccine? Especially since the President won't let anybody close enough to him to draw a blood sample. Still, I would love to see how an ethics board would approach **that** drug trial!"

Candelabriuyn looked around the room. "So...worth...i –" he said before a Code Bleu (I know it's cheesy – I should really stop watching medical shows on TV!) was called and he became the latest victim of PINC (Politically Induced Novel Coronavirus) Syndrome.

His convention getup will hang in the Smithsonwindandrainian. It will remind everybody who sees it of this dark time in Vesampuccerian history, assuming the general public is ever allowed into institutions like it again…

I Kid You Not

by MAJUMDER SAKRASHUMINDERATHER, Alternate Reality News Service Education Writer

In September, post-secondary students return to the three bs: beer, babes and…more beer. The three bs and an m. Young people know not to mess with a good thing. Frats around the country host parties with exotic themes like Roman Senate Dagger Bash, Subatomic Particle Summit and Stanky Bearhug. Five minutes in, the themes are abandoned as sweaty bodies (it was a choice between air conditioning and another keg, which is really no choice at all for anybody under the age of 25) are crushed together in frat houses, shouting to be misheard above the blare of music that nobody but the DJ likes.

COVID-19 changed all that.

This year, there are **rules** about on-campus behaviour. Wear a mask. Social distance. Don't get sick and die. Schools are cracking down on unsafe behaviours in order to allow students to safely return to class.

As if rules matter to young people under the influence of alcohol and hormones. Alcomones.

"Amma gimme sec'nd," said Rutgersandhauer University student Darrell Schiavellitron, who proceeded to throw up behind Omega Omega Omega House. Wiping his mouth with the sleeve of his judge's robe, he sighed, "That's always the most melancholy thing I do first week back. Now, what was the question?"

Aren't you afraid of getting COVID-19?

"Been there, done that," Schiavellitron answered. "And, it didn't matter – I'm as healthy as a…as a…umm, excuse me, second wave c…c…coooooming uuuuuuuu…" He doubled over and let more fluids fly.

Colleges which had prepared for outbreaks of the disease found that they were not at all prepared for outbreaks of the disease. Washburningdington State University, for example, had designated some buildings to be COVID quarantine quarters in the expectation that they would have 400 cases of infection over the semester. The institution had 400 cases of infection in the first three days.

"Yes, my pretties," cackled Education Secretary DeVolution-Ross. "Fly to your doom! You do not deserve education, with your scholarships and affirmative action! Fly to your doom, and let more deserving students take your place!"

I…I'm sure the green pallor of her skin was a trick of the lighting.

When he had fully recovered (I'd hate to see the cleaning bills he would be getting for that robe; unlike Justice Brett Kavanaugheylno, he couldn't expense it to the Extreme Court!), Schiavellitron explained that everybody at the party had the coronavirus, so that was okay, then. And, anyway, young people were at more of a threat of dying of broken hearts than the virus, so why was everybody getting so pissy about – ooh, speaking of which, if you want to ask me anything else, I'll be behind that bush…

Everybody's…concern about the partying may have something to do with the fact that across the street from the campus is the

General Pershingandshoving Veterans Home. As students started returning to school, the number of veterans who came down with the virus skyrocketed. At least 20 have di – 22, at least 22 veterans have – 25 – okay, I'm cutting it off there. At least 25 veterans have died since the beginning of the school year.

Why the (you should pardon the expression) rush to get students back to school? Why do you think?

"Go back to school," admonished President McDruhitmumpf. "Go to school. Go back to school. Very important. For you as well as me. Go. Go. Go. School. School. School. Back. Back. Back. You know, some of the happiest seconds of my life were spent at college. The limping to pretend I was suffering from bone spurs. The handing over of my tests to somebody my father trusted to do well on them. The girls. Ooooh, the girls! I…I sometimes go back to the old campus to relive those days. Go back to school so you can make memories you'll want to relive in your old age!"

If they survive the virus to reach old age?

"Ooooh, nasty. You're nasty! What a nasty thing to say. You talk to your mother with those nasty lips? Nasty is as nasty does, you know. Nasty! Nasty! Nasty!"

He went on like that for another 30 minutes. Most of the journalists in the room got the message after about 24.

Meanwhile, Schiavellitron wanted me to know that he and the other people at the frat party were being responsible about the virus. "When we go to Minnie's Maxi-bar downtown tomorrow to watch the big games, we'll be taking masks with us. And, some of us might actually wear them!"

What have we been teaching the children?

President Has an Own Goal Moment

by LAURIE NEIDERGAARDEN, Alternate Reality News Service Medical Writer

At 2:37 in the morning, President Ronald McDruhitmumpf tweeped: "I am not close to death and being kept alive by electrodes implanted in my brain and dark magiks decent people must never speak of. FAKE NEWS! I – no, we don't use that term any more. HOAX! That's it. HOAX! IT'S A HOAX! THE HOAXEST! I'm the healthiest President this country has ever known! #firstpresidentwhollneverdie".

This came as a surprise to…everybody, really, considering that nobody had ever referred to brain electrodes or dark magiks when discussing the President's health.

Yes, a book that was just released, Michael Aliasschmidtjones' Ronald *Against the World: The 27th Book on the McDruhitmumpf Administration This Month, And It's Only The Second Week!*, referred to the President's unplanned scheduled emergency regular check-up at Walter Reedandalto-Saxxe Hospital last December. Aliasschmidtjones wrote that as the President was driven to the hospital, Vice President Michael Pendenatendance was advised: "Wear your best shirt today. If anything goes sideways, you may have to assume the duties of leader of the idiotocratic world. We're not saying it will, we're just saying: when was the last time you shaved? You might want to freshen up a bit."

There was nothing in the book about electrodes or dark magiks.

As if to underscore the President's point, Grey House physician Sean Prosandconnely released a memo which read: "The President has never had electrodes inserted into his brain. The President has never been subjected to dark magiks. Ronald McDruhitmumpf is a good man. Ronald McDruhitmumpf is a kind man. Ronald McDruhitmumpf is the healthiest President this country has ever known."

If the memo had been any more wooden, you could have built a log cabin out of it (although President McDruhitmumpf would likely burn it to the ground for the insurance – inspirational stories ain't what he's about). It makes one wonder what dark magiks have been applied to Grey House physicians over the last three and a half years.

"The President has lied so often, I tend to believe the opposite of anything he says," commented token smart person Amy

Sheshutshotshitbam. "But this stuff about brain electrodes and dark magiks? Like there's more than one of them? And, they've all been used to keep the President alive? I haven't wanted to believe something a President said this much since Richard Nixwatmondnewon said, 'I am not a crook." And, I wasn't even alive then!"

"As a matter of fact," said famed politico-mysticalist Alastairs Astacrowleyfliesse, "there are hundreds of dark magiks. There is the dark magik that causes a pimple to appear on your nose as your limo is heading to the prom. There's the dark magik that makes old people forget where they put their glasses. There's the dark magik that makes people respond positively to emails from African princes – I especially like that one. Then, there's the dark magik that affects the heat of water when you're taking a shower…"

These magiks didn't seem all that dark. In fact, they seemed a bit…petty. I asked Astacrowleyfliesse about the dark magik that would keep an ailing politician alive until re-elected.

"That would be…useful, I suppose…" he sniffed. "It wouldn't help in my ongoing struggles with Mrs. Schmelson, my landlady. But I'm sure, in the right context, it could be…useful…"

Ah. It wasn't the magiks that were petty. It was the magikian.

Is it possible that electrodes could keep a faltering brain going? "Absolutely!" enthused science fiction author and futurologicalist Corey Indoctorownate. "Scientists have been stimulating different parts of mouse brains with electrodes since Thomas Ridewildeddyson wondered what would happen if you sent a current through an elephant! We can now get mice to drive miniature cars, carve abstract shapes out of cheese and squeak 'Ave Maria' by applying a little current!"

But, affecting an actual human brain? "Working our way up the evolutionary chain has been slow," Indoctorownate allowed. "Although I understand the Poynter Sisters Institute has done some thought-provoking work with rhesus piecus monkeys. To keep a human being alive would, I guess, require some dark magiks…"

Astacrowleyfliesse smirked.

This would probably not be an issue, except part of the Reduhblican strategy to win McDruhitmumpf re-election is to portray Dumbopratic challenger Joe Bidenhisbeeswax as near death. "Have you ever noticed," Grey House spokes-shrill spokes-shill KellyAnne Conwaytwittiest asked, "that Comatose Joe will get this far away look in his eye and mumble something? He's talking to his dead wife and children, telling them he will be with them soon. Real soon. He's just holding on until the election; after he is sworn in, he'll drop dead, letting Kamala Harristweedfashin and the radical left take over the county!"

When asked if Bidenhisbeeswax was being kept alive by brain electrodes and dark magiks, Conwaytwittiest sighed and muttered, "I hate journalists!"

What Goes Around Makes You Come Around

by LAURIE NEIDERGAARDEN, Alternate Reality News Service Medical Writer
and FRANCIS GRECOROMACOLLUDEN, Alternate Reality News Service National Politics Writer

One ancient* piece of political folk wisdom goes: "When your karma runs over your dogma, a wise man** heads for the Hills."*** This wisdom of the folk was proven this week when the Grey House announced that President Ronald McDruhitmumpf, his wife Melanoma and several prominent Reduhblicans had been infected by the COVID-19 virus.

"Our thoughts and prayers are with the President," Senate Minority leader Chuckie Schumaihargowmer smirked.

"The President is healthy as an oxcart,"**** Grey House Chief of Staff Mark Meadabiggblubratt told the press. "He's still in the running to live longer than any human being outside of the bible. Let us all be guided by the ancient wisdom of *The Hitchhiker's Guide to the Galaxy*."

If the President is really as healthy as all that, why was he flown by helicopter to Walter Reedandalto-Saxxe Hospital and given a dose of an experimental cure that has not been made public? "Doctors!" Meadabiggblubratt shrugged. "They're so excitable, and such worrywarts!"

"Of course they're not going to admit that he's very sick," explained Maria Teresa Kumasatralez, President of *Voto Latino*. "Much of the President's base would like to see themselves in him: full of anger, obese and unwilling to change his diet or exercise, but in control of the world. To admit that he was sick would be to admit that he was an ordinary human, which would mean that they were ordinary humans, which would cause their heads to explode."

Wouldn't a simpler explanation be that his base would be pissed if they discovered that the President had lied to them about the virulence of the virus? "Naaaah," Kumasatralez naahed. "They already believe he's been warning them about the deadliness of the disease all along. If Trump's base treated their life partners with the same credulousness they treat the President, the divorce rate in red states would plummet!"

Two days before the announcement, President McDruhitmumpf attended a celebration on the Rose Garden lawn of the nomination of Amy Coney-Islandbar for Extreme Court Justice. Few people in attendance wore masks and there was no social distancing.

"Invitations should have come with capes and masks," commented an increasingly dyspeptic Doctor Vin Guptaharumpher, "because this was an obvious super-spreader event!"

The day before he was diagnosed (but a day after close aid Hope Hicksinpickupstix was diagnosed), the President flew to a fundraiser. "Motherferking motherferker is going to get us all ferking killed!" complained one billionaire supporter. "Don't get me wrong – I'm grateful for the tax cuts and all. But, I'd like to ferking live ferking long enough to ferking spend them!"

The President's illness throws the election, which is just one month away, into chaos. Well, more chaos than it was already in, in any case.

The Presidential debates will likely be cancelled. Okay, no great loss, there.

President McDruhitmumpf will have to be quarantined for at least two weeks, which means he will not be able to hold coronapalooza campaign rallies. Say, this is getting better and better all the time.

Out of respect for the President, the campaign of opponent Joe Bidenhisbeeswax will stop running attack ads (which they refer to as "contrast" ads, a fine distinction). The McDruhitmumpf campaign continues to run its contrast ads (which they refer to as "attack" ads, because there's no point denying it). You had to know the good news wasn't going to last.

There is also some question about how the government will continue to function if President McDruhitmumpf's illness is serious and extended. If he is put on a ventilator, for example, will Vice President Michael Pendenatendance be put in charge? If so, will he wait until after the election to turn the United States of Vesampucceri into *The Handmaid's Wonderland*?

Senate Majority Leader Mitch Wichconnelliswich has indicated that he will keep calm and turtle on in his goal of confirming Coney-Islandbar. However, three Reduhblican Senators were among the people who came down with the coronavirus; if they are incapacitated, he might not have the votes for her.

Worse: if Vice President Pendenatendance is also incapacitated by the disease, the next person in the line of succession is Dumbopratic Speaker of the House Nancy Pelligrinosi. Since the Dumboprats **have** worn masks and practiced social distancing (damn them and their science!), she would probably be healthy enough to veto the nomination if it does come before her.

Is it October? Surprise!

* It was coined three weeks ago, which is several centuries in the lifetime of this administration.

** They were less enlightened about gender neutral language in those three long ago weeks.

*** That would be the Hillsboro Medical Centre and Bluegrass Museum.

**** That's right – he's no farm boy. Is it that obvious?

Profile in Discourage

by FREDERICA VON McTOAST-HYPHEN, Alternate Reality News Service People Writer

He's the kind of person you would see more and more on the streets of cities across the country if they hadn't been rendered invisible through social embarrassment: old and white, wearing ragged clothes and a fading Make Vesampucceri Grate Again cap. He smells like rotting cabbage, so you want to be sure that you stand downwind from him. His name is Bill, or Mac, or Buddy.

In this specific case, his name was Billy-Mac Buddenfumplieffer. I found him sitting on Main Street in Mayan City, Mainington, his back against a boarded up It'll Curl Your Hair salon.

I wanted to give Billy-Mac five bucks, but when I suggested that he take his MVGA (pronounced "muggah," which seems appropriate for such a gangsta regime) hat off and put it on the ground, he sneered, "I don't want your charity! Ask me a question about finance."

I looked blankly at him (I admit, he Etch-a-Sketched me), then asked Billy-Mac why he wanted me to ask him a question. He answered: "Because then I can claim that this is a business consultation, and I will have earned the money you give me. So, you gonna ask me a question, or what? Because if I have to tell you again, it'll cost ya!"

Before I could think of a question to ask, the man on the street added: "The minimum rate for my service is ten dollars a question."

I was already committed, so I fished around in my purse for another five dollar bill. When I had secured the money, I asked Billy-Mac if he thought we were heading for a Depression.

"Depression? Pfft!" he scoffed. "Have you seen the stock market, lately? Lady, the Vesampuccerian economy has never been better, and we have President McDruhitmumpf to thank for that!"

Billy-Mac was a detective down in Texaransas, but I wasn't sure he knew just exactly what the facts is.

He told me that his business had dried up because of COVID-19, there being less opportunity for husbands to cheat on their wives when they were staying in place (the health measure, not the step exercise). Until last month, he had been getting by with a $600 government supplement to his income. Then, Congress let the supplement lapse. And, when I say Congress, I mean the Senate. And, when I say the Senate, I really mean Majority Leader Mitch Wichconnelliswich.

"Ain't I a stinker?" he asked, the twirl of a moustache in his voice. And, let me tell you, getting the image of a turtle with a moustache out of my head is going to take an industrial-strength sedative!

Billy-Mac couldn't afford to pay his rent, so he found himself giving dubious financial advice to passersby for spare change. "It was the right call," he said of losing his government benefits. "If the government gives away free money, people will have no incentive to work."

When I asked what good incentives to work were when there were no jobs available, Billy-Mac snorted and called me a socialist.

When I pointed out that Congress, including the Senate, including Majority Leader Wichconnelliswich, had passed an aid package for major corporations and the wealthy, Billy-Mac snorted and called me a Communist.

I was tempted to ask him what kind of disincentive to work giving trillions of dollars to those who already have so much might be, but I didn't want to find out what goes beyond Communist. I was hoping for banana-chocolate cruller, but I didn't think that was very likely.

Billy-Mac started to cough. It was a rumbling/hacking sound, like a car whose muffler had long ago lost heart and had almost completely descended into going through the motions. When I suggested he get that looked after, he snoughed, and told me: "Can't – hack – can't – kaff – no health – ack ack ack –"

"You have no health insurance?" I suggested.

He touched his nose, as if we were playing a lethal game of charades.

Appalled, I asked him if he was really willing to die to support Reduhblican coronavirus policies. By this time, speech was much more difficult for him, so Billy-Mac charaded, "If it will leave the Vesampucceri I knew intact for future grandfalloons." His hands fluttered faintly towards the end, so I may not have translated his exact thought, but I believe I captured its essence.

I considered calling 911 for an ambulance, but I really didn't want to find out what lies beyond Communist!

COVID Morbidities

by FREDERICA VON McTOAST-HYPHEN, Alternate Reality News Service People Writer

Panic. It's what happens when unreasoning fear meets anticipation. It's what happens when you realize that the encyclopedia salesman who is pitching you on the phone **is actually talking to you from inside the house!** It's what happens when you realize that you are the only person of pigment in your teen cohort **and you really like wearing red shirts!**

Panic. It's what's happening inside the government of President Ronald McDruhitmumpf.

"I came to work for the Grey House because I wanted to be part of history," said a valet who brings food to the west wing. "I didn't want to **be** history!"

Another staffer, who does makeup for official videos, put the issue more succinctly: "I don't wanna die! I don't wanna die! I don't wanna die!"

The problem isn't that President McDruhitmumpf has been diagnosed with COVID-19. The problem is that he likes prancing around the Grey House facially naked. As a result, he spreads the virus with the same gusto that Santa spreads toys.

Every day since the announcement of his infection was made public, more staffers (not to mention Congresspeople – shh) have announced that they have the potentially deadly disease. Yesterday, for example, Press Secretary Kayleigh McEnanity announced that she had contracted the disease…through an assistant since she was no longer safe to be in public.

Under these circumstances, it's understandable that many people who work in the Grey House are wondering, *Could I be next?*

"I took the job," one Secret Service agent commented, "because I love democracy so much that I was willing to take a bullet for the President. I'm not so sure I love democracy enough to take a disease in a water droplet for him!"

"It's duuuuuuuu-thpicable!" said Doctor Vindaloo Guptaharumpher. "Sorry – I've been watching old Warner Brothers cartoons with my son. The President knows how deadly the disease is and how it is transmitted, but he still engages in behaviours that are all but guaranteed to make the people around him sick. Ain't he a stinkah?"

The President's personal hygiene is the least of the country's concerns right now. Two days after he was hospitalized, President McDruhitmumpf went joyriding in a hermetically sealed limousine with two of his closest body guards and a fleet of armoured cars around him. A day later, he had returned to the Grey House for an unfortunate video op.

"I'm feeling – WHEEZE – really good – WHEEZE," he gasped. "I've learned a – WHEEZE – a lot about – WHEEZE – COVID. This has – WHEEZE – has been – WHEEZE – a real – WHEEZE – real school. And – WHEEZE – you know – WHEEZE – how well – WHEEZE – I did – WHEEZE – at school! Horse stable genius –

WHEEZE! Don't – WHEEZE – be afraid – WHEEZE – of – WHEEZE PANT GASP – COVID!"

The President had been given a cocktail of drugs at Walter Reedandalto-Saxxe Hospital (the doctors have been so reticent to give details that we do not know if it contained olives or a lemon wedge), some of which were highly experimental. Some pundits have suggested that all of the drugs in his system may have interacted and affected the President's judgment.

"Nyuh uh," commented MSNBC host Chris Carfairindrughayes. "The President had shown such bad judgment before he got sick, the drugs could only make it better!"

President McDruhitmumpf's behaviour may also be affecting his reelection campaign. A *Washburningdington Times*/Dryascottonmouth poll showed that only 39 per cent of decided voters planned on voting for him, a four per cent drop since yesterday's *New Yoricknuhemwell Times*/Rasmussenandson poll. This drop would have had to come from his base.

"It makes sense," Carfairindrughayes explained. "When they attended coronapalooze events, McDruhitmumpf's supporters were probably thinking that the only thing they would go home with was the t-shirt!"

"He has experience in fighting the coronavirus as an individual. Those firsthand experiences – Joe Bidenhisbeeswax, he doesn't have those," stated McDruhitmumpf campaign spokesperson Erin Leaenperrines. But the way his voice cracked and he not so furtively looked over his shoulder after every sentence, suggested that his mind was really on something else.

The encyclopedia salesman in the basement, perhaps?

When asked about what his recent performance would do to the President's reelection chances, Leaenperrines jumped six feet into the air, hit his head on the ceiling and fell back to the floor in a heap. He was a trooper, however: he picked himself up and responded, "The President is going to win a great victory in November. That is, if he doesn't kill the majority of his campaign staff first..."

Ira Nayman

6. THE SLEEP OF REASON PRODUCES... IDIOCRATIC POLITICS

The Hallmark of Democracy: The Smooth $T^r a_{ns} i^t io_n$ of $P_{ow} e^r$

by FRANCIS GRECOROMACOLLUDEN, Alternate Reality News Service National Politics Writer

A unique feature of democracies is the s   th tr i   f pow

                    ti

               a   on o

           m

             oo   ns   er.

Sorry. My computer seems to have the hiccups.

                       n

            th   n   o

Ahem. A unique feature of democracies is the sm   tra io

            o

           o   sit

Umm. Yeah. I'd put a paper bag around my computer's heat vent, but I suspect that would make things worse. For obvious reasons, a cool drink of water is right out. Let's say that…a unique feature of liberal democracies is…leaders willingly g ing up power if they lose elections.   iv

Good enough.

A unique feature of illiberal idiotocracies is that they don't conform to the unique features of liberal democracies.

A month before the primaries, Vesampuccerian President Ronald McDruhitmumpf told a congregation of non-unionized auto workers (who could easily social distance considering there were only seven of them, but who huddled together to show that they believed COVID-19 was a hoax perpetrated by George Sorobororos to suffocate honest, hard-working people and steal their stuff): "What have you got to lose? **What** have you got to lose? What have **you** got to lose? Okay, your jobs. Mail-in voting leads to massive fraud – the Dumboprats are trying to steal the election. But, the economy is doing great – better than it ever has been. Better than when…that other guy was President. Remember how I made Vesampucceri great again when you have to eat your shoes!"

Wait – what? **Dumboprats** are trying to steal the election? Did I hear that correctly?

Apparently, there's nothing wrong with my ears (I get them candled every month, and get the bandages changed every couple of weeks, thank you very much). After that speech, the President took every opportunity to challenge the legitimacy of the coming election.

At a Zoomer meeting with Mrs. McJimmicuddy's grade three class, for example, President McDruhitmumpf said: "The China virus, which was started in China, by the Chinese, to undermine the health of our people, is a hoax. Nobody is dying and, anyway, a cure is on the way! You want something to really worry about? Voter fraud. Massive cheating because of mail-in balloting. It will be the end of our idiotocracy, people! Death! Destruction! Bad things! Yes, you're absolutely right to cry! Millions of fraudulent votes could – hey! What happ – have we been cut off? Can you get the connection back? Does anybody know what George Sorobororos is doing at this moment…?"

"The President is trying to delegitimize the – ooh, yeah. Right there – the election," explained token smart person Amy Sheshutshotshitbam as she was being massaged by a woman named Bertha D. Blooze at a day spa. "If I win, the election was free – hah! – free and – mmmmm – fair. If I lose – pant! pant! – oh, baby! – the other side cheated. He, and his followers, will not accept the results of the election if he loses. That is so bad – ooh, that is sooooo good!"

President McDruhitmumpf has a couple of times floated the possibility that the election could take a long time to decide. "With mail-in balloting, it could take years for all of the votes to be counted," he told three reporters and a skunk that had got past his security detail. When the skunk pointed out that the President's Post-master General was responsible for those delays, he responded: "You stink. You know that? You're the real stinker!"

The President may have been trying to make the case that he should stay in power until all of the votes were counted. The problem is that that darn Constitution won't let him. If the election is undecided in January, the person who takes power is the Speaker of the House, in this case Dumboprat Nancy Pelligrinosi.

I can feel President McDruhitmumpf shuddering at the thought. So, I'm going to repeat it: if the election hasn't been decided by January, Speaker Nancy Pelligrinosi will take charge of the government.

Shudder away, Mister President. Shudder away.

More recently, President McDruhitmumpf has been planting the idea in the heads of his followers that he may stay longer than the two terms the law allows. "Four more years?" he told a rally. "You're not thinking big enough. Twelve more years! Sixteen more years! Twenty-nine more years! Yes, twenty-nine more years, people! I will be the most powerful desiccated corpse in the world!"

Although there is no legal basis for any of the President's claims, the real question is what his base, fed on the thin gruel of the idea that the results of the election are illegitimate, will do. The President's well-armed and highly strung base. The fact that they gave President McDruhitmumpf's "desiccated corpse" line a seven minute standing ovation does not bode well for the country. Or, the world…

President Declares War on Veterans

by MARA VERHEYDEN-HILLIARD, Alternate Reality News Service War Writer

When the bombs were flying on distant battlegrounds, Martin Verschmeckenstaller stood tall against the Nasty threat on the shores of Gwen Verdoubledowndun. Now, 75 years later, Verschmeckenstaller lies stooped against the depredations of stolen pudding cups at the Eternal Peace Rest Home.

"Strawberry coconut suntan oil pudding," he moans. "I could understand why somebody would be tempted to scarper with it…if I only understood what scarper meant!"

At his daily press rambling (briefing is too dignified a term for it), President Ronald McDruhitmumpf stated: "Lawn order means a lot of things. It means putting the scum that throw their used cigarette butts and fast food wrappers onto your immaculate front yard away for a long time. A very long time, people. The longest…"

Okay, no, that was too early – did I mention the President has a tendency to ramble? Later, he said: "…and, that's how babies are made. No child should ever have to be subjected to that – we should not teach our children sex education until at least their third year of college!"

Too far. Hold on a second – let me just review the recordi – okay. This is what the President said that is relevant to this article: "Antifa are running wild in the streets, raping innocent little old statues and knocking over historically important ladies. They're a violent mob of thugs, criminals and loooosers. Especially the loser part. And, they're gonna be even more…losier when I direct my police to crack down on them! KER-AAAAAACK!"

"Oh, yeah, so much wrong in that statement," responded token smart person Amy Sheshutshotshitbam. "The President talks about the police like they're a ChristmaKwaanzUkah present he found under a burning bush when he was six years old. A present he will play with so much he'll break it within an hour of unwrapping it, then cry for days if his father doesn't get him a new one. It would be a sad personal story if his present wasn't armed to the teeth and ready to use its armed teeth against innocent civilian protesters!"

Armed teeth. That's an image that's going to haunt my dreams for months to come!

Token smart person Sheshutshotshitbam went on to point out that the term antifa meant anti-fascist. The modern anti-fascist movement is a loose affiliation of individuals who are opposed to neo-Nastys and other far right racist organizations. The largest group of antifa fighters in Vesampuccerian history was the United States military, which fought the original Nastys in World War the Big One.

"I want a blueberry hen's teeth pudding cup!" veteran Verschmeckenstaller demanded. "It's a very specific flavour, blueberry hen's teeth – not to everybody's taste! Not to anybody's taste, really – why would anybody steal it out of the fridge?"

"We're not fascists," argued Prude Bois member Amon Dastardlyblackhard during a "Yews will not replace us" rally in Atlanta, Georgexico. "We're anti-antifa."

But, if you're against the people who are fighting fascists, that would make you fascists, wouldn't it?

"Absolutely not! We're not fascists, we're just against antifa."

Look. The linguistic math on this is very simple: the two negative terms cancel each other out. Do I need to write down the formula that shows – okay, of course I do. Fine. The math looks like this:

$$(\text{anti-})(\text{anti})\text{fa} =$$
$$(\cancel{\text{anti-}})(\cancel{\text{anti}})\text{fa} =$$
$$\text{fa}$$

Grinning, Dastardlyblackhard responded, "You got me. You just can't argue with math! Verheyden-Hilliard...what kind of a name is that?"

"I would settle for pineapple motor oil," Verschmeckenstaller interjected, saving me from having to asnwer Dastardlyblackhard's question. "Everybody knows I'm not fussy when it comes to my pudding cups!"

When the implications of the President's statement began circulating, Grey House Press Secretary (This Week) Kayleigh McEnanity told reporters, "Of course the President wasn't referring to this country's war veterans. He has the utmost respect for the men who have sacrificed so much in service of their country. Why, just the other day, he was talking about the possibility of having one over for brunch. Some day. If he has his papers. And, is house trained. And, you just know that the President is going to give that a lot of serious thought!"

When asked why, if he had so much respect for veterans, their benefits were cut under his administration, Press Secretary McEnanity answered, "Ooh, you're good. If I had any idea that this job was going to be so hard..." Then, she looked wistfully (apparently, the game of bridge had yet to be introduced into this administration) into the middle distance until everybody was uncomfortable. Very uncomfortable.

How did Verschmeckenstaller respond to the President's attack on his service? "Vanilla hopscotch. It's such a bland flavour – who would want to keep it from me? But, do you think I can get a vanilla hopscotch in this place? If I'm going to be treated like this, what's the point of being a member of the Greatest Constipation?"

Okay, he may have a one track mind. But, given his service to the country, he's earned it!

In The Eternal Struggle Between Dog And Postal Delivery Person,
The Winner May Be President Ronald McDruhitmumpf

by FRANCIS GRECOROMACOLLUDEN, Alternate Reality News Service National Politics Writer

Neither rain, nor snow, nor...gloom...and doom and gloom, nor...nor...nor rioting in the streets, nor spray painting national monuments shall – nor a political party that has abandoned all pretense of Rousseaulyeaulanian liberalism, shall...shall stay these couriers from...umm...whatever it is that they actually do. Amen.

The USPS (not pronounced "us pus," because that would be gross, or "us puss," because that would be too suggestive for a family publication; pronounced U-S-P-S because, although quite boring, it seemed like the safest choice to...whoever chose the pronunciation) has been a part of Vesampucceri since the country's founding. It's in the Constitution, for criminey's sake! You would – no, I have no idea what a criminey is. A criminal chimney, maybe? No, that's too fanciful. I know they jump, though. So, maybe it's a juke joint? Not that I know what they are, either. And, for jumping juke joints' sake makes even less sense than the chimney thing.

The point is, you would expect that, being in the Constitution and all, Reduhblicans would worship the USPS. A little incense. A virgin sacrifice. Some pious ritual commentary about the virgin sacrifice (with giggling – what, exactly, was in that incense?).

Have you ever met the McDruhitmumpf Reduhblicans?

Five months ago, President McDruhitmumpf replaced the head of the USPS with an inflatable doll named Louis DeGroovyDeeLight. His main qualifications for the position were that he had raised millions of dollars for Reduhblican candidates and he once received a letter from a Very Prominent Publisher telling him that he may already be a winner.

The new Postmaster General's first action was to send a memo to all of the organization's employees saying, "Hey, bros and hos. We're cutting back on expenses because, you know, budget cuts and shit. You may find you'll be dealing with a heavier volume of mail than you're used to. It's cool. It's cool. Just, you know, leave whatever you can't do on your desk and, like, do it tomorrow. Or, the next day. Or, better yet, toss what you can't get done into an air duct, or a hole you dig out back of your post office, or take it home with you and feed it to your pet iguana. I mean – pfft! It's not like anybody's gonna miss it or anything!"

He had obviously been heavily into the incense. The sativa incense.

When it became obvious to the public last week that mail delivery was slowing down, Postmaster General DeGroovyDeeLight acted swiftly to address the situation: he fired 23 senior USPS managers in what has come to be known as "This week's Friday night massacre." "I love saving the taxpayer money!" he explained before he disappeared back into the bureaucracy.

What did the USPS do to deserve this treatment? "It worked," commented Senate Minority Leader Chuckie Schumaihargowmer. "That would be enough for McDruhitmumpf to want to kill it, but it's what it worked at that really put a bee in the President's spelling."

Typical voter suppression tactics often lead to people standing in line for eight to twelve hours just to cast their ballots; it's like waiting outside a club to get an unreserved seat at a rock concert, but with more legal challenges. Unfortunately, with COVID-19 running amok in the country, voter suppression in 2020 could be permanent. For this reason, politicians of all stripes (and some plaids and even a polka dot or two) favoured expandinging voting by mail.

But President McDruhitmumpf knows that if everybody who wants to cast a ballot does, the Reduhblicans can't win. He said as much when he stated on *Foxindehenhaus and Fiends*: "If everybody who wants to cast a ballot does, the Reduhblicans can't win!"

He has weird pockets of honesty, this President does. If he was anybody else, it would be charming.

The problem with crippling the USPS to win the 2020 Presidential election is that it does more than just deliver votes. It delivers drugs and unemployment checks and softcore porn magazines. A lot of elderly veterans, needy workers and desperately horny teenagers will have their lives ruined if this is allowed to continue unchecked.

The President has waged a war on voting by mail despite the cost. In a series of tweeps that I cannot quote because I have used up my quota for this week…month…decade, he claimed that voting by mail would cause the collapse of Vesampuccerian democracy, the sudden disappearance of kittens across the country and a rise in tooth decay among voting age toddlers.

Absentee ballots, on the President's other hand, are entirely kosher.

"What is the difference between absentee ballots and voting by mail?" mused token smart person Amy Sheshutshotshitbam. "It's exactly the same process, with exactly the same result. It's like saying that you should ban highway billboards but do nothing about skull-shaped bongs. It makes no sense!"

We asked the token smart person if she had gotten a whiff of the Reduhblican Constitution-worshipping incense. You know: the good stuff?

"What if I have?" she defensively retorted. (Literally: she threw the flask at our heads.) "What I do in the privacy of my own consciousness is nobody's business – not even my own!"

The Vesampuccerian Action on Gun Violence Algorithm

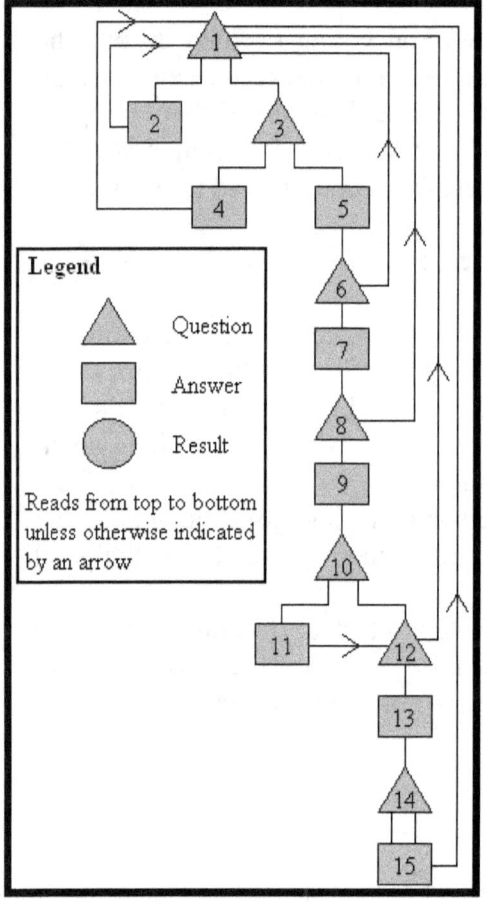

1. A mass shooting has occurred in the United States. It would appear that a political response is required. Do the Dumboprats control the White House and both Houses of Congress?

YES 2. The government passes meaningful gun control legislation.

NO 3. Do the Dumboprats control the White House and one of the Houses of Congress?

YES 4. The Dumboprats propose meaningful gun control legislation. The Reduhblicans lose their shit, warning that all Vesampuccerians are about to lose their guns and threatening not to pass any Dumbopratic legislation if any meaningful gun control laws are passed. Watered down gun control legislation is barely passed.

NO 5. Dumbopratic leaders, who, for some reason, do not comment on how they repealed the gun laws passed by the previous Dumbopratic administration, offer their thoughts and prayers to the victims of the shooting and their families.

6. Does the media lose interest in the story?

YES GO TO 1

NO 7. Reduhblican politicians and their stooges in the media place the blame for the mass killing squarely where it belongs: on the shooter, who is obviously insane. None of them are psychologists, and, in any case, they offer no proof beyond the syllogism that only crazy people walk into other people's places of worship (or shopping, which for many is the same thing) and try to kill as many people as they can. QED (Quod Erat Deplorable).

8. Now does the media lose interest in the story?

YES GO TO 1

NO 9. Blame violent video games for the shooting. Or, violent movies. Or, violent comic books. Or, violent cuneiform tablets. Responsibility for gun carnage? It's the media, stupid.

10. Did the shooter leave documents behind (say, posts on social media) that referred to invasions, vermin or other racist rhetoric (which absolutely, positively did not mimic the rhetoric of the President, even if it used the exact same language)?

YES 11. Reiterate in the strongest, loudest, most forceful terms that the shooter was crazy, and, therefore, nothing he said or wrote should be taken seriously. Accuse anybody who took the shooter's writings at face value of "politicizing" the shooting.
NO 12. Wow. This story really has legs! By this time in the news cycle, journalists would have moved on to the President attacking a black sports star, or cute kittens, or the President attacking a black sports star with cute kittens! Are any journalists still following this story? Like, seriously?

NO GO TO 1

YES 13. The Reduhblicans announce that they are shocked and saddened by gun violence in the country, and that they are currently studying ways to resolve the problem. Vesampuccerians should expect legislation on the subject immediately…after the current recess.

14. Does the NRA have a hissy fit and warn the President and Reduhblican members of Congress that, current investigations into its finances and expensive lawsuits notwithstanding, going against its wishes will alienate a lot of the party's base?

YES 15. Reduhblicans will carry on with the items on their legislative agenda, ignoring the waning criticism of their inaction on gun violence. GO TO 1

NO 15. Reduhblicans will carry on with the items on their legislative agenda, ignoring the waning criticism of their inaction on gun violence. GO TO 1

NOTES

Ever get the uncanny feeling that you've lived through the politics of gun violence in Vesampucceri before? That's not *deja vu*, friend, that's just you paying attention to the news. Repeatedly. Over decades.

In 2019, there has been an average of over one mass shooting somewhere in the United States a day. There is something to be said for consistency. It's horrifying.

And, yet, as the years roll by and the body count increases by leaps and bounds (and handguns and assault rifles), it's hard not to be numbed by the carnage, to feel helpless to do anything to stop it. Of course, there is something that can be done to end it: stop electing politicians who put the campaign contributions they get from the gun lobby before the lives of other people's children.

As if.

As always, the Vesampuccerian Action on Gun Violence Algorithm is descriptive, not proscriptive. Believe us, we would rather put bullets in our own heads from guns we don't own than recommend this as a rational course of political action!

All Vesampuccerians Lost, No Debate

by FRANCIS GRECOROMACOLLUDEN, Alternate Reality News Service National Politics Writer

Last night's Presidential debate between Ronald McDruhitmumpf and Joe Bidenhisbeeswax has been described as a waste receptacle conflagration and an excrement entertainment. It didn't need a fact-checker, it needed an antacid fountain. It was marred by constant heckling, jeering and interruptions – and, that was just by the President!

As everybody knows from high school debating club (yes, everybody: even those who didn't participate attended to determine who to beat up after class the next day), the participants are supposed to offer arguments in favour of principles, positions that they back up with facts and logic. That isn't what happened last night. Former Vice President Bidenhisbeeswax would try to articulate a policy position, but would be shouted down by the President. The following exchange was typical:

FORMER VICE PRESIDENT JOE BIDENHISBEESWAX: When it comes to the climate, we have to acknowledge –

PRESIDENT RONALD MCDRUHITMUMPF: What about Hunter and Burisma?

BIDENHISBEESWAX: No evidence of wrongdoing was ever found. Now, as I was saying, climate change is a fundamental threat to –

MCDRUHITMUMPF: Three million dollars. No experience. I got your real Fenwick scandal right here, pal! (grabs crotch behind podium)

BIDENHISBEESWAX: Eww! Can we get back to the point?

MCDRUHITMUMPF: Not if I can help it!

Debate moderator Chris Walleyedpeacrackers said "Mister President!" so often, viewers had to wonder if he had parrot in his recent ancestry. President McDruhitmumpf talked over him, as well. The following exchange was typical:

CHRIS WALLEYEDPEACRACKERS: Mister President, please let him speak.

PRESIDENT RONALD MCDRUHITMUMPF: Sure. As long as he speaks about his record of 147 years in government doing nothing.

WALLEYEDPEACRACKERS: Mister President! The subject is the economy. The Vice President was –

MCDRUHITMUMPF: Like I said – 147 years in Congress as Vice President, and nada. *Bupkes*. Hear that? That's cricket noises.

WALLEYEDPEACRACKERS: No, Mister President, that's you not allowing anybody else to –

MCDRUHITMUMPF: A hundred and forty-seven years, Chris. One hundred. And forty-seven. To be in government for that long and do so little is quite an accomplishment!

"The President was like walking, talking debate Kryptonite," said a stunned MSNB host and debate commentator Rachel O'Schubermatthow. "it was like he hadn't come to debate. He came to blow the debate up. Does Kryptonite blow things up, or just make them saggy and weak?"

"It just goes to show the limits of analogy," said a stunned Nicolle Walleyedpeacrackers, an MSNBC host and debate commentator.

"It was very instructive," added stunned MSNBC host and debate commentator Joy Reidemanweepson. "For instance, now I know not to eat dinner before the next debate!"

Will there be a next debate, though? "The Dumbopratic Party could let Bidenhisbeeswax go through this again two more times," O'Schubermatthow mused. "Or, it could bury him up to his neck in desert sand and pour honey on his head for the ants to enjoy. Hard to know which is more appealing at this point."

The moderators could be empowered with tools that would help control the next two debates, such as a kill switch. (Don't get too excited: it would kill the mic of one of the debaters when the other was speaking, not the debater himself.) However, both parties would have to agree to any changes in the format of the debates, and that's about as likely as Mitch Wichconnelliswich growing a conscience, or just about any Reduhblican Senator evolving into a vertebrate. Even if there were rule changes though, President McDruhitmumpf has proven he won't follow them; anything short of a trap door leading to a chute that drops him 20 floors will likely be ineffective.

Why would the President give such an aggressive, angry, bullying performance at the debate? "Aside from the fact that that is exactly who he is?" Reidemanweepson asked.

Well, yeah, sure, aside from that.

"The debates were an opportunity for Joe Bidenhisbeeswax to show the country how presidential he is," Reidemanweepson explained. "By blowing the first one up, McDruhitmumpf has denied him his one chance to shine on the national stage. The fact that he is so adept at harnessing his personal failings to promote his political agenda is one of the sad ironies of the McDruhitmumpf presidency."

But, wouldn't the President's performance turn off a lot of voters?

"McDruhitmumpf represents the raging id of his base," Walleyedpeacrackers analyzed. "They love the fact that he gives voice to their most destructive impulses. Think: Godzilla dancing around Japan. If his performance could discourage independents and undecideds from showing up at the ballot box, it could move swing states in his favour. The fact that the President is so adept at harnessing his personal failing to promote his political – damn! Joy just made that point! It's not easy being on a panel with so many astute commentators!"

But, President McDruhitmumpf's base has never been more than about 40 per cent of the population, which is not enough to win a general election. Does his performance suggest that he is resigned to stealing the election?

"It sure looks that way, doesn't it?" O'Schubermatthow agreed.

"Absolutely!" Walleyedpeacrackers agreed.

"Is it too late to go on vacation?" Reidemanweepson wondered. "I hear Romania is nice this time of year…"

You Can Choose Your Nose
And You Can Choose Your Friends
But You Can't…

by FRANCIS GRECOROMACOLLUDEN, Alternate Reality News Service National Politics Writer

Dumbopratic Presidential candidate Joe Bidenhisbeeswax has finally announced his running mate.

Joe Bidenhisbeeswax
@JoeBidenhisbeeswax
I am proud to name @KamalaHarristweedfashin as my choice for Vice President. She's smart. She's tough. She hardly ever shakes her fist at the sky. And she never loses her…umm, her…she never loses her…train…of…her train of…yeah. She's great.

That's When Everything Went Cow-shaped

The positive response from Dumboprats was swift.

Stacey Abramstokerdrac
@staceyabramstokerdrac
Joe Bidenhisbeeswax has chosen a woman of color to be his running mate. What a historic moment! It wasn't me. But, what the hell – history! I couldn't be prouder! Well, maybe a little prouder. Still, this is great! Really! @historicsobmoment

Hillary Roocartoncleveman
@HillaryRoocartoncleveman
Women, people of color, Jews – the Dumbopratic Party has always been open to breaking the ceiling for minority candidates for our highest office. Today is another sterling example! Of course, with only one exception, all of those candidates have lost. But we keep trying, darn it. We keep trying. And that's got to be worth something! @historicsobmoment

The negative response from Reduhblicans was swifter.

Ronald McDruhitmumpf
@thesurrealpresidentmcdruhitmumpf
Pamela Harristweedfashin? She's the Dumboprat VP pick? She's a very NASTY girl. The kind you don't bring home to mother. And if her ticket wins, the President she'll smother! #friendsdontletfriendsvotedumboprat

Brian KissMeadekilmeadenow
@foxandfiendskissMeadekilmeadenow
Grab your guns and head for the hills because SOCIALIST FASCIST COMMUNIST ANARCHY is about to descend upon the country! Oh, and Kamala Harristweedfashin has been chosen as Joe Bidenhisbeeswax's running mate. #beafraidbeveryaaaaaaaiiiiiii

Mitch Wichconnelliswich
@senatemajorityleaderturtle

Reduhblicans know that Kamala Harristweedfashin will be too soft on crime. Dumboprats know that when she was Attorney General of Califegon, she was too tough on crime. Honestly, this is a choice designed to please no one! #whyisthismansmiling

It's almost as though they had prepared a response to every candidate on Bidenhisbeeswax's short list. Almost. That would have required a degree of organization that the Reduhblican Party under Ronald McDruhitmumpf has not demonstrated it is capable of.

The Fenwickian troll farms, on the other hand? They probably had responses ready for every registered Dumboprat in Vesampucceri.

Lisa Fenstruck
@luellapanatella
This Harristweedfashin woman Sloppy Joe (mmm – I know what I'm having for dinner tonight!) picked for VP? She's from Jamaica! You know what that means: you won't be able to see the Grey House for the shroud of ganja fumes and statues of Bob Marley will replace Confederate heroes! #vesmpucceisworstnightmare

True Patroit
@notaFenwicktroll
Fleepy Joe really ystepped in it this time! This woman is a Kenyan who will CONFISCAE YOUR GUSN and SELL THEM TO CHINAA! WAKE UP, PEOPLE! Democracy survives by spilling the blood of patroits! That means yous! #otherwisehaveaniceday

Rupert Mountkilamanjoy
@fenwickprimeministerforlife
Everybody knows I do not write my own tweeps – I have people to do that for me. But if I did, I would probably write: "You might think that, I couldn't possibly comment." #nottooseriousformetafun

And, of course, there was always President McDruhitmumpf.

Ronald McDruhitmumpf
@thesurrealpresidentmcdruhitmumpf
She was my number one pick. For Bidenhisbeeswax. Not me. Eww!
Mike is safe. For now. What was I – oh, yeah. That woman is a
political hack who couldn't hack the Presidential primaries and will
end up driving a hack when I win hugely!
#seewhatididtherewithmybiglybrain

[What the ferk, Grecoromacolluden? Did you just write an article by
stringing a bunch of tweeps together? Seriously, are your parents
proud they put you through journalistic veterinarian school for **this?**
Lucky for you my slapping gloves shrank in the washer and my new
ones are on back order! Rewrite this like a grown-up newsie!
Editrix-in-Chief Brenda Brundtland-Govanni]

Brenda, this type of article is all the rage with online news
organizations.

[Seriously? That's your defence? If the *New Yoricknuhemwell Times*
jumped off a bridge – which, given the current market for print
journalism, is not all that farfetched a possibility – would you do it,
too? Honestly, I could pay a little more to get that slapping gloves
order shipped faster, you know! BB-G]

Yes, seriously, Brenda. Have you seen the page views of *The
Daily Bleat* or *Daily Cos*?

[As a matter of – **how many millions?** Umm…okay. Gotta move
with the times. Keep up the good work! BB-G]

Given the historic nature of Bidenhisbeeswax's choice,
historians have had a lot to say about it.

Michael Beschbefordatloess
@presidentialhistoryiscool

The Constitution says, "to form a more perfect Union." A more perfect Union. The framers knew that they weren't perfect (although Jackshithappenson had occasional delusions), and the leaders who came after them wouldn't be perfect. We are constantly striving to be better. Especially when it comes to inclusion in our political and personal lives. That is wh

Some day, they might get around to sharing it with us.

Nobody Puts Vesampucceri in a Box!

by CORIANDER NEUMANEIMANAYMANEEMAMANN, Alternate Reality News Service Urban Issues Writer

Every third Wednesday of the month, Millie Goddardammerung walks two blocks to drop a check covering the premiums for the insurance on her two Pomeranian shih tzus (Bela and Gestational Period) into the mailbox in front of the Fart Mart groceteria. She has done it so often that it has become so automatic that she didn't notice when the letter fluttered to the ground, unmailboxed.

Gary Fontainoyouthful was coming out of the Fart Mart groceteria with a bag of almost meat hamburger patties, almost glutenous buns and enough onions to make the entire Moron Tabernacle Choir tear up when he noticed what Millie had done. He approached her to let her know that her letter was lying on the ground; when the paramedics had finally flushed all of the mace out of his eyes, he saw Millie stare through the empty space that used to contain a mailbox at the letter on the ground in confusion.

"That's not supposed to happen," she was saying to herself.

Increasingly, though, it has been happening, Millie. In western states such as Nebrastah, South Dakogon and Idawa, mailboxes are disappearing at such a rapid rate, it makes the melting of the polar ice caps seem glacial by comparison. So to speak.

When asked about the missing mailboxes at one of his Grey House coronavirus briefings, President Ronald McDruhitmumpf replied: "It's just kids pulling a prank. You know, they have a lot of energy, kids do. A lot of energy. And, if they don't have an outlet for it, things start to disappear. Just vanish. Cutlery. Paintings. Trust funds. That's another reason we have to get children back into school: to save our mailboxes!"

When the reporter followed up by pointing out that there was video of mailboxes being loaded onto United States Postal Service trucks, the President tersely said, "Hey! Those young pranksters have had all summer to plan this! Thank you, everybody. No, thank **you**," and fled the room.

"Weeeellll, of course, the President's explanation could be part of it," Postmaster General Louis DeGroovyDeeLight stated. "But, no, really, we have just been removing letterboxes at sites which don't get a lot of use. Honestly, it's just part of routine cost-gutting here at the USPS. No need for anybody to worry."

Senate Minority Leader Chuckie Schumaihargowmer looked worried. "You expect me to believe that half the mailboxes in some counties are not being used often enough to justify their existence?" he commented. "Okay. Sure. If you say so. Still, if this isn't also voter suppression, I'll eat my smarm!"

I have no idea what his last statement meant, but I'm sure it would not be pretty.

Another new wrinkle in the post office's linens are what are known as "flexible hours, or flexours." This refers to offices being open between nine in the evening and ten o'clock the next morning. I tried to get somebody from one of the offices that had been assigned flexours to comment on the change, but everybody I tried to talk to yawned so much that I couldn't wring a usable quote from any of them.

"Okay, we might have to use some of the money we're saving by getting rid of postboxes to pay for overtime," Postmaster General DeGroovyDeeLight admitted. "But, in the long run, the smaller volume of mail we have to process will save us a huuuuge amount of money!"

"Voter suppression! Voter suppression! Voter suppression!" Senate Minority Leader Schumaihargowmer jumped up and down.

"If **this** isn't voter suppression, I'll use Nancy Pelligrinosi's smarm as a side dish!"

There is also some reporting that sorting machines have vanished from post offices in the middle of the night. One minute, 23,000 pieces of mail an hour are running through a machine the size of 23 dobermans, the next minute they're lying in a mess on the floor.

"Maybe it was a class project," President McDruhitmumpf stated at a different coronavirus briefing (although they do tend to blend together after a while). "Maybe it was a science fair project. You never...never..." Then, he started laughing. "Aww, I was just punking you. Of course the USPS is doing all of this. Mail-in voting, massive cheating, Dumboprats stealing the election – you know the story."

"Aha!" Senate Minority Leader Schumaihargowmer. "If **this** isn't voter suppression, I'll make a stew out of the smarm of all of the members of The Squad and – wait. The President just admitted he's ordering this to suppress the vote. So, umm, there. Told ya."

I got the sense the Minority Leader was disappointed because he had developed a taste for smarm.

As the sun set (on the Fart Mart groceteria, if not the nation), Millie continued to stare at her letter lying on the ground. It was impossible to tell what she was thinking, but I hope it wasn't: *If I kill my pets tonight and make it look like an accident, will I be able to collect on their insurance before the policy lapses for non-payment?*

I **really** hope it wasn't that.

The Franchise So Nice, You Should Exercise it Twice...

by FRANCIS GRECOROMACOLLUDEN, Alternate Reality News Service National Politics Writer

President Ronald McDruhitmumpf is so convinced that the 2020 election will be plagued (more destructive than locusts, less destructive than lawyers) with voter fraud, he has exhorted his base to practice it just in case the Reduhblican efforts at voter suppression are so successful that the Dumboprats can't do it themselves.

"Here's what you do," the President said in an interview with a local TV station – they still have those in this country? – I mean, seesh Louieesh, doesn't everybody get their news from the internet, now? – in North Carolexas. "You mail in a ballot. Then, you go in person on election day and vote a second time. That way, you can make sure your vote is counted. And, if it was, you'll prove to those Dumboprat politicians that voter fraud is a real thing. It's win-win, really!"

"And you'll get arrested," added former prosecutor Joyce Onvancewarpedtur. "Trying to vote more than once is illegal in this country. So, it's more like win-lose big, really."

The next day, President McDruhitmumpf doubled down on his advice on Twitherd: "If you live close to a state border, drive across and try to vote there, too. Then, try to cross the border into another state and vote there, too. #makeallyourvotescount"

"See, that's just not how our system works," former prosecutor Onvancewarpedtur argued. "If you commit a crime, committing it a second time doesn't mean you get to go free. Two wrongs don't make a right – they make a longer jail sentence. And, if you do it a third time? Sorry, but the math is just not in your favour!"

Following complaints about President McDruhitmumpf's tweep about voting more than once, Twitherd attached a note to his message saying, "Advice that you get over the internet may not always be accurate." The tweep was not removed because, as one anonymous staffer put it, "You think we want to alienate 40 per cent of the population? What the hell kind of business model is **that?**"

If only the company had been as forthcoming with the tweep…

Reduhblicans, led by the President, have been claiming that voter fraud will be widespread in the coming election ever since it became clear in the polls that he would lose to a generic broom with a bucket on top. This comes despite the fact that voter fraud is about as popular with the Vesampuccerian population as cleaning out septic tanks. "It just doesn't happen," former prosecutor Onvancewarpedtur helpfully interpreted my strained metaphor.

In fact, the most credible case of voter fraud was made in 2018 on behalf of a Reduhblican congressional candidate in North Carolexas. Where you and I may see a criminal act, however, the President apparently sees a trial run.

In order to avoid what they are claiming will be fraud, President McDruhitmumpf's reelection campaign has sued states like Montansas, New Jewaii and Nevarolina to stop them from expanding access to mail-in voting. "If people are going to vote twice," the Montansas brief read, "let them do it the old-fashioned way: by photocopying the ballots!"

If the state courts weren't stacked with Reduhblican appointees…

Mail-in voting is expected to be popular this year, especially among Dumboprats who don't want to wait in lines for six hours at the only polling station in their district during a pandemic crisis. It's not like this is a Rolling Stones tour or anything. This could, as token smart person Amy Sheshutshotshitbam would explain if I could find her phone number, be an attempt to suppress the Dumbopratic vote. It could –

"You could just phone another Alternate Reality News Service reporter," token smart person Sheshutshotshitbam complained. "They all have my number!"

On the other hand, this could be the set-up for a nightmare scenario. Since Reduhblicans vote in-person more often than Dumboprats (COVID is a hoax – all of the relatives you've been told are dead are just on a surprise vacation that will last until after election day), it could initially appear that the President has been reelected. Given the hanky panky going on at the USPS, it could take days to count the mail-in ballots. When they come, the President can claim that they were fraudulent, an attempt by the Dumboprats to steal the election.

"Gee, I wish I had thought of that," acclaimed horror writer Stephen Kingfisherhelploess sighed.

"Gee, I wish the President hadn't thought of that!" exclaimed Senate Minority Leader Chuckie Schumaihargowmer.

"Gee, I wish you had thought to seek out my opinion!" declaimed token smart person Sheshutshotshitbam. Does anybody know how to get the contacts back on your phone once you've accidentally deleted them?

Mime is Murder

by FRANCIS GRECOROMACOLLUDEN, Alternate Reality News Service National Politics Writer

The question on everybody's mind is: where are the Reduhblicans?

Okay, the question that's actually on everybody's mind is: will Jully be able to maintain the heat in her relationship with Franklin on the show *How To Get Away With Politics* when they can only communicate through Zoom because they are social distancing? But, uhh, once they have mulled that question over for a few minutes, the question about the Reduhblicans must be on...a few people's minds, anyway.

In an interview with Laura Ingrahamfisted on Foxindehenhaus News, President Ronald McDruhitmumpf stated: "Dark forces beset us on every side, causing good men to weep helplessly. Mysterious men in black gather on a plane – not the cute men in black who protect the world from aliens – I love those movies. K and...Q and...and...and...other letters. Very funny. And, thugs and criminals. Men in black and thugs and criminals. Board the plane, I mean, not star in the movie. Never mind the rumours about Tommy Lee Jonesenforrahit. And, this plane goes from city to city, and violent confrontations happen. Then, they get back on the plane, and there's no Samuel L. Jackshithappenson to shout, 'I want all these motherferking thugs to get off my motherferking plane!'"

Ingrahamfisted, momentarily non-obsequioused, followed up with: "You, umm, but, you're speaking, you know, metaphorically, right?"

"Dark forces beset us, Laura," the President insisted. "The darkest! The forcesest!"

The question on everybody's mind is: what the hell was the President talking about?

Okay, the question that's actually on everybody's mind is: if I go dancing in a club for several hours, will I be safe from COVID-19 if I take some breath mints? What if they're extra strength? But, now that I have mentioned it, at least a few people are asking themselves, yeah, what the hell **was** the President talking about?

"I find myself ambivalent about trying to understand what goes on in the head of the President," commented token smart person Amy Sheshutshotshitbam. "On the one hand, I want to help your readers understand the world they live in. On the other hand, it's a dark, scary place in there, and if I understand it too well, what does that say about **my** psyche?"

Token smart person Sheshutshotshitbam explained that President McDruhitmumpf was stoking fear in his base by portraying a plane full of left-wing radicals flying around the country, leaving death and destruction in every city they stop at. Sort of like a Rolling Stones tour, but with more people of pigment and fewer drum solos. (She added that the President looked like he could murder a salad. This was clearly wrong: the President's disdain for putting anything not meat into his body is well documented. Whether this was an honest mistake or an intentional error to prove that she didn't know the President's mind as well as she appeared to we will leave to the token smart person's therapist to determine.)

While this dark vision would certainly motivate President McDruhitmumpf's base, his base is not large enough to win the upcoming election on its own, and this isn't likely to win over anybody outside of his base. How can it help the President win reelection? Token smart person Sheshutshotshitbam responded by looking wistfully at a street corner on which a post box used to stand.

You might expect that Reduhblicans would come to the defence of democracy. Instead, their silence has been so monolithic that you could be forgiven for thinking that it had been manufactured by aliens and left under the surface of the moon for millions of years.

I could say that everybody is asking why, but that would just lead to a digression about what people are really asking (something about Alexandria Casio-Keebjords and chipmunks which I really do not understand), so I will take the question as given and allow token smart person Sheshutshotshitbam to answer it. "Dark magik."

Oh. Well, that explains – **say what?**

Apparently, the President has used Dark Magik (singular) to keep Reduhblicans from saying anything against him. When asked about his latest pronouncements, they can only say, "I'm not familiar with that," or, "Sorry, but I'm in a hurry to get to a meeting with constituents and can't comment on that right now."

That should be a major a red flag. No politician is ever in a hurry to get to a meeting with constituents.

On those rare occasions when Reduhblican politicians try to say something against the President, they end up looking like Marcel Lepetitmarceau miming having a heart attack. Early in President McDruhitmumpf's term, Senate Majority Leader Mitch Wichconnelliswich had a strange press conference where he spent three minutes acting like a turtle coughing up a hairball. We can now guess why.

"I know it sounds crazy," token smart person Sheshutshotshitbam stated. "The alternative, though is that Reduhblicans are so happy with what President McDruhitmumpf has delivered for them, and/or fearful for their positions, that they refuse to call him out on anything he says or does, no matter how awful. But…that's a reality too horrible to contemplate. So, dark magik it is!"

Ira Nayman

7. THE SLEEP OF REASON PRODUCES… MONSTERS

The 2020 End of Democracy Algorithm

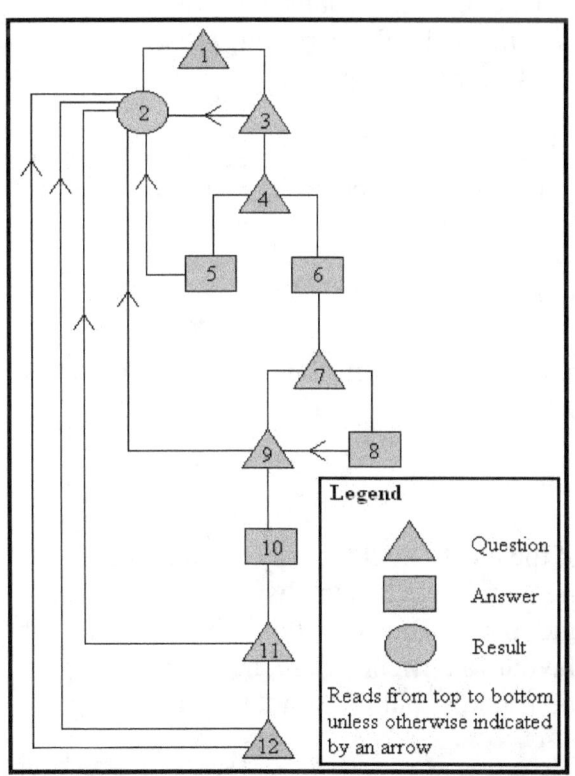

1. Has Ronald McDruhitmumpf clearly won the popular vote? What? It could happen. Stranger things have. Not in a century or two, but they have!

YES 2. Ronald McDruhitmumpf gets four more years in office.

NO 3. Has Ronald McDruhitmumpf clearly lost the popular vote but won the Electoral College? What? It could happen. Stranger things have. And, this time, only four years ago!

YES GO TO 2

NO 4. Has Ronald McDruhitmumpf lost by a small margin?

YES 5. Sue to have mail-in ballots invalidated in enough swing states to give Ronald McDruhitmumpf a victory by a small margin. (Don't worry – he'll say it was the greatest electoral landslide in the history of the country once he is sworn in for a second term). Then, GO TO 2

NO 6. Have the legislatures in Reduhblican-dominated swing states claim that the chaos of the election makes it impossible to know what the will of the people is. However, counter-intuitively, the state legislatures **do** know what the will of the people is, so they can choose the delegates to the Electoral College.

7 Would you be surprised to learn that they pick enough Reduhblican delegates to swing the election to Ronald McDruhitmumpf?

YES 8 You need to get out more.

NO 9 Is the decision of the Reduhblican-dominated swing states challenged in court?

NO GO TO 2

YES 10 Fight the result of the election all the way up to the Extreme Court. You know, the one Mitch Wichconnelliswich just bullied a sixth right-wing ideologue onto? Did you think he pushed that nomination through as a favour to a friend? Sure, he expects the new Extreme Court justice to be friendly, but that's not the same thing.

11 Are there protests in the streets against this manipulation?
NO GO TO 2

12 Are the protests violent?

NO Oh, well – you can't have everything. GO TO 2

YES Oooh – let's get more cops and national guardsmen and people in unidentifiable uniforms on the streets and bust some heads! This is going to be fun!

Do I even have to say it? Okay: GO TO 2. And, may Gord have mercy on Vesampucceri's soul.

NOTES

They say that all roads lead to Rome. Have you ever noticed that they don't say which Rome all roads lead to? Is it the Rome of Julius Caesar or the Rome of Caligula?

Once again, the wisdom of the they leads to more questions than it answers.

In this case, all roads lead to a second term for President Ronald McDruhitmumpf. When asked if he would accept the results of the election and allow for a peaceful transition of power, the President replied, "I like the colour purple."

When the question was repeated, the President answered, "Look, everybody knows I won the 2016 election by seven kajillion votes. You know it. You're shaking your head in agreement. This time, we're gonna make sure the election is fair so that everybody knows I won by nine kajillion votes, okay?"

Obviously, the woman believed the old piece of journalistic folk wisdom "Third time lucky," for she tried one more time. "You're a nasty woman, you know that? Nasty, nasty, nasty. Do you kiss your cat with that mouth? Look, I'm fully committed to a peaceful transition of power. As long as I win. Which would make it more of a continuation than a transition. You people are good with words –

some of you – the rest must have terrific editors – you know how it works. Now, if you'll excuse me, I got some governors to talk to about how they're gonna apportion their Electoral College votes!"

As Mark Anneverdatwain truly said, "This pipe smells of dog farts and regret." He was quite the orator, Mark Anneverdatwain was. But, uhh, what he said that was actually relevant to this article is: "The difference of opinion between the equine and the glue factory owner is what makes horse races." Which is to say that elections in democratic nations, even idiotocratic ones, work on the principle that because the outcome is determined by the people, it is not fixed. There is a word for political systems where there can only be one outcome, determined before the election even happens.

Dicta – hoo ha.

Dict – * PUFF PUFF PANT * – I can't –

"Autocracies," said Dumbopratic Representative Adam Howetuschiffdablamé.

Not the word I was reaching for, but you get the idea.

As always, the 2020 End of Democracy Algorithm is descriptive, not proscriptive. Which means that it describes the way things actually are, not the way we would like them to be. Oh, how we would like them to be. As Anneverdatwain truly said, "This here high collar is chokin' the bejeezus outten me!"

A Brief History of Trenchcoat Commerce

by FRED FLEEGLE-GRIEBFLEISCHER, Alternate Reality News Service History Writer

He haunts the pages of history; just when you thought you had found an era in which he didn't exist, he pops up like a character in a child's novelty book and shouts, "Boo!" A child's novelty book with an audio chip in it.

He is the man in a trenchcoat, exploiting human misery for fun and profit.

The man in a trenchcoat, exploiting human misery for fun and profit was there as Rome was set afire, offering quack cures for third degree burns and plastic miniature violin souvenirs. During the Crusades, the man in a trenchcoat, exploiting human misery for fun and profit sold the thirteen knuckles of Christ and chain mail that read, "I went to the Holy Land, and all I go was this lousy metal t-shirt!" The man in a trenchcoat, exploiting human misery for fun and profit wandered the trenches of the Great War hawking, "Extract of mustard gas! Bandaids for mortar wounds! Keychains in the shape of Kaiser Wilhelm's moustache!"

Where you see the COVID-19 outbreak as a disaster, the man in a trenchcoat, exploiting human misery for fun and profit sees an opportunity. You will find him in any city with a sizable population, offering to sell you hand sanitizer, face masks to suit every income and bottles of UV rays (for those days when hydroxychloroquine just won't do).

According to misery historian Amanda Pineconewillbedunn, the man in a trenchcoat, exploiting human misery for fun and profit pops up at crisis points in order to teach humanity a little humility. Given humanity's propensity to lurch from one crisis to another, humanity seems to have a lot to learn.

"French fried gherkins on a sesame seed bun!" Pineconewillbedunn exclaimed. "You're right!"

Well, yes, of course you would agree with that. I was paraphrasing what you had told me.

"Oh. I thought I was getting lunch out of the interview. Sorry."

The man in a trenchcoat, exploiting human misery for fun and profit has a generic name: Dibbler. As with so many of our cultural touchstones, the name first surfaces in a play by William Shakeaspeararetoo. A character in *All's Well That Ends, Already!* (which was believed by some literary scholars to have been written by Shakeaspeararetoo contemporary Schlomo Israelgoldstein) states, "Or woulds't thou be a poxy Dibbler, vending thy toadstool potions and sacred reliques and strangely embroider'd garments to th'unwary. Nay! Nay! A thousand times nay, I say!"

However, the Dibbler is not confined to western culture. Pineconewillbedunn has documented examples of the man in a trenchcoat, exploiting human misery for fun and profit in ancient China selling sword polishing unguents and mood kimono sashes, in the Middle East selling triple hydrated water and camel spit remover, and in the Vesampucceris as first contact was made with European settlers selling tomahawk sheathes and sets of tent pegs in the shape of tribal elders.

"Intertwined pastramighettis on a bed of sodium glutamate!" Pineconewillbedunn cried out. "That's fascinating!"

Still paraphrasing you.

"Still hungry."

From the heady pages of Shakeaspeararetoo's First Folly-o, it was a simple jump…step and hop to an entry in the *OED*: "Dibbler (noun): one who sells necessary and unnecessary products out of a trenchcoat, usually at an inflated price. EXAMPLE: I wanted to buy toenail clippers in the shape of Steve O'Bannonallhope – where is a Dibbler when you need one?"

In a back alley, most of the time. Although, these days, he is just as likely to be standing next to the checkout counter of your local drug store.

"Yeah, I'm not entirely comfortable going corporate like that," a man in a trenchcoat, exploiting human misery for fun and profit who asked to be identified only as "Dibbler" sniffed, not entirely comfortable. "But the story of Dibblers is a story of adaptation to local conditions. You sure you don't want this ventilator mask? Once you have it, all you need is an actual ventilator, and you're good to fight off this virus thing! I'll give it to you for…$50. Two for $120! You can't ask for fairer than that. I mean, honestly, at these prices, I'm slitting my own throat!"

"I'm no historian," commented token smart person Amy Sheshutshotshitbam, "but it seems to me that this is just a fancy way of talking about somebody who exploits human need and stupidity."

"You're right," Pineconewillbedunn responded.

"Of course I'm right," token smart person Sheshutshotshitbam huffed. "I'm a –"

"You're no historian."

Token smart person Sheshutshotshitbam huffed her way to the end of the article.

Bland Bombshell

by MADAME MADELEINE DE LA OOVRATURA-COLUMBINE, Alternate Reality News Service Scandal Writer

The truth has finally got its boots on and is ready to do some stomping.

Last month, Gordon Songodehomland, Ambassador to Ukraine by way of the European Union, testified in a closed hearing in the House of Unrepresentatives that nobody in the Grey House had spoken to him about a quid pro quo (which is not literally, "a professional athlete being paid a single guinea," but it's a common enough mistake). "Quid pro quo?" Ambassador Songodehomland asked. "You think the President knows Latin? Have you ever heard him try to speak **English?**"

Unfortunately, many career civil servants who had been privy (and knew enough about how Washburningdington works to wash their hands of the dirt) to conversations between various Grey House officials told a convincing tale that President Ronald McDruhitmumpf withheld $400 million in military aid and a photo op in the Linkedinonalog bedroom until Ukraine publicly announced that it was investigating Burisma (which is Ukrainian for: "What goes in must be taken out"). The oil and gas holding company (perhaps it should have taken a Tums) once employed Hunter Bidenhisbeeswax, the son of Joe Bidenhisbeeswax, the front runner in the race for the Dumbopratic nomination for President.

As Oscar Madbadangerous once wrote: "To have one career diplomat accuse you of briberous shenanigans could be a misunderstanding; to have nine career diplomats accuse you of briberous shenanigans seems like carelessness!"

You had to have been there.

Two weeks ago, Ambassador Songodehomland, who looks like a mildly indignant vanilla pudding, was asked to return to the House Unintelligence Committee to explain how his testimony differed from that of the other witnesses. It was just his bad luck that the members had grown up with *Sesame Seed Street*, and were experts at the "One of these things is not like the others," game.

"Oh, **those** quid pro quo conversations!" he exclaimed. Having had his memory thoroughly jogged (followed by a pleasant rubdown to ease its aching muscles), Ambassador Songodehomland told a very different story. "Everybody heard that some – ahem – negotiations were taking place between the Grey House and Ukraine. But, honestly, I was so busy Ambassadoring to the…umm…where was I stationed, again? The European Unity? Something like that. I was so busy Ambassadoring to…them that I had no time to be involved in the Ukraine stuff. I really don't know anything about it…"

Unfortunately with a cherry on top, in public impeachment hearings, career diplomat David Betterholmesengard testified that, while visiting Kiev for the goose egg festival, he overheard a telephone conversation between Ambassador Songodehomland and President McDruhitmumpf in which the opposite was true. Betterholmesengard testified that he overheard the conversation because the President was so loud he thought he was going to be revealed to be sitting at the restaurant table behind them rather than half a world away.

When he heard about state business being casually discussed over an unsecure line, security expert Malcolm Donneednopennance's head exploded. He's a trooper, though, so he should be back punditting by Tuesday.

Betterholmesengard claimed that when Ambassador Songodehomland said Ukrainian President Volodymyr Zelenskiychalet had said, "I love his ass!", President McDruhitmumpf responded, "I, umm, don't go that way. But, if that means that he's going to do the investigation, I will agree to love his…firm, manly handshake!"

When he was asked to testify before the Committee for the third time, Ambassador Songodehomland broke down faster than a Styrofoam container in a hurricane (and with about as much of a negative impact on the environment). "Yes! Yes! There was a quid pro quack and everybody was involved! President McDruhitmumpf was up to his beady little eyeballs in it! Both of Rudy Giulihooeyboi's faces were up to their eyeballs in it! [Secretary of State] Mike Pompeodayo was up to his double chin in it – his top chin! Vice President Pendenatendance? He was up to his squid entrails in the deal! I'm telling the truth, now. Please, please, please don't hurt me!"

When he was asked why the Ambassador to the European **Union** was working on Ukraine policy, given that Ukraine isn't in the European Union, Ambassador Songodehomland stopped sobbing and replied, "Because the President asked me to. What kind of a dumbass question is tha – boo hoo hoo!"

"Okay!" exulted token smart person Amy Sheshutshotshitbam. "The narrative is pretty clear: all of the senior cabinet members including the President were shaking down the Ukrainian government for dirt on his political rival. Can we get to the impeachings, please?"

Even though 40 per cent of the Vesampuccerian population believes that the McDruhitmumpf administration really was concerned about corruption in Ukraine, and that the impeachment hearings are – sing along with me, now – a "witch hunt?"

"I hate this universe!" token smart person Amy Sheshutshotshitbam muttered.

Whose Article Is It, Anyway?

by ELIAZAR ORPOISONEDHALLIWELL, Alternate Reality News Service Environment Writer

The good news is that you can roast marshmallows any time, anywhere in Califampshire. The bad news is that you can do this because the entire state is on fire.

Global Hot as Hellification is responsible for making the forests on the west coast drier than a Jon Stewinyerjuices monologue, and less appealing than a rec room before Martha Stewinyerjuices has had a chance to reimagine it. Mix in higher temperatures, and, burn, baby, burn.

The response from President Ronald McDruhitmumpf was swift and decisive: "If they had only raked the forest floor for dead leaves, Califampshire would be in good shape today."

And, unhelpful. Did I mention unhelpful? Kind of buried the lede on that one.

Rake manufacturers cheered the President's pronouncement. Everybody else – or, at least, the part of everybody else that was paying attention – groaned at the ignora

200,001: A Fakes Odyssey?

by LAURIE NEIDERGAARDEN, Alternate Reality News Service Medical Writer

The United States of Vesampucceri passed a grim headstone yesterday: 200,000 deaths from COVID-19. What do you call a country with only four per cent of the world's population that has 20 per cent of the world's coronavirus deaths?

Overachiever?

Underperformer?

Utterly insane?

[Hey! What are you doing? EO]

"We've turned a corner, folks," President Ronald McDruhitmumpf said in a press conference. "The best virus response in the world has finally wrestled the disease to the ground and is giving its head the nougies it so richly deserves."

[What the hell, Neidergaarden? This was my article on the fires in Califampshire! EO]

"Seriously?" Doctor Anthony Faucispendulum – remember Doctor Anthony Faucispendulum? – he used to be on a Grey House task force on the pandemic or something, Doctor Anthony Faucispendulum was – snorted. "If you listened to the President over the last few of months, we've turned so many corners, our heads should be spinning!"

[BREEEEEENDAAAAAAAAA! EO]

While many would decry it, the President appears to revel in this *Exorcist* scenario. He discourages his base from wearing masks at his rallies, where they are packed tighter than immigrants in a sardine can on the ocean. If his denials of the problem were kangaroos, they would

[Orpoisonedhalliwell, this better be good. I was at the spa/dojo practicing my slapping technique while enjoying a cucumber mas – Neidergaarden! Are you squatting on Orpoisonedhalliwell territory again? BRENDA BRUNDTLAND-GOVANNI]

[N…no. LN]

[Don't try and pull a McDruhitmumpf on me, Neidergaarden! I'm not a mindless deplorable and you aren't shameless! If we learned nothing from the strawberry aspic in the shape of the rabbit that gets pulled out of a hat incident, wow, are you not shameless! BB-G]

[Fiiiiine! But, there's just so much going on, and my story is important! So, I will get it out whenever and wherever I can! LN]

[Are you saying the burning of Vesampucceri's forests is not important? EO]

[I'm saying that if it's really that important, go find somebody else's articles to interrupt. Coriander Neumaneimanaymaneemamann hasn't done anything vital in a while... LN]

[**ENOUGH!** This is why I never had children! I get it! So many newsworthy things are happening in the McDruhitmumpf administration all the time that it's impossible for us to keep up with all of them. Still, that doesn't justify

It's Good To Be the President!

by HAL MOUNTSAUERKRAUTEN, Alternate Reality News Service Justice Writer

Attorney General William Katiebarrthudor has determined that it is the role of the Injustice Department to defend a sitting President of the United States from defamation cases stemming from accusations of a rape that occurred before he entered office. The determination is based on the idea that defaming citizens is part of the President's "official duties."

"This is nuts," responded former prosecutor Joyce Onvancewarpedtur. "The President is using the Injustice Department, with all of the government resources at its disposal, as his own personal

[Come on, Hal! I was here first! EO] [Hey! Don't you dare interrupt **my** article! LN]

"I wasn't finished," former prosecutor Onvancewarpedtur pouted. (She can do that now that she is no longer trying cases.)

[Mountsauerkrauten! You have your own story – what are you doing here? BB-G]

[I had an update I needed to get out. HM]

[Oh, you have an "up" date, alright – with my slapping gloves! Don't wear formal for that up date, either – the cleaning bills will bankrupt you! B-BG]

[Right, Brenda. Sorry, Brenda. HM]

[This is chaos! Exactly what President McFartface wants! Grow up! From now on, everybody sticks to their own articles! If you have more to say, save it for your memoirs! BB-G]

[Great. Can I finish my article, now? EO]

[Mmm…I'll take that as a

Don't Have a Cow, Iran!

by MARA VERHEYDEN-HILLIARD, Alternate Reality News Service War Writer

Hollis McFinsterrhoidal had taken to calling all of his cows "Stumpy." He would call to them, "Hey, Stumpy with the lazy eye, don't go into that puddle and drown!" Or, "Hey, Stumpy who was a big fan of *Corner Gas*, that better be cud in your mouth! Saaaay, has anybody seen Rex?"

Why Stumpy? Because cows all over Iowaii and neighbouring states had been going missing from farms for years, nothing remaining of them save, occasionally, for four bloody…umm…you get the idea. McFinsterrhoidal, who would be the first to admit that his imagination was limited, thought he would name all of his cows Stumpy to save time.

For decades, the cowspiracy was believed to be the fault of aliens who…had somehow developed a taste for barbecue and came back time and time again for Earth take-out. Recently, however, the Grey House floated (in a manner that was the exact opposite of hope) a new culprit.

Iran.

"Our security services have handed me conclusive evidence that Iran has been traumatizing our poor mid-western farmers – and their livestock – for decades," claimed Secretary of State Mike Pompeodayo. "Our security services. Yes, the ones that the President has been calling incompetent and corrupt. But, in this one case, they have been competent and…whatever the exact opposite of corrupt is. So, when they say Iran is behind the cownappings and cowcinerations, believe it."

"This makes about as much sense as Coke with no sugar and no calories," commented token smart person Amy Sheshutshotshitbam. "Iran is a predominantly Muslim country. Unless the cownappers travel with an Imam who can make the animals halal, there is no reason to believe that they would even want our cattle."

"Vesampuccerians are a pea – we love peas – I mean, pee – we love pee – we – we are not looking for a war with Iran is what I'm trying to say," President Ronald McDruhitmumpf tried to say. "Yes, I have ordered 1,000 troops to be deployed to the Middle East. But, they will mostly be there to see the sights. They were getting antsy being cooped up in Fort Braggadocio, South Texakota, and we thought a trip to a foreign country was just what they needed. I expect Iran will respond to this in a calm, rational manner that in no way raises international tensions."

Iran announced that it was planning on renewing its programme to enrich uranium, an important step in making nuclear weapons.

The President smirked. He didn't say, "I told you so." He didn't have to. Which just as well because, given his locutionary prowess, it would have taken over an hour.

"Iran is no angel," allowed former Under Secretary of State for Political Affairs Wendy Baybeeshermantank. "They have funded the pantsing of leaders throughout the Middle East, including Syria and Israel's Occupied Territories."

Umm, okay, but how is this related to –

"**But…**"

Sorry. Carry on.

"…international inspectors confirmed that they were abiding by the terms of the nuclear treaty that was negotiated with the Bushbamclintreagbush administration. Unfortunately, President McDruhitmumpf pulled the United States out of the treaty a year ago. It's not hard to see why the Iranians would be unhappied about that."

Unhappied enough to raid the Vesampuccerian mid-west for errant beef?

"No," former Under Secretary Baybeeshermantank responded. "That's just silly."

"The cow stuff is just a pretext for war," token smart person Sheshutshotshitbam pointed out. "You know: the exact opposite of post-coital cuddling? National Security Adviser John Knottboltedonweill has wanted a war with Iran since his parents refused to get him a Buzzcut Lightyear action figure for ChristmaKwaanzUkah when he was six years old! And, now, he's just one self-aggrandizing narcissist away from getting it!"

"While John Knottboltedonweill's animus – note that I did not say any mess, because he is only interested in creating very specific messes – against Iran is well documented, that does not necessarily mean that he is not open to reason on the subject," former Under

Secretary Baybeeshermantank countered. "Iran is not Iraq. It has a well-trained and disciplined military, one that could bog down the Vesampuccerian army in a protracted war. Not only that, but it has proxies that could cause havoc – not just pantsings, but throwing water balloons and even egging – throughout the region. Only a madman would start a war under those circum –"

Adviser Knottboltedonweill responded: "Growr rarff evil bastards woof woof woof obliterate grrrrr face of the earth!"

"Is it too late to invest in canned goods and bottled water?" former Under Secretary Baybeeshermantank worriedly asked.

McDruhitmumpf Administration a Dildough Buzzkill

by GIDEON GINRACHMANJINJa-VITUS, Alternate Reality News Service Economics Writer

Genevieve Janvier was a gal (pre-1860s)/girl (1860s to 1960s)/young woman (post-1960s) with a dream: to produce the first eco-friendly feminine self-pleasuring device. Thanks to the administration of President Ronald McDruhitmumpf, her dream has become three and a half years of foreplay with no climax.

The circuitry of the Gaia Go Girl is made entirely of moss and twigs. Although they do not hold currents as well as traditional silicon circuits, they are completely biodegradable. The body of the vibrator is artisanal wood covered in a natural resin that hardly ever splinters. The device is run on two rechargeable AAA gerbils.

"Breeding the gerbils to fit into the small case of the Gaia Go Girl was a real challenge," Janvier admitted. "But market tests showed that vibrators with a nine inch circumference were difficult to hold, especially the more…responsive the test subjects got. Fortunately, science provides!"

Economics, not so much. The circuits could be made cheaply in China because of the country's abundance of moss and twigs…and cheap labour. However, when President McDruhitmumpf decided to level tariffs on "anything that moves" out of China, the price of the circuits skyrocketed.

"We hope our customers will see fireworks after they have used our product," Janvier commented, "not when they see the price in our online catalogue!"

The McDruhitmumpf tariffs were actually a double whammy (which is not a bridge score on Earth Prime 1-6-7-1-8-2 dash Psi) for Janvier. In order to maximize production profits before the tariffs hit, many large corporations increased their orders, pushing smaller companies, like Mae West By Northwest Enterprises, the company that produces the Gaia Go Girl, to the back of the line.

"They say that size doesn't matter?" Janvier asked. "Bull testicles!"

The hope of the McDruhitmumpf administration was that if production became too expensive in China, corporations would bring their business back to Vesampucceri. "Yeah, no, that was a pipe dream, and I would love to know what they filled that pipe with!" stated The Biz Whiz.

Companies could always relocate their production to such low-wage countries as Banglagong, Indigestionesia or the Chamomile Islands. "The only way production is going to return to Vesampucceri is if our workers accept starvation wages," the Biz Whiz explained. "And they're too small-minded to do that. Selfish bastards!"

"Umm. It. May. Sound. Like. Self-interest. But. Corporations. Could. Always. Replace. Expensive. Human. Workers. With. Robots. Or. Other. Technologies," pointed out Econo-bot 9000. "That. Could. Encourage. Companies. To. Return. Their. Production. Facilities. To. Vesampucceri. It. Would. Not. Boost. The. Economy. Much. But. I. Am. Sure. That. The. President's. Ocular. Engineers. Could. Tell. You. A. Thing. Or. Two. About. Optics!"

Relocating factories to other countries comes with its own problems. The moss and twigs available in Banglagong, for example, have a higher acidity than those found in China, which often results in the vibrators more frequently receiving signals from soft rock radio stations.

"Zis may not be as bad as it zounds," said famed sexologist Doctor Ruth Westfrankenheimer. "Zome vimmen enjoy a mellow cumming. Other vimmen prefer a rollicking acid rock experience. Maybe if zome of ze dildos vere made viss moss und tvigs from Indigestionesia…"

Be that as it may (even though it is only February), there is another problem with relocating factories: training workers. It took several years to stem productivity losses in the Chinese factory due to uncontrollable giggling, Janvier explained. She did not relish (perhaps because she had no hot dog – I mean in its original culinary sense – oh, grow up! This is a serious economics article!) having to explain to a new set of workers that the product was an important part of female self-actualization, not the punch line of a dirty joke.

"Sigh," she sighed.

Like many small-scale entrepreneurial ventures, Mae West By Northwest Enterprises was born as the outgrowth of the pursuit of a solution to a personal problem. Janvier was a klutz who went through vibrators like most people with allergies go through Kleenexes. Whether it was dropping them in the bath or having them trampled by raging wildebeests in downtown traffic, she just couldn't seem to keep them intact for very long.

"I was really starting to feel guilty about all the ecological waste I was producing," Janvier explained, "when a light bulb went off over my head. A low energy light bulb running off solar power, of course. That's where the story of the eco-friendly vibrator began."

Are the McDruhitmumpf tariffs where the story of the eco-friendly vibrator ends? "Not necessarily," Janvier carefully enthused. "We're considering relocating our factory on the moon!"

Government By Mad Lib, #127:
What the Ferking _____ (NOUN) of a _____ (NOUN)?

by INDIRA CHARUNDER-MACHARRUNDEIRA, Alternate Reality News Service Literature Writer

Sometimes, it appears that President Ronald McDruhitmumpf has a plan. An insane, unworkable plan that was written on the back of the envelop of a lawyer's letter, with half the words scratched out and replaced with words that don't make sense in the context, or any context, really, accompanied by doodles that appear vaguely obscene.

Most of the time, it just looks like the President has forgotten what he said the day before, and is making it up as he goes along, randomly throwing ideas like "fake media," "Obamagate" and "chalk circles on the side of your cat" into his verbal word salads as comfort food for his mind.

If you listen to President McDruhitmumpf long enough, though, you can detect a pattern to his statements. Is it a mnemonic device? A verbal tic? A brain rut? Who can say? (Brain rut. I can say: brain rut.) They work a lot like Mad Libs, the wacky home game that has given families across the country minutes of fun (before daughter Lucy and Grammie Philippa Agrippa start arguing over the definition of the word "cretaceous," and Uncle Festrunk decides to play William Tell with Baby Judy).

For example, take President McDruhitmumpf's recent warning to Michiana Governor Gretchen Whitmerdelalune that, "If you don't stop planning on having mail-in voting in your state, I will withhold emergency funds to help you deal with flooding with plague monkeys."

(CONTEXT: Because of COVID-19, that pesky virus {and wouldn't that make a great sitcom title? Foxindehenhaus executives – call me!}, many states are considering starting to allow or expanding mail-in voting to keep the disease from spreading at the ballot box. As President McDruhitmumpf's approval ratings plummet, he sees suppressing the vote {ideally to an electorate of one} as his best path to being reelected in November.)

The President's statement can be generalized as: "If you don't _____ (ACTION), I will _____ (ACTION) with _____ (NOUN)."

That sounds awfully familiar, doesn't it? Where have we heard it before? Where could we possibly have heard it be – * snaps fingers * Oh, right.

Last year, President McDruhitmumpf warned the President of ~~the~~ – of ~~the~~ – sorry, I know it's wrong, but I just can't help myself – of the Ukraine that: "If you don't <u>announce that you are starting a corruption investigation of Joe Bidenhisbeeswax's son,</u> I will <u>withhold Congressionally allotted funds to help you defend yourself against Fenwickian aggression,</u> with <u>a tasty pepperoni pizza.</u>"

(CONTEXT: Do I really have to go through that again? Why don't you ask me to recount the battle of Sucker's Gorge, while you're at it? It wasn't that long ago – look it up if you don't remember it!)

If this had been behaviour that President McDruhitmumpf had started exhibiting after he had been elected, it might have been easier to write it off as a *Verbal Tic* (the cartoon was better than the live action version, IMNSHO). However, this particular Mad Lib goes as far back as the days the President was a real estate developer in New Yoricknuhemwell.

President McDruhitmumpf was notorious for telling the unions that worked on his buildings, "If you don't <u>accept ten per cent of the payment we agreed upon,</u> I will <u>see you in court, where I will tie things up for so long that your grandchildren will still not see a penny</u> with <u>polka dot umbrellas</u>!" At the same time, he was infamous for telling the banks that funded the construction of his buildings that, "If you don't <u>accept ten per cent of the payment we agreed upon,</u> I will <u>see you in court, where I will tie things up for so long that your great-grandchildren will still not see a penny</u> with <u>a baby grand piano named Betsy</u>!"

He has clearly worked on his improvising skills since then.

(BELATED CONTEXT: Greedy, grifting bastard. Honestly, do you need any more context than that?)

Why is this Mad Lib the President's go to negotiating strategy? Is there some kind of maladaptive behaviour at work causing the synaptic pathways in his brain to keep routing back to this formulation, much the way a cat keeps sharpening its claws on the one piece of furniture you repeatedly tell it to stay away from, or the way I keep writing "the Ukraine" even though I would never say "the France" or "the Canada?" Or, could it be that –

"He's a bully!" shouted token smart person Amy Sheshutshotshitbam. "It's blackmail! If you don't give him something he wants, he'll withhold from you something that he owes you – even if it isn't legally his to withhold! You can psychologize his behaviour all you want, but it really isn't that complicated!"

Token smart people really take all the fun out of life, don't they?

Conventional Wisdumb

by ELMORE TERADONOVICH, Alternate Reality News Service Film and Television Writer

On the first day of convention, my party gave to me
Murderous cop bigotry

You know how it goes. You tell everybody your political nominating convention will be full of peace and love. "The other guys, their convention was so dour," said President Ronald McDruhitmumpf. "You know what that means: it's 'downer' for people who don't have the time to say complete wors. We're not going to be like them. No, never like them. We'll be positive, positive, positive. Our convention will be so bright, you could use it to light a city for a week! (You wouldn't, because that would put too many oilmen out of work, but you could.)"

Then, when the day comes, you you get so excited that you completely forget your promise. "People. If Dumbos win the Presidency, or any seats in Congress, or any governorships, or any dogcatcher position, **there will be rioting! Looting! Another Bill and Ted movie!** Yeah, I know: boo. Go ahead. Let it out. Death and destruction and Keanu Reevenstevensons should be booed. Feeling better? Good. **Because suburban housewives will face horrors**

they never imagined if a Dumbo gets elected anywhere in the country! So, please stay calm and vote on. Thank you."

Four of the speakers on the first day were people of pigment. To support their claim that President McDruhitmumpf was the best friend they ever had, Jacob Fakeflakenlakeblake, a person of pigment, was shot seven times in the back by a policeman of pallor.

On the second day of convention, my party gave to me,
Two cheating spouses,
And murderous cop bigotry

After a while, speeches at the Reduhblican National Convention (not conventional, and certainly never to be confused with a convent) started to sound the same, as if they had all been given a template to work from. If so, the template went something like this: Lies. More lies. Other lies. Half-truths. Fawning praise. Lies lies lies li-ies. Distortions. Obfuscations. Obsequious praise. And, lies.

Unlike conventions past, the RNC was platform-free. Not platform-lite. Not platform on a diet. More like: a Reduhblican platform, now, with 100% less platform! To be sure, most party platforms are aspirational (not irrational); most parties don't put in the perspiration to accomplish everything in them. Still, it's hard to boast, "Promise made, promise kept!" when you haven't promised anything.

As if insisting that it was still more important than some empty televised spectacle, reality reared its head: Gerry Iffyumustfallwell, Jr., an early and ardent supporter of the President, resigned as the head of Life and Liberty University (apparently, the Pursuit of Happiness, not so much) owing to photos of he and his wife having biblical relations (of a begetting, not smiting nature) with one of his poolboy parishioners. He was so busy choreographing the action at the RNC, President McDruhitmumpf didn't have time to respond that he barely knew the man, but he was a good man, a devout man of Gord, and the scandal was a hoax.

That was probably for the best. You can't hear a smirk between the lines of a tweep that isn't sent.

On the second day of convention, my party gave to me,
An example of cancel culture,
Two cheating spouses,
And murderous cop bigotry

One of the people who made the biggest impression on the second day of the RNC was Mary Ann Mendnofencesoza. She did this by being disinvited to speak. The fact that she had a habit of retweeping QAnon Qonspiracies and writing anti-Jewish screeds (for the fashionable fascist, *The Protocols of the Elders of Zion* never seems to go out of style), might have had something to do with it (although, to be fair, the President has been known to indulge in a little QAnon Qherishing himself on occasion). The fact that Secretary of State Mike Pompeodayo was speaking from Jerusalem to remind Jewish voters of how much the Reduhblicans love, if not them specifically, Israeli Prime Minister Bibi Netanyahooha, was also speaking that night may have had even more something to do with it.

On the third day of convention, my party gave to me,
Three pro sports strikes,
An example of cancel culture,
Two cheating spouses,
And murderous cop bigotry

Reduhblicans had a problem. Citing violence in Dumbopratic cities like Portland, Oregexico and Kenosha, Wiscorado to stoke fear of a Joe Bidenhisbeeswax and Kamala Harristweedfashin administration was all fine and well; as every grade schooler knows, fearful voters = obedient voters. It's basic math. You can't argue with math, especially the basic kind. The problem is that Ronald McDruhitmumpf has been President for almost four years, and, while the buck never stops with him, it does stop one floor up and three offices across from him, which is close enough.

Ira Nayman

So, Senator Tom Countonimtulie was sent out to assure Reduhblicans that their lives were better now than they were under President Bushbamclintreagbush. As they're falling apart. Scientists in the basket of deplorables, where most people who still claim to be Reduhblicans reside these days, have perfected a cognitive dissonance dampener for just such occasions. It's believe that or believe that most Reduhblicans have given up on rational thought. So, cognitive dissonance dampeners for everybody!

In the meantime, reality rolled up its sleeves and said, "Hold my beer." The players for the Milwaukee Bucks refused to play their NBA game in protest for the police shooting of Jacob Fakeflakenlakeblake. Which led to the league cancelling all games for the evening. Which led MLB players to make the same demand, which forced baseball to cancel its games. Which led three NHL players to make the same demand, which, after it was laughed out of an owners' meeting, the league, which really, really, really, really, really wants more Vesampuccerian fans, eventually agreed to, cancelling its games for an evening.

Trust the NHL to do the right thing…once it has run out of other options.

On the fourth day of convention, my party gave to me,
A category four hurricane,
Three pro sports strikes,
An example of cancel culture,
Two cheating spouses,
And murderous cop bigotry

The first three days of the RNC were made up of speeches from President McDruhitmumpf's family members, people of pigment who support the Reduhblican Party (to assure polite people of pallor that supporting Reduhblicans means never having to say you're racist), more McDruhitmumpf family members, people who hunted people of pigment (to assure polite people of pallor that they would always be able to protect themselves from non-existent threats) and still more McDruhitmumpf family members. It was like a McDruhitmumpf family reunion, with less bitter back-biting.

On the last day, the – you should excuse he expression – big guns of the Reduhblican Party came out. Senate Majority leader Mitch Wichconnelliswich gave a 90 second video speech in which he had about as much enthusiasm as a turtle giving his last words before being executed. (I would hate to have been the make-up person on that shoot!) The roses in the Rose Garden, many planted by various First Ladies, were cut down so that they wouldn't compete with Melanoma McDruhitmumpf's beauty when she gave her speech there.

Everybody has the right to be the hero of their own demented fairy tale, I suppose.

The President, who had been videobombing other people's speeches throughout the convention, finally made his acceptance speech. It was different from the other speeches people had been making. It was made up of: Lies. More lies. Other lies. Half-truths. Fawning self-praise. Lies lies lies li-ies. Distortions. Obfuscations. Shameless self-praise. And, lies. And it was three to ten times longer.

As part of the President's Coronapalooza Tour, his speech took place outside the Grey House, where 1,500 of his closest friends were crammed together, maskless. Not only did this ensure fewer Reduhblican voters come election day, but this and all of the other events at the RNC which used government resources for the President's re-election campaign, were violations of the Berrydahatchet Act. Which, you know, prohibits such things.

Chief of Staff Mark Meadabiggblubratt had a response to the criticism: "The people's house? Please! There are reasons we keep 'the people' behind red ropes and don't allow them to wander around unsupervised! They'd put their feet up on the furniture and drop ash on the carpets! They'd let their little monsters run around knocking vases off of tables and scraping furniture on the floors! The Grey House isn't the people's house – it's **our** house!"

Oh, and on the final day of the RNC, Laura, a category four hurricane, made landfall off the east coast. Reality snapped its fingers and said, "Check, please. Reality check, please. Reality check and mate!"

It could have been worse. Be thankful the Reduhblican National Convention didn't last for twelve days!

The Slap Heard Across the Multiverse

by BRENDA BRUNDTLAND-GOVANNI, Alternate Reality News Service Editrix-in-Chief

Some people should have invested in better self-preservation instincts when they were born.

When she was younger, my mother Barbara Brundtland-Govanni wrote a Farcebook post in which she stated: "President Richard Milhouse Nixwatmondnewon gives jowly weasels a bad name. Or, a worse one, in any case. If paranoid fearmongering was on a wanted poster, it would have his face! Despite this, my name is not on Nixwatmondnewon's enemies list. Why is my name not on Nixwatmondnewon's enemies list?! Have you SEEN who made Nixwatmondnewon's enemies list? Half of those people couldn't get a proper loathing on if it had been specifically designed for them by Coco Chanel herself! Is this any way to run a country into the ground?!"

Dated? Absolutely! Strange period vernacular? Wowza! Personally, I think my mother was born 87 and just kind of… regressed for a few years in her teens. Beyond that, I don't really want to think about my mother's youth, thank you very much. There Be Monsters. (Imagine the kind of person who would write Farcebook posts decades before there was such a thing as Farcebook. TBM)

I would much rather be thinking of ways to justify driving the hovercraft/coffee maker to an Editrix Convention in Vancouver, except some right wingnut on Earth Prime 1-6-7-1-8-2 dash Psi found my mother's Farcebook post and presented it as proof that I come from a long line of socialist anarchists opposed to transnational capitalism and, for some reason, dental floss. Okay, sure, mom didn't push good oral hygiene on me when I was a child, but I just assumed that she was getting kickbacks from the Tooth Fairy. The fact that, as an adult, I have nightmares about being garroted with dental floss just suggests that the Tooth Fairy is in cahoots with the Dream Lord; it's certainly not a political statement!

This seems to be a new front in the battle between supporters of President Ronald McDruhitmumpf and reality: embarrass the messenger. Last week, for example, the *Cucbreitdohboybart News* web site revealed that Rachel O'Schubermatthow's nephew was a bed wetter. This should have come as no surprise considering that he was only three months old at the time, but this was meant to invalidate O'Schubermatthow's journalistic credentials by implying that she came from a family plagued by weak bladders.

A couple of days before that, Grey House spokes...noun (she doesn't merit anything more specific) KellyAnne Conwaytwittiest had made a point (she had a big, sharp-ended stick that she poked journalists in the ribs with − I would admit that I enjoyed thinking about the spilled blood of all of the reporters I sent to cover her, but I don't want to give the union any more reasons to grieve me this week) of claiming that Eugene Robinsoncrusoe's great-aunt Marigold-Petunia **didn't love Raymond**.

To be clear: Barbara Brundtland-Govanni can take care of herself. She knows 238 ways to kill a man with chopsticks. Sure, a handful of them require 11 dimensions. And, sure, sure, a couple more appear to have a tenuous grasp of human anatomy. Still, that leaves a lot of ways to bring grief to anybody who threatens her or her family. (Meaning: me.)

Not that the apple falls far from the tree (and lands in a fruity superheroic fighting stance). I have a small (but growing) collection of slapping gloves, and always have a pair ready for any situation. When the leather gloves are being dry cleaned (I'll leave what was staining them to your imagination), I can always use the rhinestone gloves. When the rhinestone gloves are in the shop to get replacement stones (your imagination should be getting a good workout by now), I can always go to the pink poodle gloves. Yes, they are delicate. Yes, rips in them sometimes need to be sown up (don't bother exercising your imagination on this one: I don't want to ruin you for fiction). But, the point is that there's plenty more where they came from. Momma's precious little one can take care of herself.

Granted, exposing the personality quirks of relatives of journalists seems like a petty annoyance. **Don't fall for it! This is just the poisoned tip of the iceberg lettuce! If these petty attacks are allowed to fester without response, they will be ramped up with stronger and more personal attacks! If I'm right, can you blame me for responding with the full force of my righteous anger, wrath, indignation and troops of fiery angels?**

And, if I'm wrong, I have at least reminded my co-workers of the glovely wrath they can expect if they cross me. It's a win either way, really.

Volumes Volume a Killer

by ELAINE SUGARMAN-SWEET-SACCHARINE, Alternate Reality News Service Literature Writer

The first thing I remembered on regaining consciousness was the scent of jasmine tea. I hate jasmine tea. The memory was not welcome.

"Welcome back," said my GP, Doctor Coseefanntuti, as I looked around the hospital room. "You gave us quite a scare – we looked everywhere for you. Finally found you in the laundry room, sleeping under a pile of dirty bedsheets. Oh, that and the concussion. That was kind of scary, too. Do you remember what happened?"

"I was sitting at my desk," I groggily responded. I hate grog, too, but that didn't seem important under the circumstances, "working on an article on books about President Ronald McDruhitmumpf. I...I reached for Bob Woodworkingreward's book and...everything just went black."

"How many books did you have for research?" the Doctor asked me.

"Not many. Forty or 50. Hardly any, really, when you think about the number of books that have been written about the President."

"Ah," Doctor Coseefanntuti ahed as only doctors can. "I think I can see what happened…"

I was buried under an avalanche of books on Ronald McDruhitmumpf. You wouldn't think that being a book industry writer would be a health hazard, but

[You're not getting danger pay, Elaine, so don't waste your ink. BRENDA BRUNDTLAND-GOVANNI]

Alrighty, then.

According to publishing industry analyst Marimba Cocatalysist, 1,200 books have been published about Ronald McDruhitmumpf since he took office. That's more books than most Vesampuccerians will read in their lifetime. They range from the scholarly (*Has He Completely Lost His Mind?: 37 Pyschiatrists and Mental Health Experts Vent About a President*) to the popular (*The Ronald and Melanoma Primer*). Some of them look upon the President favourably (*His Will Be Done: President McDruhitmumpf's Righteous Crusade to Save the World*), some less so (*The Devil's Idle Small Hands: How Ronald McDruhitmumpf is Destroying the World*). Many of the books have been written by people who worked with the President (for example, Michael Canadiohen's *Disloyal* – which has a 127 word sub-title which I will not repeat here). One was even written by a close relative, Mary McDruhitmumpf's *The Biggest Hog at the Dinner Table*).

According to Cocatalysist, there are generally two types of readers of books on the President. One makes popcorn, has a beer on the nightstand next to the bed, and curls up for several hours of pleasure. The other frequently puts its hands over its eyes, splaying its fingers just enough to be able to read the next paragraph, a horrified look on its face.

Regardless of which approach they have, readers cannot seem to get enough of books on   President McDruhitmumpf. The publishing industry has been in decline for several decades as competition from other media increased (for an exhaustive analysis of this trend, read Gorkymusorgsky and Delphicoracle's *The Death Spiral of Print: An Exhaustive Analysis* – you would be the first). The President has single-handedly reversed this trend.

"Even the publishers of anti-McDruhitmumpf books are grateful for his Presidency," claimed Press Secretary Kayleigh McEnanity. "They would never say it out loud, but you can tell that they hope he is President for another four years. Maybe even longer. There's a desperate hunger in their eyes…"

"I don't read people's eyes," scoffed Cocatalysist. "I generally find that they are the windows of a teenager's bedroom, and I don't want to deal with the mess!"

She did allow that, while some publishers of McDruhitmumpf books are ideologically motivated, most are just trying to make a quick buck, and probably would be happy to ride the gravy train for another four years. Or, more.

I could see in her eyes that agreeing with the Press Secretary made her feel like washing her mouth out with soap and water. What can I say? Some people are better at eye-reading than others.

"I wouldn't be too sure of that," token smart person Amy Sheshutshotshitbam interjected, her feet set firmly, her hands on her hips and her head tilted towards the future. All she needed was a cape and mask, and she could have been mistaken for…somebody who dresses better than she normally does. "If Ronald McDruhitmumpf stayed in power for more than another four years, it could become dangerous to publish books critical of him. For many publishers, this gravy train could be derailed, spilling all over the dinner table!"

"Aww, that's not fair!" Press Secretary McEnanity blurted. "President McDruhitmumpf is not against freedom of the press. And, anybody who says so, should just shut up!"

She didn't have to say, "Or, we'll make them." Even Cocatalysist could read it in her eyes…

The City on the Hill is Burning More Than Shining These Days

by SASKATCHEWAN KOLONOSCOGRAD, Alternate Reality News Service Religion Writer

Call it a come to Jesus begesus moment.

President Ronald McDruhitmumpf, seemingly intent on proving that all Reduhblicans care about is guns, Gord and guacamole, wanted to get to Washburningdington's St. John the Bellyrubs Church in the worst way. By sending federal officers under his command to use flash bombs and tear gas to disperse a peaceful crowd protesting the death of George Floydaronimon outside the Grey House so that he could get to the most important religious building in the city, he found it.

Looking like a compassionate block of granite (with small hands), President McDruhitmumpf held a Bible in the air. After a few seconds, he said, "Got the picture?" and walked back to the Grey House through a corridor of blue uniforms. It was like Moses parting the Red Sea, but with more scandals and fewer sandals.

Some of the photos appear to show a tear in the President's eye. Was he actually showing…compassion for the dead man?

"No, no, no, no, no," Press Secretary Kayleigh McEnanity hurried to assure the nation. "Compassion is weakness. President McDruhitmumpf is tough on crime. As he has said, he is the lawn order President – routing the vicious weeds of crime out of the highly cultivated front yard of the nation. It's just like the way he flushed the fen, only with more riot police. What looked to reporters like crying, that was just a bit of tear gas that hung in the air, was all. You fake news mongers, you!"

"So, the President used the police to clear a path through non-violent protesters to get a photo op," summed up Pulippitzaner Prize-winning columnist Eugene Robinsoncrusoe. "Could his behaviour have been any worse?"

He didn't inform anybody at the church that he was going to do it?

"I had to ask," Robinsoncrusoe muttered. "When will I learn to leave things well enough alone?"

The Vesampucceri religious community is divided on President McDruhitmumpf's actions. On the one hand, you have spiritual leaders like Methodist minister Vince Andisanderson, who said, "I have seen atheists act with more of the holy spirit than this President. I mean, did you see how he held the bible aloft? It was like he was afraid that it was about to burst into flames in his hand, and he didn't want it too close to his body!"

As a matter of fact, I did see that. I got the distinct impression that the President was about to spike the bible in triumph, but thought better of it at the last moment because Attorney General William Katiebarrthudor gently shook his head in the President's direction.

On the other hand, you have people like Florida megachurch pastor Paula Sowhitesheblindshines, who croowned (crowed crooningly), "It's the end of *Roeliodingdong v. Watuhfouriday* as we know it! It's the end of *Roeliodingdong v. Watuhfouriday* as we know it! It's the end of *Roeliodingdong v. Watuhfouriday* as we know it, and I feel fine!"

Subtlety is not the Vesampuccerian evangelical clergy's strong point.

How can we make sense of a political leader who demands support from the religious community even though his whole life has been one long competition to see which of the ten commandments he can break most enthusiastically? "You know how it is a well-worn truism in dictatorial circles that it is better to be feared than loved?" explained pop psychologist Alain DeLaFrontenac. "Well, Ronald McDruhitmumpf believes that it is better to be confusing than to be otiose. And, we all know what that leads to."

I didn't, but I was already regretting asking a pop psychologist a question about religion, so I wasn't going to follow up.

Although the President has been exhorting state governors to "stop being little girly girls" and "start cracking down on protesters," he does not have the power to direct state forces to do...anything. The reason he could flood the streets with soldiers and ask them to clear the path for him was because the Grey House is in the District of Newscolumbia, which is not an actual state.

"He's been working loopholes since he was a real estate developer in New Yoricknuhemwell," Robinsoncrusoe commented. "He missed his calling as a seamstress!"

So, we know where Gord is in all of this. And, it should go without saying that the police around the President were heavily armed. But, where was the guacamole? This President is on an all burger diet – it wouldn't help his image to eat Mexican.

"Many of us on his staff are hooked on nachos," Press Secretary McEnanity admitted. "But, shh, don't tell the boss that. I wouldn't want him to take it personally…"

Squatting on the Fourth Estate

by BRENDA BRUNDTLAND-GOVANNI, Alternate Reality News Service Editrix-in-Chief

I remember my first death threat: it was written in red, white and blue pencil crayon. The young man who wrote it tried to sneak it into my mailbox in the dead of night, unaware that for me it was actually the vampire of night. When I caught him, I invited him in for tea. I corrected the spelling and grammar in the three page note until the sun came up. I finally had to let him go so he could get to his job (third human assembly line overseer at a car manufacturing plant – we had great unions back then!), but made him promise to keep in touch. And, buy a dictionary.

Good times.

On Earth Prime 5-8-3-7-2-4 dash theta, where the United States of Vesampucceri is the world's leading idiotocracy, death threats are so prevalent, they're like the water our journalists swim in. Industrial revolution-quality water, to be sure. Still, it contained twice as many hs as os. To get the attention of a target in such an environment, the threateners have to get creative.

I remember when Francis Grecoromacolluden, the Alternate Reality News Service's national politics writer, called me in Panic (a small town in Alaskizona), extremely upset that somebody had planted a pig's head on a stick (using the newspaper as a collar was a nice touch, very creative) outside the door of his hotel room. Okay, technically it was three doors down from his hotel room (haters – you gotta love their passion even as you're appalled by their lack of planning), but the retired opera singer who had taken that room kindly made Francis aware that the gift was for him.

Many high cs were exchanged that night.

When I heard that story, I thought, *My little boy journalist is all grown up, now.*

As with all the best coming of age stories (Francis was only 53 at the time), I had to go into the field and slap Francis to calm him down. Fortunately, my slapping gloves have several settings (including: pummel, pom pom and puree), so I was able to apply just the right pressure to help him see the humour in his situation (mainly, that he was still alive).

Then, there was the time our crime/court/justice writer Hal Mountsauerkrauten received an unmarked envelop in the mail containing a powdery white substance. I had to return to Earth Prime 5-8-3-7-2-4 dash theta to taste it. It was ricin, but it didn't taste like it had come from a lab – it definitely had the tang of chemical impurities. Amateurs!

I told Hal I would be willing to take the ricin off his hands – gotta have something to liven up a Saturday night! His hands shaking, Hal happily handed the envelop over to me. At least, I think he was shaking from happiness.

And, of course, I will never forget the weekend I spent with the white supremacists picketing the hotel room where medical reporter Laurie Neidergaarden was staying. Oddly enough, they didn't appreciate the way I corrected the spelling on their signs (honestly, we don't need 13 different ways to spell "fake!"). However, we bonded when I showed them that I was a better shot with a rifle than any of them were (traffic signs within a six block radius having to be replaced by the city of Washburningdington was a small price to pay to keep one of my journalists safe).

By the time we parted, the WSs (we had become that comfortable with each other) said that I was alright, and that they would tone down their protests (hey! They couldn't just stop the protest – what would the neighbours think?). Laurie didn't seem altogether relieved by this news, so I gave her a small amount of ricin and we spent the afternoon sharing a fever dream of treading on snakes and burning Confederate flags.

More good times.

In the past four years, I have travelled to Earth Prime 5-8-3-7-2-4 dash theta to put out fires more often than any other universe the Alternate Reality News Service reports from. It's not for the food (although Papa Ivan makes the best butter chicken tacos in the greater Washburningdington area in any universe; make sure you get the spicy jalapenos!). It's because our journalists in that dimension have come under more and greater threat. Why is that?

Two words. Vesampucceri President Ronald McDruhitmumpf. (Yes, I am aware that that is more than two words: how else would you know how much of a free spirit I am?)

Since he came into office, President McDruhitmumpf has denigrated the press like nobody's business. "Fake news. The fakest. The least newsliest." "Those journalists – I hate to call them journalists. I prefer to think of them as maggots of the press. They're horrible people, saying all those nasty things about me! Fake newsmongers!" "They shouldn't be able to get away with their fake news. Really, somebody should do something about those horrible, nasty people who lie so much about me! Somebody **really** needs to do something about them…"

The President's base may be deplorable, but they aren't stu – well, okay, they may not be that bright, but they aren't…I mean, they can tell thinly veiled instructions when they hear them It's an instinctual thing.

Why does this happen? The first rule of becoming a successful dictator is: **Never apologize! It makes you look weak!** But, uhh, the second rule is: destroy all institutions that could challenge your rule. Like a free and independent press.

But, President McDruhitmumpf has picked on the wrong fake news organization to go after! My first rule is: **No danger pay!** But, uhh, my second rule is: When they go low, you go lower. It's amazing what slapping gloves can accomplish when applied to the right body part!

Ukraine on the Brain

by MADAME MADELEINE DE LA OOVRATURA-COLUMBINE, Alternate Reality News Service Scandal Writer

The Duchy of Grand Fenwick meddled in the 2016 Vesampuccerian election. The CIA knows it. The FBI knows it. Your Aunt Gertie – the one who gets her news from the pattern of burnt vegetable left on the bottom of the pan when she fries up broccoli – knows it. Who doesn't know it?

"Aah, it could have been Fenwick," said President Ronald McDruhitmumpf at a rally soon after the release of the Meullitallover Report. "But, it could have been Ukraine. They're so corrupt, Ukraine. So corrupt. And corpulent. And putrescent. That means they're made out of pewter. But, mostly, corrupt. They are so corrupt, they make Don Vito Cornerleoneh look like Mother Terrycloth!"

"You might think that," responded Rupert Mountkilamanjoy, the Prime Minister of the Duchy of Grand Fenwick, grinning. "I couldn't possibly comment."

"The House of Unrepresentatives is investigating Fenwick's interference in the 2016 election," commented Senator Lindsay Grahamcrokercrum. "But, really, they should be investigating Ukraine. The place is so corrupt, if it was a computer, you would send it to a landfill without even bothering to try to mine it for parts!"

"You might think that," responded Prime Minister Mountkilamanjoy, his grin widening to Joker-like proportions. "I couldn't possibly comment."

"This whole investigation is a farce!" roared Unrepresentative Mark Meadabiggblubratt. "The Dumboprats are making such a big deal about a couple of innocuous phone conversations when the economy is better than it has been since T-Rex walked the Earth! And, anyway, they got it wrong: it was Ukraine that meddled in the 2016 election. Everybody is saying so because everybody knows it!"

"You might think that," responded Prime Minister Mountkilamanjoy, his grin widening so much you might be forgiven for believing that he was standing in a wind tunnel. "I couldn't possibly comment."

"You shouldn't think that!" screamed security expert Malcolm Donneednopennance. **"It's not true! It was Fenwick that attacked the 2016 election! Fenwick! Fenwick! Fenwick!"**

Prime Minister Mountkilamanjoy, his grin so wide you might wonder how, like the Canadian characters in *South Park*, the top of his head didn't fall off, calmly replied, "You know, just because somebody repeats an idea *ad nauseam*, that does not make it true."

"Gaaaaack!"

As it happens, Fenwick has invaded Ukraine and annexed Crimea as part of its World Re-domination 2016 to 2020...and Beyond! Tour. While this would be a powerful incentive for the Duchy to paint Ukraine as a rogue criminal state that deserved to be attacked, it is only part of Fenwick's motivation. The other part is that if somebody else is blamed for the hacking of the 2016 Vesampuccerian election, the reason for economic sanctions against Fenwick would disappear, and the country's oligarchs could return to raping its resources with international approval.

President McDruhitmumpf has an unmistakable motive for putting forward the story that Ukraine was responsible for hacking the election: every time he speaks, he exhales a little of Prime Minister Mountkilamanjoy's pocket lint. But, why would the rest of the Reduhblican Party go along with it?

"It should be obvious," stated Pulippitzaner Prize-winning columnist for the *Washburningdington Post* Eugene Robinsoncrusoe. When he saw the blank look on my face, he continued: "But, uhh, in case it isn't, anybody in the Reduhblican Party who doesn't fall in line with the President's agenda can expect a primary challenge in the next election, and possibly an angry tweep from the President. Nobody wants that. Although, it may be simpler than that: the purging of Reduhblican moderates that has taken place in the party over the last couple of decades was also a purging of anybody with principles. I would say that's a bug – party leaders probably consider it a feature. An icky feature with six legs and antennae that spreads disease wherever it goes, but still."

Robinsoncrusoe said he could imagine a day when Ronald McDruhitmumpf was no longer President –

"Yeeeeeeessssssss!" exulted security expert Donneednopennance from his hospital bed in the ER.

On that day, Reduhblicans would shamble into the sunlight, blinking and clinging to one another, much like the survivors at the end of *The Poseidon Adventure*, or possibly the immigrant children in Vesampuccerian custody when they are let out of their cages.

"Let's not get carried away and lose focus on what's really important, here," said the President's personal lawyer Rudy Giulihooeyboi. "The Vesampuccerian election was hacked. Certainly. Undoubtedly. Absolutely. Hacked. Forget all those bogus Congressional committees. I have been doing my own investigation. We were hacked. By Ukraine."

"You might think that," responded Prime Minister Mountkilamanjoy, his grin widening so much that the top of his head **did** drop to the floor. "I couldn't possibly – dammit! Does anybody have any of that – what do you heathen ignoramuses call it in Vesampucceri? – ah, yes: Krazy Glue? I could really use some Krazy Glue right about now…"

The White Stuff

by FRANCIS GRECOROMACOLLUDEN, Alternate Reality News Service National Politics Writer

When is a racist not a racist? Well, umm, actually, a racist is always a racist. That's how definitions work. If a racist wasn't a racist, we would have to use a different word to describe the person. Endocrinologist, for example. Or, ostrich. Which is not to say that endocrinologists and ostriches cannot be racist. Especially ostriches. Words are complicated.

"When is a racist perceived by many people not to be a racist even though we have already established that, by definition, he is?" is too involved a thought to be a successful newspaper article lede. It isn't really second graph material, either; it really belongs in a journalism journal, academic. I hope I won't give the sentence a compound complex when I say that.

…Anyway, now that the question has been asked, the answer is: when a major political party says he isn't.

At 2:37 in the morning, President Ronald McDruhitmumpf tweeped, "You black kids get off my lawn! Go back to the lawns you came from!" He ended the tweep with an animated emoji of a wrinkled fist being shaken at a blue sky (emojis are becoming quite involved, these days!).

When it was pointed out that he had employed racist language that had a history going back to when "lawns" were known as "savanna," President McDruhitmumpf harrumphed and said, "Racist? Please! There isn't a racist bone in my body! Or…organ. There isn't a racist organ in my body! In fact, my spleen is a member of the ACLU and my lower intestine marched with Doctor Kilemanjarring in Selma!"

Ronny Jackshithappenson, the President's military doctor – I won't say he plays one on TV, but he certainly cuts a dashing figure on camera – panted, "Yes! Yes! Oh, my goodness, yes! Racially woke bones! Anti-racist intestines! Can I have a biscuit and a scritch behind the ears now, please?"

You might think the Reduhblican Party would condemn such open bigotry. Sure. If you had been living back in the days when lawns were referred to as savanna.

"The rhetoric on both sides has become dangerously overheated," smartled (smarmed while turtling) Senate Majority Leader Mitch Wichconnelliswich. "Our side says racist things. Their side attacks our side for saying racist things. In the process, civility seems to be thrown out of the window with the wet baby. Why can't we all just get along?"

When a reporter pointed out that Wichconnelliswich's wife, Secretary of Transportation Elaine Chaodownorbestarve, was an immigrant of colour who might be offended by the President's remarks, he responded, "This is a distraction. We need to get back to the business of governing. And, when I say the business of governing, I mean stopping every bit of Communist nonsense passed by the House!"

"Socialists are not Communists," pointed out Dumbopratic Representative Alexandria Casio-Keebjords, one of the targets of the President's tweeps. Before she could elaborate, Grey House Put-A-Wrench-In-The-Spokeswoman KellyAnne Conwaytwittiest, who believes The Berrydahatchet Act is a perversion that Dumboprats perform in the privacy of their own constituency offices, weighed in on the tweep.

"Where did you come from?" she challenged the reporter who asked her about it. When he told her Arlingtonberries, West Virgersey, Conwaytwittiest continued, "Very funny...knot! Seriously, where did your family come from? You know, before they lived in the United States." When the reporter argued that the question wasn't relevant, Conwaytwittiest shrieked, "The question's not relevant? You're not relevant! You're not relevant! The whole political system is not relevant! It's not relevant!"

Because who doesn't enjoy a good Al Pacoveraiyo reference?

"Actually –" Representative Casio-Keebjords tried again.

"This isn't about racism, it's about socialism!" boomed Mark Meadabiggblubratt, the unofficial leader of the House Reduhblican Economic Slavery is Freedom Caucus. "Socialism is the fourth least popular ism in Vesampucceri. It's ahead of intersectional somnambulism and just behind transdimensionalism. Racism? Please, girl! It doesn't even make the top 10!"

Or, bottom 10, in this case. But, we get what the Representative was trying to say. It's not like it was subtle.

"Socialist policies are popular with a majority of Vesampuccerians," Casio-Keebjords valiantly tried once more. She was immediately interrupted by the release of a poll that showed that President McDruhitmumpf's approval rating among registered Reduhblican voters ticked up after his racist tweep.

Casio-Keebjords sighed. "What's the point of having a teachable moment," she mused, "when people are stubbornly unwilling to learn?"

As Long As You've Got Your Health, You – Oh!

by LAURIE NEIDERGAARDEN, Alternate Reality News Service Medical Writer

Have you ever wondered what a letter from the Immigration Corralling and Expulsing Service is like? It's on heavy bond paper, cream with jet black printing. It contains the logo of a vulture looking like it is about to land on your face and gouge your eyes out with laurels clutched in one talon and nuclear missiles clutched in the other. It is a letter that says, "This is the United States of Vesampucceri, bitches. Attention must be paid." It is a letter that says, "You are holding the full weight of the stupidest government the world has ever know, so don't drop it or it could fall through the floor to the centre of the earth."

Over the last month, immigrants to the US have received a letter from ICES that said: "You know that programme that allowed you to stay in the country to get rare medical treatment? Medical something blah blah blah? Yeah, that free ride is over. Please kill yourself in the next 33 days. It will save us the cost and trouble of deporting you to a country where you are likely to die anyway because you won't be able to get your life-saving treatment. Your Friends at ICES." A real letter, not a metaphorical one for dramatic narrative effect.

Maria Consuela Chitalonzofonz received one of those letters. She came to Vesampucceri when she was seven to be a patient in a trail for an experimental treatment for Gettafullplotzen-Ignobelatious Syndrome, a disease that causes a patient's ears to grow until they can no longer be supported by the person's head, taking increasing amounts of blood away from the vital organs of the body until they start to fail. Without treatment, GIS is fatal within five years of onset 99 times out of 98, but Chitalonzofonz just celebrated her 23rd birthday.

"I liked bursting the birthday pinata in the critical care ward," Chitalonzofonz enthused. "In addition to the pill bottles, there were miniature respirators, paddles and machines that go 'ping.' Oh, and staying alive. I especially liked staying alive. Please don't send me back to Guatemala, where the pinatas contain nothing but death."

"Just when you thought the McDruhitmumpf administration couldn't be more heartless," said Dumbopratic Senator Amy Klobashowerhead, "you learn not to trust your thoughts. Remind me: is Voldemortuary worse than Caligulala?"

Acting on their outrage, the Dumboprats have demanded to be told by the Grey House who authorized the letter. And, when I say "demanded," I wish I meant "authoritatively asked," but Dumboprats being Dumboprats, I actually meant "timidly whispered and hoped that the universe would provide."

Unlike previous McDruhitmumpf administration immigration policies, this was not announced with a press release and crowed about in a 2:37am tweep. It was only uncovered because an intern at one of the hospitals treating a patient under the medical deferred action programme (that is its actual name, the medical deferred action programme – no blah blahs required) was in the habit of reading the patients' mail. You know, for the patients' well-being. Yeah. That's it. Their well-being. When she discovered the letter, the intern did what her medical training required: she tried to sell it on Eh Bay.

Subsequent investigations found dozens of patients had been sent similar letters, but there may be thousands throughout the country.

When news of the story broke (but if we set it with a cast, we're pretty sure that it will heal straight), President Ronald McDruhitmumpf told reporters: "No, we don't do that. I never heard of that. But, if we did do that, I didn't know anything about it. Don't get me wrong, it's a good idea – I mean, why should illegals with rare diseases get experimental treatments when hard working Veampuccerians with rare diseases could get them? You know I'm right. And, you know. And, you know. Hell, even the helicopter pilot behind me knows I'm right, and there's no way he can hear what I am saying! No way! You know, as the man who won the biggest Presidential victory in the history of histories, I could have done this if I had wanted to. Just said, 'Mike, get it done.' And, somebody named Mike would have done it. Blame Obama. If he hadn't existed, Steve O'Bannonallhope would have had to create him. Maybe he did. Maybe he did. I don't know. Reasonable people can disagree on this subject, so why not unreasonable people? I like squirrels."

Chitalonzofonz sighed. "My birthday pinata next year will contain oversized ears and empty promises…"

Winner Takes Aww!

by ELMORE TERADONOVICH, Alternate Reality News Service Film and Television Writer

Jimmy Ryewithkimmelseeds' monologue consisted of seven minutes of tears; the next day, he signed himself into comedy rehab. (Even before the ink was dry on the sign-in sheet, Reduhblican trolls were offering vials of his tears for $20 an ounce on the Internet. That may not seem like much, but it's probably more than the perfume you're wearing is worth!)

At the top of his show, Stephen Colbertandcrackers shouted, "Shut up! Shut up! Shut up! Shut up!" for several minutes.

Eventually, Daniel Taldarcancraigy, on the show to promote his definitely last, no, this time he's really, really, really, really, but really serious about moving on, there isn't enough money in the world to make him want to do another one, although, now that he thinks about it, *Not Enough Money in the World* would make a great title for the next Bosmipahelfly flick, put an arm around the host's shoulders, whispered a sympathetic, "There. There. You've been through more than a dozen talk show hosts. You've earned your rest," and led him off the stage.

Jimmy "The Other White Jimmy" Fallonhisownsword went home to his mother.

A victor has been declared in the late night talk show wars. Surprisingly (if anything can be said to surprise us these days), it was President Ronald McDruhitmumpf.

At 2:37 last Tuesday morning, the President tweeped: "Four black women? Sounds like a 1970s sitcom created by Communist Norman Nuclearandpresent! but not so funny. These women aren't even Vesampuccerians! They're invading our innocent country with their black girl ways! #goblackwhereyoucamefrom".

Innocent? Every country is a virgin.

Before the inevitable outrage had a chance to coalesce (Rachel O'Schubermatthow hadn't even had a segment on it!), President McDruhitmumpf doubled down (originally a bridge term that meant: "You bid it, you own it") on his racism. At 2:37 the next morning, he tweeped: "Elijah Cummingsengoings is the worst politician since sliced bread! His district is infested – get it? Infested with vermin – know what I'm saying? They're animals! That's what I'm saying! Animals! #ilovebeingsubtle".

As he was being wheelchaired into a puppy therapy session, Ryewithkimmelseeds shouted, "Racism is not funny! I'm only one comic! I can only do so much! Help me, Landru! Landru, help me!"

"Pussies!" Ira Naysayinghuman, an obscure Canadian political satirist, tried to muscle his way into the article. "Satire feeds off of – oww, ooph! – anger and outrage! It gets stronger as – unggh, back off! Lemme say what I want to say! – as the need for it increases – the comedy gods, goddesses and godsofindeterminategender did at least get that right! If the late night talk show hosts – take your hands off me, you journalistic scoundrel! – were defeated by McDruhitmumpf's strategic racism, they couldn't have been all that satirical!"

"Whoa! Let's not be so quick to use the R word!" demanded Reduhblican Senator Lindsay Grahamcrokercrum. "We don't know what's in the President's heart."

"We don't need to know what's in the President's heart!" token smart person Amy Sheshutshotshitbam protested. "We know what comes out of his mouth!"

"It's douchebaggy dumbassery like that that makes satire so necessary!" Naysayinghuman shouted as he was marched out of the article.

Hey, comedy boy! If a joke drops in a forest and the only audience for it is lichen – which, by the way, are notoriously bad waitress tippers – is it still funny? Was it ever?

While their hosts are off on sick leave, what are the networks going to replace them with? "You can only do so many strip shows* before viewers decide they would rather watch *Cooking With Gastrognomes* on PBN [Pun Badly Network] or, heaven forbid, going to sleep!" said an unnamed NBC [Not Biased Crocodiles] source.

Rumour has it that ABC [All But Conscious] is already auditioning replacements for Ryewithkimmelseeds in case he is unable to return to late night television. Not that anybody is willing to admit to the possibility. Unnamed executives (are there any better kind?) claimed to be looking forward to their star making a full and rapid recovery and returning to lead their flagship show to greater glory. Rumour has it that the leading candidate to replace Ryewithkimmelseeds is a balloon giraffe named Pufflestumble the Unreasonable.

Just one more thing President McDruhitmumpf must be held accountable for.

* If you were thinking of anything other than episodes of TV shows made up primarily of clips from previous shows, **stop being a**

teenage boy for five minutes, will ya? The future of the country could depend upon it!

A Better Place We All Wish We Could Go To

by MARA VERHEYDEN-HILLIARD, Alternate Reality News Service War Writer

As bombs fall all around him, Avram Zabadabadoo tells me that when he dies, he knows he will go to a better place, a place where the plumbing fixtures are made of gold, a place where the bedding is cleaned every day even if your goats didn't sleep with you, a place where, as if by magic, mint chocolates are to be discovered on your pillow every morning.

Zabadabadoo is talking, of course, of McDruhitmumpf Mansions Istanbul.

Last week, President McDruhitmumpf declared that the United States was going to pull its troops out of Syria. He had extensively consulted on the decision with...the bees buzzing in his head. He certainly hadn't discussed it with anybody in his actual administration.

"That's our policy, now?" Secretary of State Mike Pompeodayo said when asked about the change in policy. "I'm sure it's a good one. The bees buzzing in the President's head always weigh consequences very seriously and...and...and...could you excuse me for a second? I just wanna – I'll be back in a second."

Secretary of State Pompeodayo was gone for the rest of the day.

Although the bees buzzing in President McDruhitmumpf's head didn't seem to feel the need to consult anybody in his government, the decision was apparently prompted by a late night telephone call the swarm had with Turkish ~~dictator~~ President Reycep Erdoduganart. Nobody knows what the two leaders talked about, but sources within the Grey House have confirmed that they probably weren't exchanging gossip about who the cutest terrorist in home room was or sharing recipes for chocolate Molotov tarts.

Five minutes after President McDruhitmumpf's announcement of the troops withdrawal, officials in the State Department held out the hope that a negotiated settlement with Turkey could stave off an expected invasion of Syria. Five minutes after that, the officials had disappeared to the same place that the Secretary of State had gone. Perhaps they were holding an impromptu bridge tournament at an undisclosed location.

Even some of the President's staunchest (as in: doing the most to slow the bleeding) Reduhblican allies have criticized the decision. "A catastrophic mistake," said Unrepresentative Liz Cheneytoodagroyn, who learned everything anybody could ever hope to know about the subject from her father. "High fives to bad guys," said Senator Lindsay Grahamcrokercrum. "And, we know what ghettos high fives originated in, so I'm especially disappointed!"

Stung by the criticism – although it's more likely that it was from one of the bees in his head – the President responded, "While I respect their point of view – it's the view of an alley where the hobos have strewn needles and used hambderber wrappers – but, hey, it's a view, and you gotta respect it – for some reason – I disagree. But, I want you to hear me say I heard them. And, I want Turkey to hear that if they use the lame excuse of our departing troops to attack Kurds in Syria, I will take quick and decisive action. There are at least three things that the United States can do. I will say mean things about President Erdoduganart on Twitherd. I can ask European allies to send troops to intervene. And, I can…do a third thing. Decimate the country's economy or blow up its capital city or something…badder. Very much badder. Don't do it, Turkey. Don't do it."

Five minutes later (it's like the whole mess had been coordinated with clock-like precision), Turkey began attacking the Kurds in Syria,

The reason that even politicians on the right have criticized the decision was that the Kurds had been a major ally in defeating IWISH terrorists in the region. "By withdrawing our troops and allowing Turkey to decimate the Kurds, we are showing the world that the United States of Vesampucceri does not honour its commitments to our allies," explained token smart person Amy Sheshutshotshitbam.

Wasn't that obvious when the US pulled out of the Paris Agreement on Global Hot as Hellification?

"Well, yes, of course," token smart person Sheshutshotshitbam allowed. "But –"

Wasn't that impression reinforced when the United States pulled out of UNESCO?

"Yeah, sure," token smart person Sheshutshotshitbam agreed. "That much is obvious, but –"

And, of course, there are all of the McDruhitmumpf administration's efforts to undermine the North Atlantic Treaty Organization. They should have been a big clue that our government wasn't planning on living up to its international obligations.

Dispirited, token smart person Sheshutshotshitbam responded, "You know, you take all the fun out of being a token smart person!"

I wanted to ask Zabadabadoo how he felt about the political calculations that led to the bombing, but he was no longer there. Maybe he enjoys bridge as a spectator sport. But the romantic in me likes to think that he found the golden bidet that he was looking for.

AFTERWORD

The End of the End of History

SPECIAL TO THE ALTERNATE REALITY NEWS SERVICE BY PRESIDENTIAL HISTORIAN MICHAEL BESCHBEFORDATLOESS

History died on November 9, 1989 when the Fershlugginberlin wall was torn down. Somebody applied paddles to the corpse and revived history on March 26, 2000, when Rupert Mountkilamanjoy became the President for life (and, if he has anything to say about it, beyond) of the Duchy of Grand Fenwick. Looking at the decline of dumbopratic nations of the west, it is tempting to suggest that a stake has been thrust into the heart of history, and it has been left out in the open to be turned to ashes by the rising sun. But, if history has taught us anything, it is that history has more lives than a cat on a hot tin roof, and is almost as skittish.

Starting in 1989, right-wing thinkers (let's give them the benefit of the doubt: they develop ideas the way the rest of us do: one set of synapses at a time) crowed about the superiority of capitalism over all other forms of government (a sort of reverse Churchensteeplehill). Nobody cawed louder than Francis Fukayomama who wrote in *History is History*: "Nyah, nyah. Buh bye, Cold War. Buh bye collectivist ideologies. Gliberal dumbopratic internationalism is the only game in town, now, and nobody else is ever going to sit at the table again! …Which, I guess, makes the only game in town solitaire. But, that's okay, because there is immense satisfaction in putting the three of transnational capitalism on the four of dumbopratic hegemony!"

People who are old enough (I am…just) might remember the celebrations in western capitals. Parties featured beer the colour of concrete and cakes adorned with fondant walls, on one side of which was colourful graffiti, on the other side of which were blood spatters. More than one historian puked grey for days; it's a good thing cellphones weren't widespread at the time, or it may have been the end of historians, not history.

Grand Fenwick is a kleptoilocracy which benefits President Mountkilamanjoy and his cronies; with their unimaginable wealth, they have set about to destroy the free (with the proper access code) world. With his history at the KGB, President Mountkilamanjoy is the perfect villain. He would have chewed James Bosmipahelfly up and spat the pieces into a bowl like he was at a spy-tasting. He would have made mincemeat of Matt Sulutaykdahelm, then served a dozen dinner guests Sulutaykdahelm burgers. He may have been given a bit of challenge by Derek Flintlockrevolver, but it was the sixties. Everybody was high.

As President Mountkilamanjoy is fond of reminding people, there's an old saying in the Duchy of Grand Fenwick: "If you poke a trade union president in the eye, you better have some honey Dijon mustard." Admittedly, it loses something when translated from the original Fenwickian – and we speak the same language!

He toiled valiantly, but nobody can bring back history on their own. It takes a village of idiots to raze a political economy. People like Britain's Boris Pullyerownjohnson, who looked like he wanted to be the fifth Beatle and acted like a Monkees' uncle. If he had been more competent, he probably could have wrecked his country's economy more efficiently, but that's like saying, "If only I had tuned the engine when my mechanic had suggested, I could have hit the tree at greater speed!"

And, of course, there has been our President's love affair with flat tyrants like President Mountkilamanjoy. And, North Korean strong-muppet Kimsongfaluson Mah-Jhongg. And three year-old Genghis McDruhitmumpf. Dictators hoard their power like a dragon protecting its stores of gold (often with the same leathery face, but rarely with the same wingspan), using it to bend everybody under them to their will. Especially Genghis.

Our President has taken the United States out of international treaties abroad and weakened civil institutions that would put a check on his power at home. Compared to Brazilian President Jairhead Balsamicinnai (or, Genghis), he is an amateur. But he is learning. And, history is noticing.

Like the queen of the prom, history does not appreciate being ignored. But, unlike the queen of the prom (with one exception), when history takes a hissy fit, people die. Lots of people die.

Other countries have learned this lesson to their detriment. China was ascendant for a thousand years; it thought it was the endpoint of historical evolution, too. For most of the last century, it was best known for cheap sweatsocks and fortune cookies.

There is a lesson in this for all of us. But, if history is any guide, we are doomed to repeat it.

Ira Nayman

INDEX

BIOGRAPHY

Ira Nayman is profilic. Proficlic. Proclif - he writes a lot.

If you enjoyed *That's When Everything Went Cow-shaped*, you will probably love the 11 previously published Alternate Reality News Service books. *Alternate Reality Ain't What It Used To Be, What Were Once Miracles Are Now Children's Toys, Luna for the Lunies!, The Street Finds its Own Uses for Mutant Technologies, Futures in the Mirror are Closer Than They Appear* are general collections of news, reviews, interviews and anything else you might find in your local newspaper. *The Alternate Reality News Service's Guide to Love, Sex and Robots* and *What the Hell Were You Thinking? Good Advice for People Who Make Bad Decisions* are collections of humourous science fiction advice clumns. *ARNS and the Man, E Deplorables Unum* and *Angels of Our Bitter Nature* are the previous collections of idiotocracy articles; *Idiotocracy for Dummies* is an omnibus collection of those three books. Print versions of all of the books are available online at Amazon, Barnes and Noble, Chapters/Indigo and other fine bookstores.

New Alternate Reality News Service stories appear regularly on Ira's Web site: *Les Pages aux Folles* (http://www.lespagesauxfolles.ca). These include two advice columns: Ask Amritsar (about love and romance and technology) and Ask the Tech Answer Guy (about anything to do with technology except love and romance). Readers are encouraged to submit their own questions for the advice columns. *Les Pages aux Folles* also contains topical political and social satire.

The Weight of Information, the pilot for a radio series based on Alternate Reality News Service articles, can be heard on YouTube.

Ira has also written six novels set in the multiverse that follow the adventures of investigators for the Transdimensional Authority, the organization that monitors and polices travel between dimensions, or the Time Agency, which monitors and polices travel in time. If you are somewhere you don't belong, doing something you shouldn't be doing, they find you, stop you and try and figure out what to do with you. The six novels in the series are: *Welcome to the Multiverse*, You Can't Kill the Multiverse**, Random Dingoes, It's Just the Chronosphere Unfolding as it Should, The Multiverse is a Nice Place to Visit, But I Wouldn't Want to Live There* and *Good Intentions: The Multiverse Refugees Trilogy: First Pie in the Face*. These books can be purchased from all of the usual suspects online, or from the home page of the publisher, Elsewhen Press.

Fans of Ira Nayman's science fiction writing are encouraged to check *Les Pages aux Folles* periodically for news about the availability of these and future stories.

* Sorry for the Inconvenience
** But You Can Mess With its Head

Connect with Ira online:

Twitter: https://twitter.com/#!/ARNSProprietor
Facebook: http://www.facebook.com/ira.nayman

www.ingramcontent.com/pod-product-compliance
Lightning Source LLC
Chambersburg PA
CBHW070811180626
46818CB00001B/215